Then, all at once, there were streams of orange-red tracers shooting high into the rainy blackness, slowing at the top of their arcs, drawing parabolas over the Scrims. Strung beads of fiery fully automatic bursts went lofting every which way; red star clusters and other signal flares went up; somebody started shooting illumination rounds out of a fireball mortar. People were throwing their helmets aside and starting to scream like lunatics.

Burning never found out who had fired first; maybe no one Ext had. In any event, there was no joy in the fireworks. No soldier who had fought a night battle under live rounds could feel much good from them. But there was release.

More and more Exts opened up, launching rockets and grenades, waving 'ballers around over their heads, and squeezing off .50-caliber rounds as fast as they could. Burning couldn't make out a single coherent word among all the raving, shrieking, and howling. Caution had been flung to the winds . . .

By Brian Daley
Published by Ballantine Books:

GAMMALAW
SMOKE ON THE WATER

THE DOOMFARERS OF CORAMONDE
THE STARFOLLOWERS OF CORAMONDE
A TAPESTRY OF MAGICS
TRON
REQUIEM FOR A RULER OF WORLDS
JINX ON A TERRAN INHERITANCE
FALL OF THE WHITE SHIP AVATAR

HAN SOLO AT STARS' END
HAN SOLO'S REVENGE
HAN SOLO AND THE LOST LEGACY

STAR WARS: THE NATIONAL PUBLIC RADIO
    DRAMATIZATION
THE EMPIRE STRIKES BACK: THE NATIONAL
    PUBLIC RADIO DRAMATIZATION
RETURN OF THE JEDI: THE NATIONAL PUBLIC
    RADIO DRAMATIZATION

SMOKE ON THE WATER

Book One of GAMMALAW

Brian Daley

A Del Rey® Book

THE BALLANTINE PUBLISHING GROUP • NEW YORK

A Del Rey® Book
Published by The Ballantine Publishing Group
Copyright © 1998 by The Estate of Brian Daley

http://www.randomhouse.com

Library of Congress Catalog Card Number: 97-92493

ISBN 0-345-35858-9

Manufactured in the United States of America

First Edition: February 1998

10 9 8 7 6 5 4 3 2 1

In memory of my father, Charles Joseph Daley,
and of meteor watching on warm August nights

ACKNOWLEDGMENTS

The author wishes to express his heartfelt thanks to the following people, who aided and abetted him over the many years: Officer Michael Kueberth and Cpl. Garland Nixon of the Maryland DNR Police Hovercraft *Hunter*; Dr. Yoji Kondo of Goddard Space Flight Center, Greenbelt, MD; Calvin Gongwer of Innerspace Corp., Covina, CA; Ray Williamson, formerly of the Office of Technology Assessment; Professor Conrad Neuman, Oceanographic Department of the University of South Carolina; Drs. Frank Manheim and Allyn Vine of the Woods Hole Oceanographic Institute; Masaaki Hirayama, for the crash course in Korean history; skipper Richard J. Severinghaus and men of the USS *Annapolis*; the boys and girls of *sensei* Tom Fox's "American Rock and Roll Karate," for massive intrusions of reality; physicist Dr. Charles Melton and the late Dr. Al Giardini of the University of Georgia; Drs. John Camerson and Eric Seifter, for both their concern and their efforts on my behalf; and to Lucia Robson, Owen Lock, and Jim Luceno for their love and support.

Some features of the LAW 'chetterguns are drawn from the research and recommendations of Lt. Col. Morris J. Herbert, formerly Assistant Professor of Ballistics and Associate Professor, Department of Ordnance, U.S. Military Academy, West Point.

ACKNOWLEDGMENTS

The ocean encompassed everything, and everything could be understood in terms of it. Everything true about it was true about life in general.

Robert Stone
Outerbridge Reach

God's gonna trouble the water.
from "Wade in the Water"
Traditional Spiritual

SMOKE ON
THE WATER

CONCORDANCE

CHAPTER ONE

Digging his own grave was the most peaceful thing he'd done in a long time. Past exhaustion, past any hope of survival, Burning engaged the hard mountaintop soil of Anvil Tor with his entrenching tool. Better to die in a shallow fighting hole, he had decided, than in some dark muddy corner of the command bunker. He labored with an exactitude born of the Exts' war against the forces of LAW. Once ingrained, the Skills kept a hand-eye vigilance of their own.

Burning already had his field of fire marked out, the scrub cleared away with measured whacks of the e-tool's machete edge. The hum was still in his ears despite the fact that his helmet phone's gain was turned down and the lapped neck-shirt was open so that he could hear what was going on around him.

The hum had followed him around for weeks, building steadily in the background since he had faced the reality of their situation. There was simply no way the Exts could survive, much less prevail against the Periapt forces. When the last Ext fell dead, the LAW moguls and the proxy detachments that had been bribed or pummeled into shifting allegiance would control every square centimeter of Concordance.

The hum was like the vague precursor of a quake or an incoming tidal wave; it coursed in his ears all the time now, waking and sleeping.

The mindless exertion of digging in made it less painful to contemplate the string of disasters that had driven the Exts onto Anvil Tor for a last stand; it dulled Burning's awareness of his own culpability in the whole sickening business and helped shut out the heartrending sounds from the plain below.

3

The winds that scoured Anvil Tor's cliff face carried shrieks and screams and the din of turncoat mop-up weaponry. Occasional major detonations punctuated the white noise as fuel reservoirs and missiles in wrecked Ext armor exploded.

A string of three blasts made Burning pause for a moment. They couldn't have come from his men and women—any that had been left behind were surely dead by their own hands. Shortly he began to hear the far-off jubilee of victorious First Lands Alliance and Concordance Liberation Army units as they sounded sirens and vehicle horns and fired delirious volleys into the air.

Burning grunted as he pitched a bit more of the hard-baked dirt aside, then stopped to check the sky. The clouds were continuing to close in, and so LAW airpower might be hampered a bit. He doubted that the Periapts would screw up their courage for a nighttime ground assault, though a clash in the dark, perhaps in driving rain, would certainly suit the Exts.

His drill instructor in the student reserves would have approved. *Damn fine infantry weather!* she might have said.

But Burning was not about to applaud a couple of clouds. To hell with the everlasting glory of the infantry, he told himself. That day alone he'd had to give two good people the knife—people who had been relying on him to supply another glorious Ext victory. A few of the survivors were so far gone that they *still* expected it.

"Burning!" a voice called.

He glanced up and immediately returned to digging.

"Allgrave Orman," the voice drawled, mocking the name and the title. "It's about your sister. Seems she's wandered off from the operations bunker."

Burning—born Emmett Orman, the tenth and current Allgrave of the Exts—planted the e-tool. On Anvil Tor it was not especially bizarre to see Zone wearing a major's trefoils instead of a lieutenant's stars or, for that matter, a sergeant's stripes. As Ext units were attritted, field promotions had become daily, even hourly commonplaces. Hell, what would it matter now if General Delecado bucked the patho bastard to field marshal? When one came right down to it, Zone's new rank was no more unmerited than Burning's being named All-grave, which he owed to a chance of lineage and had been granted against his will.

"I gave word that Fiona was to be watched," he said at last.

Sucking at his teeth, Zone offered a languid salute. His raw-boned muscular body never even approximated the position of attention, but almost nobody else's did anymore, either.

"Sweetmeat was doing just that, sir, till he stumbled into a LAW recon floater packing a coilgun."

"How long has Fiona been gone?"

"Excuse me, Allgrave, but I've had better things to do than watch over her. She hasn't passed through the perimeter, if that's any consolation to you."

Zone's hollow-eyed stare was different from the thousand-meter gaze so many Exts wore those days; Zone's was more daring. And he had always had a special bad eye for Burning, one that said, Yeah, you're *right* to be afraid of me, and we both know why. Only I'm not gonna put it into words just yet, and you're too rule-bent to.

Burning stepped out of the fighting hole, adjusting his battle suit and then taking up his boomer. The heft of the big battle rifle gave him pause for just a moment. Why not just toad-crank Zone now, square away accounts while he had the chance?

Two years earlier the idea would have appalled him, but the LAW conquest had changed that. In any case, it wouldn't be the first time Burning had boomed another Ext as a matter of wartime necessity. But Zone was staring straight at him, maybe expecting it. Then, too, Zone was the best fighter on Anvil Tor, perhaps in all the Broken Country, and he was going to be needed soon.

Burning slung arms. "Where are the Discards?"

Zone nodded toward the cliff face. "Over that way, maybe."

"Fiona's probably with them, but I'll check it out. If any-body needs me—"

"In fact, Allgrave, Daddy D's been yelling for you in the bunker."

"Tell General Delecado that whatever it is will have to wait."

"Don't think so," Zone said, shaking his head. "Somebody's out across the perimeter, asking to summit with you."

"Who?"

"That's the mystery of it."

The muscles in Burning's jaw bunched. "We all dug in?"

Zone spit on the ground. "Getting there. Fireball mortars, triple-A batteries, rest of the crew-served weapons. Countersonics and ECM are in place. Ran outta landline fiber, but we've got runners set up. Daddy D's got everybody consolidated, chain of command patched—half-assed, anyways."

They headed for the operations bunker, passing small groups of Ext soldiers hastily preparing fighting positions, all of them descended from the exteroceptive implant–controlled slaves who had claimed a bloody freedom when the Cyberplagues had reached Concordance and had gone on to forge themselves into the planet's most stoic and fearless guerrillas. Filthy, damaged battlesuits showed patches and unit flashes from all across the Broken Country: the Gray Flats Gang, Murderers' Col Heavy Arty, Riyoko's Ronin . . .

As they passed, a catapult paratrooper from the Rumpstake Glacier Airmphib muttered, "We get 'em at close quarters tonight, and we'll baste 'em all. Santeria Corners all over again, you just watch."

It had been the only clear Ext victory in the latter part of the war—Murphy's Law at critical mass. All Concordance and Periapt warwares had malfunctioned or canceled each other out: SAT/counterSAT systemry, airpower, antiaircraft weapons. Command and coordination nets had failed, rain had set in, and the brutal terrain around Santeria Corners had become the scene of a far-flung two-day-long gutter fight.

Even so, Burning faked agreement whenever Exts cited the battle to bolster themselves and modesty when they commended him for it. He and the command staff had been powerless to direct strategy. It had been Ext company commanders, platoon and squad leaders, and linedog privates who had given LAW a savage mauling.

The memory did nothing for Burning's morale, however. He hadn't been truly glad or grief-stricken for some time, and he often wondered if he had dissociated completely from what was going on around him. He no longer felt anything like what he presumed he was supposed to feel when friends, comrades, and kin met their end. He suspected that he was an unwell man.

"Heard some sniper rounds a couple of minutes back," Zone said casually. "Zazzing through the bushes whistling, 'Where's Burning? Where's Burning?' "

"Why don't you take the knife now, Zone, and save us the trouble of giving it to you later?" Burning kept walking. There was no reply.

A square pit ten paces on a side, the Exts' operation bunker wasn't much to look at. It was roofed with hastily felled logs and polymer sheeting and covered with mounded soil and rock. The only openings were blackout-draped observation and firing slits and two small entryways.

As Burning approached, the rain began as a light drizzle, scarcely more than a mist. The mountaintop chilled, but few of the subcommanders, runners, and others marking time near the bunker bothered to close their battlesuit collars. Without interrupting what they were saying or doing, they just shifted their boomers to sling them muzzle-down on the weak-side shoulder. Keeping moisture out of the barrels was more a reflex than a reasoned response.

General "Daddy D" Delecado was outside looking at the sky, his Adam's apple bobbing. He was a tall, stoop-shouldered man with a head of thinned-out white hair. The war had taken a lot out of him, and his battlesuit fit him like a clown costume.

"This rain'll give their pilots something extra to reckon with," he remarked to Burning.

Burning nodded out of respect. If the Periapts chose to make air strikes with all-weather fighter-bombers, a little rain wasn't going to thwart them. The enemy was just as capable of marching an artillery unit up the slopes and pasting the whole mountain for hours or days or, for that matter, employing orbital kinetic or directed-energy weapons. That was what Burning would have done in their place.

Only Bigtimers were unlikely—for the moment, at least. Ensnared by Concordance-wide intrigues, civic affairs considerations, and political priorities, LAW had to make a pretense of using measured force against the Exts. Mass surrender would have made AlphaLAW Commissioner Renquald look good, but no Ext would be taken alive, knowing what LAW had planned for them.

Daddy D motioned Burning through a blackout drape. Zone followed without waiting to be invited. Inside, the general fingered an A/V touchpad, bringing up a holo, while Burning leaned in close to the display field.

"Recon team's got a contact at a hundred meters south of LP niner."

That was well in front of the projected forward edge of the battle area, practically at the foot of Anvil Tor. "They're trying to sneak recondos past us?" Burning asked in surprise.

"Not hardly," Delecado said.

Burning was confused, and the hum in his ears was bothering him again. He wanted to locate Fiona before the whistle blew and the shit flew, and now there was this. Over the holo's shielded hardwire line came a blurry image from the recon detail. It was foggy down below, but the infrared and lightamp showed a lone figure sitting on a boulder as big as a tank.

"The contact came in waving a white bicycle flag and singing," Delecado explained. "I think you'll recognize the voice."

Audio pickup was only fair, but Burning instantly recognized the words to "I'm a Decent Extian Girl, So Get Your Finger out of That." "Lod!" he said in greater surprise.

"The little cumwad," Zone muttered.

Burning had liked his puckish cousin well enough when they were growing up, but Lod had long since quit resisting LAW unto the death. Burning opened a mike to the recon team leader and said, "Fetch him up."

At the same time Daddy D instructed all other elements in the area to stand fast at full alert. What could it be, after all, but some kind of 'scatbrained diversion?

But when LP niner's team spread out to move in on him,

Lod scrambled down behind cover. "You cannot touch me, who do not love me!" Over the A/V his tenor voice sounded even thinner than usual. "Be good enough to tell the Allgrave of the Exts that his kinsman's come to talk sense with him. Burning! Are you listening?"

"He's working some angle of his own," Delecado said. Given that they were talking about Lod, that was like predicting the direction of sunrise.

"Burning, you don't have to die up there!" Lod added. "Cousin—can you see this?"

Burning squinted at the holo display as Lod came out from behind the boulder, holding something high.

"Romola asked me to show it to you. She apparently doesn't want you dead, either."

"Close-up, zoom in!" Burning grated over the hardwire. The recce leader's boomer-mounted optical pickup showed Lod's extended hand in the crosshairs. The thing he was holding was the engagement bracelet Burning had given Romola forever ago. "Bring him here, *now*!"

But Lod skipped back from the scouts. "My tailor won't tolerate my being manhandled! I talk to Burning down here or not at all."

"Trap." Daddy D made the call flatly.

"Hold position; don't let him leave," Burning said to the recce detail. He enhanced the image of the bracelet as well as he could; if it wasn't his fiancée's, it was a perfect copy. "Make sure he's alone. I'll be right down."

CHAPTER
TWO

The wealthiest and most populous of Concordance's score of nation-states, the First Lands had once lorded it over the entire planet, especially over the Broken Country, whose citizens had been pacified by means of drugs and turned into exteroceptive chipslaves. But the reign of the First Lands had endured for less than a century when the Cyberplagues found their way across the stars to Concordance and swept away the old order.

Of unknown origin, the Cyberplagues had liberated the chipslaves from their behavior-modification implants, killing countless thousands in the process, but the survivors had dug in wherever their labor units had been deployed—typically in the planet's harshest and most unforgiving terrains. Military esprit became the social value essential to survival, and in defending their newfound autonomy, the Exts had evolved quickly into ferocious, disciplined fighters. They probed the Flowstate and used it to arm themselves with the Skills—an array of mind-body disciplines that were unique to them.

Bitterly vengeful, they had gradually reclaimed the Broken Country, and for some fifty years after the Cyberplagues an uneasy coexistence had prevailed between the Broken Country and the First Lands nations.

Until the coming of the LAW starship *Sword of Damocles*.

The military wing of the Hierarchate of Periapt—a world distant from Concordance but at the very center of things nonetheless—LAW was short for the Legal Annexation of Worlds, dispatched across the reaches of space to restore unity in the wake of the Cyberplagues and enlist new populations in the centuries-old conflict against the Roke, an alien species whose unprovoked assaults on human-colonized worlds had left millions dead.

Subjugation was LAW's first order of business, but there were many in the First Lands who had made their peace with the annexation mission for personal advantage. The lure of Periapt's wealth and the threat of its power had co-opted one nation-state after the next, until at last the Broken Country stood alone against the interstellar conquerors.

But even the Skills were not enough to offset the might of allied Concordance foes backed by LAW military technologies. Eventually even some Ext clan bastions and polities began to sue for peace with AlphaLAW Commissioner Renquald. Those who refused to lay down their arms were threatened with the unthinkable: renewed chipslavery. The threat violated certain unspoken principles of the Post-Cyberplague epoch, but LAW felt free to teach that kind of object lesson.

Even so, the threat had proved a gross miscalculation. Many who had already made a separate peace and been disarmed made preparations for suicide, and the Exts in the Broken Country vowed to hurl the LAWs from Concordance or die trying. What had been localized resistance to the annexation escalated into the most bitterly fought conventional war in LAW history.

In a way, each became the enemy the other side had not counted on.

The Exts had their porcupine strategy, curling up and releasing deadly quills until the foe got tired and went away; LAW, by contrast, accustomed to bringing small powers to heel with nuclear strikes, found itself faced with an allied population that had had an ingrained loathing of nukeweps since the Cyberplague known as HorrOrgasm had detonated four hydrogen Bigtimers on Concordance seventy-five years earlier.

Rather than risk wide-scale rebellion, LAW had gone in on the ground, using First Lands forces as proxies. And since almost every weapon system on the one side had had its countersystem on the other, finally it had come down to artillery and armor and infantry units slowly and deliberately grinding each other to bits in mud, swamp, and snow. And in the end the last of the Exts had taken to Anvil Tor to make it their funeral bier.

Daddy D knew better than to try to dissuade Burning from having a face-to-face with Lod. But when he began to call for an escort to see his Allgrave down the mountain, Burning countermanded him.

"Fiona is the only one I want in on this." The career Lothario Lod had always had an oddly chaste affection for Burning's sister, and she had maintained a filial fondness for him. Burning felt that Fiona's presence could help pry the truth from the family scapegrace.

He ducked through the blackout curtain, flipping back the cheek pieces of his helmet and half opening the articulated neck guard, which reshaped to cup the sides of his head. By gathering and concentrating the sounds around him, the helmet could provide rough source bearings.

He made his way through a copse of trees that had been stripped bare and partially flattened by a heavy explosives hit before enemy fire had ceased around noon. The air was thick with the smell of sweet heartwood sap. In a clearing beyond he skirted Daddy D's outdated hardcorps Hellhog assault chopper, which had managed to convey the general, Burning, and several officers to Anvil Tor. A few other grounded aircraft and a number of surface vehicles dotted the mountaintop, but none offered escape. All had been stripped of weapons for the coming Götterdämmerung.

He passed the rain tarp that served as a MASH, telling himself not to look in but doing so anyway. Warm blood met chilly air and steam curled from open wounds, as if the rent bodies were steam tables in a field kitchen.

With whole and artificial blood stocks gone, the meds were draining the dead to keep the more hopeful cases on the effectives list. The Exts had had to resort to that before, but on Anvil Tor casualties with ∈E's jetpenned on their foreheads by triage sorters—for "expectants"—were being harvested as well. Much of the blood would transfer diseases, parasites, and other contaminants, but nobody on the Tor was expecting to live long enough for any of that to matter.

He came close to stumbling over an improvised litter where a woman wearing the patch of the Pissant Estates Bon Vivants lay propped up. The sapper's battlesuit was rashed with bloody punctures, and her nose had been shot away. Burning realized that he was looking through the orifice in her nasal bone into the back of her throat. Blood frothed from the exposed gap as she swallowed and spit to keep her air passage clear. She came around long enough to recognize him, flash a woozy thumbs-up, and mouth something that did not sound human, though it eventually dawned on him that she was saying "Stay staunch."

He didn't know how to answer but was spared having to when two aides who were themselves wounded came to move her inside for treatment or, more likely, a jetpenned E.

The gray drizzle turned colder as he double-timed on, certain that his sister had returned to the Discards, who had adopted her as their surrogate matriarch. No other adult was truly safe among them, but Fiona was as secure there as she could be anywhere in the world. Daddy D was holding the kids in reserve for whenever their feral murderousness would be needed.

Just now two dozen of them, ranging in age from twelve down to eight, were lying doggo in a boscage west of the MASH. They were passing canteens around, along with a sipflask of gin. Some wore wraparounds to hide their eyes; others, war paint. There were necklaces of human ears, ratty dress wigs, and wildchild fetishes of bones, feathers, empty styrettes, and hand grenade pins. Many had fingers that had been gnawed down a knuckle or two, chewed off to kill the raving hunger that had been a near constant in the First Lands POW/concentration camps. The weapons they carried looked far too big for the Discards, but they were cradled lovingly and expertly. Even Daddy D refused to run the risk of forcing these true children of war to strac up.

They made Burning uneasy. Some commanders had handed captives over to the Discards for interrogation. The kids might have learned the art from the wrong side, but they had learned it well.

When Burning asked after Fiona, he got little more than blank stares. Eventually, however, a few put their helmets together and spoke in voices too low for Burning to hear, then pointed to the nearby Scrims, Anvil Tor's wind-blasted cliff face.

He shagged on and finally spied her framed against the darkening gray sky, standing on a rocky prominence that resembled the pulpit of a ship. She had her back to him, and her helmet and boomer were on the ground. Her elbows were clasped in the opposite palms, and she was gazing down at the plain. Even in a battlesuit her carriage was graceful, more like that of a Periapt fashion model or an improbably tall ballerina than like that of an Ext. The winds moaning up from below fluttered her fine blue-black locks and warrior's plaits.

Fiona heard him and turned just enough to show a quarter profile of her celebrated face and a curve of long, slender neck. "I wonder if the LAWs know the significance of this place."

From behind her Burning saw flashes through the rain and fog—turncoat railgun artillery being fired from sheer exuberance. "I imagine the Cottswolds or someone would've mentioned it," he answered. "But the LAWs care about Periapt empire, not Ext history."

From the Scrims, nearly two hundred years earlier, another group of Broken Country holdouts had leapt to avoid capture by allied First Lands armies.

"I'm glad we won't live to see what becomes of the Broken Country now," Fiona added. "What becomes of Concordance." Her voice was throaty but expressionless.

"That's what we've got to talk about," Burning said. "Now, come away from there before LAW starts lobbing harassment rounds at you." As he reached for the sleeve of her battlesuit, Fiona turned to him, wearing a tranquil smile. The gloaming offered just enough light for him to see her sloe-brown eyes, extreme cheekbones, purple-red lips, and slight overbite. But when he got a better look, he almost lost his grip on her. Her face was a swirly mask of scars that stood out like raised arabesques, scabbed and already swelling with fibrous tissue.

"What've you done to yourself?" he blurted out.

"I couldn't give them the satisfaction of killing me. So I've beaten them to it, Emmett."

Her using his birth name put him off his guard. His first thought was that she had gone tripwire and retreated into some fantasy of the past.

Then all he felt was weary bitterness. "Fiona—"

"*Ghost!*" she said, cutting him off. "You see the scars. I'm Ghost now." Her expression was serene behind the veil of incisions. She had come away from the long drop, but only a step.

She had voided her living name and marked herself dead for all to see, Burning realized. Her scars said that she considered herself to be beyond grief, pain, fear, or any enemy's ability to harm her. As far as he knew, no one had performed the ritual in three centuries. Studying her face, he recognized Ext ceremonial patterns from the history books: the Talons, Hermes's Footprints, the Strength That Lives in the Flames, Kali Weeps . . . Judging by the scabbing she had to have dosed her wounds with growth factor like the old-timers used, though where she'd gotten it on Anvil Tor, he couldn't imagine.

"*Ghost,* then." He pulled her gently from the edge.

She had always nursed her private sorrows—both of them had—despite being raised in bastion privilege. Early on Fiona had blossomed into a blithe, witty beauty with a glow to her face and a willowy figure, as different in personality as in looks from her shambling, bookish older brother. Drawing stares wherever she went, she had become the toast of the Broken Country and—for a brief, bright season—a rising star in the Concordance social firmament. About the same time the *Sword of Damocles* had arrived in-system.

With LAW had come renewed warfare, and for Fiona the detention camps, where every dignity and decency had been methodically stripped away. She had helped the younger ones—the Discards—stay alive, and they had helped her—but only at the cost of her humanity.

Liberated, she had refused noncombatant status, and

Burning—Allgrave by then, part warlord, part political leader—had been, as ever, helpless to dissuade her. She and the Discards had become a detachment unto themselves. And now, there she stood, watching him through her death scars as he guided her to safety.

"Lod's at the foot of the Tor," he said in a soft voice. "He claims to have a message from Romola. Hear him out with me."

Her lips curved sweetly, her angular beauty showing eerily through the self-mutilation. "Why not?" She shrugged out of his hold and went to where her helmet and boomer lay, pausing to search a sleeve pocket. "But this first."

She brought out a tight, thin braid of tar-black hair interwoven with twists of glittery filament—one of her Hussar Plaits from the palisade of them that hung under the outer layers of her curtain of hair.

She extended the lock to Burning. "Fiona left this behind for you to let you know she loved you."

He unsealed and removed his gauntlet to take it. "Then accept a lock of mine to give to Fiona if you see her before I do. And tell her I love her all the more."

He hit the releases on his collar, lifted his helmet free, and tucked it under his left arm. Then he unclipped his hair and shook loose the copper-red ringlets and Hussar Plaits. By that time she'd pulled her knife—a soot-black dagger that had been their mother's, one of their few mementos of her.

Burning watched it come to his throat. "Can I still call you sister?"

The jet blade veered slightly. Fiona barely had to flick her wrist, high up where his plaits were only hair, for a braid to fall into her gloved palm. She opened the torso seam of her battle-suit enough to slip it into a pocket next to her heart.

"Of course."

After they had pulled their bone-domes back on, slung the heavy battle rifles, and moved out, it occurred to Burning that the Discards had stood witness to her death name ceremony.

They were almost back to the C&C bunker when Zone stepped from behind a shot-up weapons carrier and joined them. His gimlet eyes recced Ghost from helmet to toecaps and

back. Burning bristled fleetingly but said nothing. Fiona's
death scars didn't seem to surprise Zone.

"They were all you needed to make you perfect," he said.

CHAPTER
THREE

The way Zone took up rote-step alongside Burning and Ghost left no doubt that he was accompanying them to the foot of Anvil Tor.

Burning didn't object; the guy was a limbic case, but he could smell a midnight ambush coming at reveille. He tried to keep from fruitless agonizing over Romola's safety. Bastion Gilead—one of the clans that had gone over to LAW—had given its word that it would protect Romola when the Exts had elected to continue the fight. Please don't let them have bio-chipped her, he said to himself, almost in prayer. If that was the threat, he would kill her before he himself could be killed.

With darkness coming on and the rain thickening, the three of them set the battlesuits' phase-change skin to ambient temperature to avoid being picked up by enemy thermal sensors. They kept their visors transparent and, like everyone else on the Tor, used passive detectors and targeting equipment only; nobody wanted to be the juiciest return on the enemy's scopes. The antilaser aerosols had thinned for the time being, and so they left their breathers open. That was fine with Burning, since his had ulcerated the bridge of his nose.

Employing aloud passwords, field signals, and commo authenticators, they made their way past defensive pozzes and observation posts that camouflage and gathering gloom had melded into the landscape. Zone, on point, wove a path through temporarily deactivated minefields and other kill boxes. If a drone or SAT picked up their movement and the advancing foe used their route as an avenue of attack, there would be some surprises for the turncoats.

Fiona—Ghost—with her runner's physique had always been a fair hand at fieldcraft, but now she moved with a new assuredness. Any Ext would spot it right away as a heightened affinity for Flowstate. Burning guessed that it stemmed from the death scar ceremony; ritual was a potent avenue of access to the Skills. He accepted her way of ending the anguish, perhaps even envied her a bit.

They held up in a culvert off the main road to receive a sitrep from the bunker. Opposition forces were moving into new positions around Anvil Tor, but there was no sign of an assault in the making. Enemy surveillance drones had been recalled, which made no sense; remotes were cheap and expendable.

"Perhaps they've lost their taste for attrition," Ghost speculated. "They'll use standoff weapons or a Bigtimer."

Burning shook his head. "LAW understands that the rest of Concordance is watching."

Zone nodded in agreement. He would have relished discomfiting LAW and its client states that way, even if he had to flashfry for it. "Renquald cuts just one tactical nuke fart, all his proxics'll have to be pulled home for riot control."

Ghost sighed. "How I wish *we* had even a single little half-K party popper."

But the Exts didn't. A year before, the Cottswolds had launched a futile Bigtimer attack on the *Sword of Damocles*. The Periapts not only had knocked out the MIRVed missiles but also had utilized conventional weapons to take out every threat stockpiled on Concordance—if LAW's superconducting superstorage warheads could be said to count as "conventional weapons."

When they took up their way again, Burning heard the tweedles and wonks of two surviving Wheel Weevils at their training farm a klick or so to the southeast. The owner, jockeys, grooms, and the rest were long gone. A few Exts who were accustomed to handling the giant myriapods had talked of turning them loose, but Daddy D had forbidden it. Better for the time being to leave the native beasts to blunder around the stables—the only home they knew—than to have them tripping booby traps and ambushes.

For Burning, the plaintive sounds of the animals brought to mind the carefree derby days of his youth, before his life had started going wrong. It was a pity that he was probably going to have to order the Weevils shot.

Turncoat searchlights had come on, sweeping the mountain from all sides. What with the jamming and other kinds of electronic warfare, hardwire commo lines to the listening and observation posts had been a must. The one that led to Lod served an additional function as a guideline. Burning, Ghost, and Zone followed it to where the two-person recce team that initially had spotted Lod was holding its position.

The reccers were a man and a woman from the Lightning Flats Wetworkers, a SEAL outfit. Reservists, both looked to be in their late twenties, he a sergeant first class and she a lieutenant. They had holed up behind some rocks from which they could keep an eye on Lod and pass the time. And to do that they had made creative use of an enemy KIA.

It was a LAW shocktrooper lieutenant colonel in exoarmor, pintle-mounted steadigun still attached to his torso module. An observer, Burning assumed, who had gotten too close to the action—far too close, because the top of his head had been sheared off by a boomer round.

The Wetworkers had propped the corpse against a boulder where rainwater had filled and overflowed the open skull and now made tiny splashes on the water and floating brain tissue there. Droplets ran down the cracked face bowl past eyeballs that still bulged in the aftermath of the fearsome hydropressure shock wave the impact had sent through the gray matter.

Between glances at Lod, the reservists were taking turns winging playing cards at the open-top helmet and the colonel's flooded brainpan. Burning noticed that they were using a dog-eared deck bearing the LAW logo—it had to be the shocktrooper's.

The Wetworkers put the cards down, and the lieutenant claimed the sergeant's stakes, a pair of dry—albeit filthy—socks. They crawled and duckwalked over to the new arrivals and pointed to the big rock Burning had seen in the holofield at the C&C bunker. Lod had planned ahead. Lod always did.

He was sitting on a collapsible camp stool, his white bicycle flag stuck into the mud to one side. He held over him a double-size luminous orange umbrella, probably intended to keep the Exts from mistaking him for an infiltrator and, Burning imagined, as a precaution against getting shot by turncoat troops. The bumbershoot explained the Wetworkers' sour expressions: no true reccer would feel easy around a light source like that.

But it was keeping Lod so comfortably dry that he could enjoy a perfumed Periapt cigarette in a long gold-plated holder. His mirror-polished knee boots somehow shed the rain and mud completely, and he was wearing a saucer cap with a heavily braided brim and a splendidly tailored dress uniform trench coat lined with phase-change silk, with a white ascot showing from it.

Burning didn't recognize the trappings, but they were quite a sight on the only man he knew who had been discharged from the student cadet corps on grounds of sexual profligacy. Nevertheless, when war had come, Lod had somehow wangled an Allgrave's direct commission and had served honorably until the Gileads and other bastions had begun suing for a separate peace. Using the technicality of holding a Gilead commission, Lod had soon loopholed himself out of the Ext coalition forces.

The Wetworkers and other recon teams confirmed that Lod had come alone. Burning told the others to hold fast while he dealt with Lod. The face-to-face had to do with Romola, after all.

"SOP says we check him out first," Zone said, and before Burning could stop him, he stepped out from behind cover, leveling his boomer at Lod. "On your feet and make an angel, you little suck-ass! Delta-V!"

Lod hastened as ordered, eyes wide not because of the big battle rifle but because it was Zone drawing dead aim on him. Dropping the umbrella and cigarette holder, he placed both hands behind his head.

"That'll do," Burning said as he forced the boomer's barrel aside, heading for Lod. "Everybody stand fast."

He moved into the clear with the rifle slung, raising his

helmet visor. Recovering his dignity, Lod retrieved the
umbrella, tossed the soggy cigarette aside, and pocketed the
muddy holder.

"How now, Cousin?"

His looks had not changed in the year or so since Burning
had last seen him. Diminutive and blond, he was as neotenic as
a ten-year-old, with a head seemingly too big for his body. As
for the cousin part, he was distant to Burning and Ghost at best,
having more Gilead than Orman in him. Like them, he had
spent his youth at Bastion Orman as a peripheral—a dweller by
sufferance amid the affluence and the conspicuous pecking
order.

Burning indicated the cap and trench coat, the decorations
and aiguillettes. "What's the unit?"

"Concordance Interplanetary Defense Forces, actually.
Diplomatic liaison staff attached to Commissioner Renquald's
AlphaLAW headquarters." Lod hurried to change the subject.
"Not a very pleasant bivouac spot, eh?"

Burning exhaled through his teeth. "Love it. Wouldn't swap
it for another ten centimeters of dick. Is that all you wanted to
know?"

Lod's expression changed. "Not quite. I'm here to help, and
you look to me as if you could use it."

The hum had arisen in Burning's ears again, and while he
couldn't quite tell what expression his face held, he supposed
Lod was referring to his NoMan stare. "I've seen people die
out here who wanted to live. And I've seen people live who
wanted to die."

"Which do you want?"

Without warning, Burning's bitterness rose up, and he was
too tired to control it. Lod didn't even have time to move as
Burning brought the boomer up from where it rested at sling-
arms, left hand grabbing the barrel shroud, pulling it forward,
and swinging the piece up, right hand to the pistol grip, thumb
flicking the selector to semiautomatic. The sling was made taut
against his upper left arm—a programmed infantry drill exe-
cuted with the speed and precision of the Skills.

The suppressed muzzle pointed between Lod's huge eyes.

"I might want to bring some scorch on a cousin who's wearing the other side's uniform. Unless he tells me what he's doing with Romola's bracelet."

Lod held very still.

"Where is she, Lod?"

"Not six klicks from here, Allgrave. At LAW field head-quarters with Renquald, along with Tonne-Head and some of the other Gileads, a few Cottswolds—"

"Why didn't she come herself? Have they hurt her?"

"Upon my mother's soul, no! But there's a new proposal on the table, something no one would tell me about. She's unharmed, but they wouldn't let her come here." Lod held up the bracelet again. "It's a sign of good faith—safe passage there and back again if you choose."

Burning drew closer and worked a release on the boomer's stock. A bayonet that was as nonreflective as lampblack sprang out of the front end to one side of Lod's neck. "And what's in it for you, turncoat?"

"Personal advantage, what else? MeoTheos, it's the end of an age, only you're too blind to see it. LAW's going to take dominion over Concordance, and half the world welcomes it! For me it's just a change of masters, so yes, I look to my own survival. Who else ever has? Now, I've delivered my message, and I need to dry off and seek out a drop of absinthe. My jump-jeep's five hundred meters that way." He pointed east. "You can return with me if you like."

Burning felt muddled. When he'd been e-tooling his grave, he'd had no misgivings left. If it was a trap, surely Renquald and the rest knew that the capture of the Allgrave would not force an Ext surrender. And if it was an assassination plot, it was resoundingly unnecessary.

Through the trees the hoot of a Wheel Weevil drifted down Anvil Tor. What would there be for Renquald to talk about at that late hour with LAW already holding all the cards? Or did it?

Lod turned away from the bayonet with a swirl of the magnificent trench coat. "If you want to stab me, here's my back."

Out of curiosity Burning stamped after him by the numbers

in the cadence of the drill. Lod stopped but didn't turn or plead; he just stood with his epauleted shoulders up around his ears, nearly lifting his saucer cap off.

There were other footsteps in the mud; Ghost was advancing from cover. "Allgrave, you call that an interrogation?" she said with a dark chuckle.

Hearing her voice, Lod swung around with a look of delight. "No, it's just hard to overcome a polite upbringing—"

He cut himself off and stared at her. The sight of her death scars broke his composure in a way that threats on his life had not. He knocked Burning's bayonet aside and went to lay one hand on her cheek, something she would have suffered no one else alive to do but her brother.

"You foolish . . . this is desecration!" He was almost in tears. "Fiona, you had no *right*—"

"Fiona's passed away, Lod. I'm Ghost."

He glared at Burning. "Go on showing how *staunch* you are, Allgrave, but even the noblest defeats don't keep history at bay."

Lod set off for his jumpjeep as the Weevil hooted again, and the sound seemed to flick a switch in Burning's head, causing the hum to die away. He caught his cousin by the shoulder and held him while he got Daddy D on the command push.

"Get some experienced hands over to the training farm to rig one of the Weevils with the biggest saddle they can find." He smiled at Lod. "I'm late for a meeting, and I'll be carrying a passenger."

"Oh, dear me," Lod said.

CHAPTER
FOUR

"If someone down there goes trigger-happy," Lod insisted, "what chance will we have? We'll last about as long as a PFC's re-up bonus in a Costa Hedonia bordello."

"At least I'll know they don't want me alive as much as you claim they do," Burning pointed out. He'd let his cousin chirp Commissioner Renquald's HQ to say only that he and Burning would be arriving by the Allgrave's preferred means of transportation.

Burning put his hand out. "Give me the bracelet." Lod handed it over, and Burning slipped it into his pocket alongside the Hussar Plait of Ghost's hair.

Lod looked at the Weevil that was to bear them. "I've always detested these hideous-smelling hoop snakes."

Standing outside the training farm paddock on the northeast side of Anvil Tor with Lod and Ghost—Zone having returned to the operations bunker—Burning found that the smells, sights, and sounds of the place were setting off charge after charge of remembrance in him.

Some of his earliest memories were of the racecourses and the great beasts that rolled across them, memories that included his parents and sister, among others. The odors of the Weevil wallows and the sight of handlers had Burning half expecting his father, Dunhill Orman, to emerge from the jockeys' dressing room in racing colors. Turned out in silk blouse, jodhpurs, riding boots, and helmet, he would cut a dashing figure surrounded by admiring men and women. He would smell of leather, expensive cologne, blowbacco smoke, amp brandy, and traces of one woman or another's perfume. He'd had the

25

size and red hair Burning had inherited but also enough physical courage and brash joie de vivre for three Exts. His field name, Hipshot, had been as well known in casinos and cabarets as on the military freqs.

He had been a minor Orman peer, but his renown as soldier, sportsman, and rake had drawn him the acquaintance of wealthier and higher-born Exts, women such as Siri Mahfouz Orman, who'd won distinctions of her own in military service. Siri was every bit as breathtaking as her daughter Fiona was to become, though that had not kept Dunhill from a string of infidelities.

Nor had common sense freed him from the definitive Ext vice, gambling. He'd won and lost fortunes on anything and everything. In the end his luck had gone bad, putting him so heavily in debt that he had lost face and several friends. Yet even those losses hadn't kept him from using his celebrity to front an investment fraud. Dread of dishonor—his greatest fear—had eventually driven him to blow out his own brains with a .50 'baller.

The Weevil Burning had selected for the trip to AlphaLAW HQ was finally responding to the handlers' stim impulses and shockprods. To him, the creatures had always looked like rows of immense, many-legged stone vertebrae come to life. This one moved with abrupt speed, wrapping herself belly-out around the ring cockpit like a myriapod tire mounting itself on a rim. She clamped hold of her own head with specialized tail grippers, firmly but carefully encircling what her gulled senses informed her was her own egg.

Her name was Artemis.

"Burning, there'll be hell to pay," Lod said.

Burning shrugged and handed his boomer to Ghost. "I've got unlimited credit on hell to pay, Cousin."

He hadn't been in the saddle in years. Even so, it was liberating to step onto a foot peg and swing aboard. He hoped that by surprising the enemy he could get Renquald to reveal his motives.

Artemis's banks of closely set, bowed, and immensely strong legs ruffled a bit as Burning's battlesuited leg brushed one of them. Because the Weevil's responses were inhibited by the stim circuitry, she didn't reach out to tear him apart.

The cockpit scarcely resembled one of the giant eggs. It was a narrow, minimal seat with armrest- and footrest-mounted controls affixed to a circular frame that rode ball-bearing tracks within an outer frame. The frame was greasy with brood secretion that had been loosed when the annuloid had clenched its dorsal suckers. The cockpit's gyros, inner race bearings, and track cogwheels kept it relatively upright, while the outer rails turned with the Weevil's minor shifting steps.

Burning adjusted the seat harness for maximum slack. "Sit right up here in front of me, Lod, where your new friends can get a good look at you."

Glumly, Lod accepted the inevitable. It was clear to him, in any case, that the Weevil handlers would have relished an opportunity to rough him up and bundle him aboard.

As he sat and Burning began buckling them both in, Ghost stepped closer to ask if Burning had checked his 'baller.

Burning nodded, patting the kilo-and-a-half handgun in a cross-draw holster high up on the front left side of his chest.

Lod understood what she was verifying: Burning was committed to taking his life if that proved the best option.

"Stop gibbering like a pair of utter blitzwits!" he snapped. "There's been far too much cranking of toads around here already without you two planning more!"

Burning almost smiled at that. The Ext slang's origin lay in a German expression, *tod-krank,* which on Old Earth had meant "fatally ill." In the Broken Country the phrase had come to denote terminal cases in general, and with the coming of the AlphaLAW war, "terminal" had quickly become synonymous with terminated, killed in action, corpsified.

The handlers and Ghost, a boomer slung on either shoulder, drew away. Stim circuitry or no, Wheel Weevil riding was a perilous sport in many ways. The handlers made the distress hoot of a rolling annuloid, and when Artemis answered it, Burning hit a touchpad tile. Circuitry in the Weevil's sensorium told her that her egg was in peril. She tucked her legs close, pushed off, and rolled into motion, shoving with her podia whenever they found purchase and rapidly gaining speed.

Burning steered with his body weight and piloted with the control stick. He didn't quite avoid the paddock corral gate, but the Weevil—evolved to deal with just that kind of obstacle—pushed off it automatically. The cockpit wobbled and, according to the Weevil's surges and split-second decelerations, rode the outer race forward and up or back and up but always returned to vertical.

They rolled across the training farm's access road and into the bush. Burning had no intention of descending by way of the dirt lanes the Exts had land-mined above and the enemy below. The great plated doughnut of annuloid and cockpit hit rough ground, rebounding from stump and stone. On their first extreme jounce Lod lost his grandiose braid-heavy saucer cap. Both men were thrown against the safety harness and each other.

Heavier now, the rain blurred Burning's wiperless helmet visor. He concentrated on following the course overlay he'd worked out and downloaded into the beast's mapping memory: between two enormous trees and down a sloppy wash, then along a rocky streambed that descended the tor's side in precipitous steps and low falls. He prayed that Daddy D hadn't missed any orders to secure booby traps, deactivate mines, and stand down snipers and troops at other firing pozzes. It was the kind of run a Weevil was well suited for, though that didn't keep the two men from being lashed by branches, torn at by vines, and swarmed over by every scuttling pest and noxious bug the Weevil shook loose.

Prompted by the day's events as much as by anything else, Burning thought of his last cross-country run, years earlier.

After Dunhill's suicide his impoverished widow and children had been taken into the populous household of Bastion Orman, and there Siri, Emmett, and Fiona had grown up as familial charity cases. Siri had suffered the situation in silence for the education and social grooming, the connections and entries she wouldn't have been able to provide for the kids on her own, not to mention physical security from the enemies Hipshot had made in the course of his wild life.

Eschewing remarriage, she had concentrated on earning her keep and raising her children, only to die tragically and far too young when—as had happened intermittently on every planet with a technoindustrial infrastructure—a long-inactive Cyberplague vector program had emerged from hiding. The outbreak was a mutated strain of the insidious DoomsData virus, one of the original and most destructive of the lot.

Despite 'wares scrubbers and phages, DoomsData had infected a First Lands CAD/CAM facility, though how it had lain undetected or penetrated the system, no one could say. Using the machinery, hazardous materials, vehicles, and even climate controls, the Cyberplague had slain more than 2,800 human beings before it had been contained and eradicated. Siri, who had been acting as assistant on an Orman purchasing delegation, had died trying to fight her way to the complex's control room.

In the wake of her death, Humbert Orman, paterfamilias of the bastion and onetime Allgrave, had shown Siri's orphaned children an even greater measure of the gruff warmth and inadvertent pity he doled out to them. Burning had already been made something of a loner by his lack of status, and Fiona had begun to look for her self worth in the opinions others held of her. Then had come that day at Bastian Orman's Wheel Weevil stable.

Burning had been out for a practice ride not because he rejoiced in the sport the way his father had but because he had needed to clock roll time for a cadet Skills qualification. At the stables Humbert had taken a crash that had left him unhurt but furious, and Burning, without thinking it through, had pointed out that the Weevil's belly plates had been allowed to become mite-infested and inflamed. Normally, Humbert would have controlled his temper. Publicly humiliated and shaken, however, he had instead taken a swagger stick to the groom, a half-feral boy whose own mother was dead and whose father was an abusive alcoholic brute.

Without uttering so much as a whimper, the groom had

taken a thrashing that would have made a grown man cry. Humbert Orman was beyond any revenge, but a month later Burning, out on a solo orienteering exercise, was set upon by a masked assailant who beat him senseless and heaved his body into a crevasse.

Found by chance, he was brought to intensive care and began a period of recuperation and rehab that lasted nearly two years.

The attacker had worn a fieldsuit developed by the Bastion Gilead, with which the Ormans had had a long-running and sometimes violent feud. But the Gileads had refused to respond to accusations, and save for Burning's gut conviction, there was no evidence that the abused groom was involved. The long convalescence yanked him off the usual bastion rearing track and set him even more apart from his peers.

In due time, his body healed and he resumed his pursuit of Flowstate, the Skills, and military training, as all Exts were required to do. But it took the war with LAW to turn him hard.

By then the father of the abused groom had died under murky circumstances, and the boy himself had left Bastion Orman. Years would pass before Burning reencountered him in the theater of war. The former groom's ferocity, cunning, and combat prowess had earned him nearly legendary status among the Exts, who had given him the field name Zone.

CHAPTER
FIVE

"Mother always warned me," Lod screamed. " 'Never share a foxhole with anybody braver than you are!' She forgot to say 'Weevil rides, either!' "

Artemis lofted off a little hummock and bounced through some tall weeds. The annuloid was honking for breath and sloughing a lathery trail of yellow saliva behind her but was still rolling strong.

She flattened a screen of frogwood saplings and slewed when she hit a mud hole but regained balance and headway thanks to her scores of strong bowed legs. Burning's battlesuit and Lod's trench coat were spattered with mud and rain and decked with blue tresses of hagmoss, lengths of lime-green popbead vine, and webbed flipper leaves.

Burning slipped into Flowstate calm, scanning the terrain, watching the tracking cursor on his visor display, and plying the armrest stick. The Weevil burst through a screen of dirk sticker vines that would have given even a battlesuit trouble and barreled on unscathed across a low meadow. The point where Lod had encountered the recce team was only seven hundred meters to the southwest.

Enemy positions came into view, seeming to bob insanely. There were spotlights everywhere, along with illumination banks the size of First Lands billboards. To the southeast a chemically lit trail laid down by remote on the assumption that Burning would arrive in a surface vehicle traced a safe ground route from the enemy lines to the area where Lod had left his jumpjeep.

Drawing a deep breath, he cut a course away from it and

somewhat to the northwest, telling himself, Here's where we
find out how badly Renquald needs me alive.

Turncoat and Periapt elements had maneuvered into a mean-
dering siege line around Anvil Tor. Heavily reinforced at the
foot of the mountain's sloped side, the line looked like something out of a trench warfare stalemate. It was an extravagant
show of force, and it had doubtless made the military commanders blanch to bunch up their units like that, even though
the Exts had nothing big left to throw at them.

Armor was dug in: conventional and coilgun artillery, missiles, sensors, directed-energy weapons, and too many smaller
firing positions for Burning to begin to count. The lines were
already two deep at the bottom of the Tor, and there, as everywhere, more maneuver elements were being moved up by
ground and air. Farther out on the plain remnants of what had
been the Exts' main force were still sending smoke smudge
into the sky.

A half kilometer behind the bristling gun pits and hastily
made berms loomed the LAW mobile field headquarters. Air
deployed in modules by heavy lifters when the enemy had
achieved uncontested control of the sky, the modular HQ put
Burning in mind of a luminous pile of burned-orange bubbles
trying to float free. As well as being graceful and fragile-
looking, the place was essentially assault proof.

The Weevil stunt notwithstanding, it occurred to him that
he might be playing into Renquald's hands. After all, the commissioner had already proved himself a masterful political
strategist. In the space of three years he had checkmated Concordance leaders with bewildering power plays that had
dropped the planet into his hands like a vending machine
fruit cup.

But Burning couldn't go back. Most of all it would have
been unthinkable not to answer Romola's summons, even if it
meant dying a little sooner.

The Weevil took a particularly high loft off a mossy brow,
and Burning had a momentary vision of some itchy First Lands
gunner blowing the annuloid and her riders clear out of the sky.
But no shot came, even though there looked to be a lot of com-

motion at the enemy perimeter. Searchlights slewed and came to bear, and loudhailers blared a threat his external helmet pickups did not catch.

Lod was waving frantically. "Hold your fire! The Wheelie and I want to live!"

Fifty meters in front of the ranks of lights silhouetted figures were finishing a snarewire fence, joining up the last accordion lengths. But off to the left a security lock gating arrangement was open in expectation of Burning's arrival on foot or in Lod's jumpjeep. Burning angled the control stick, leaned, and kicked the foot controls, and the Weevil changed course. Glare and commotion did not make her balk: her sensorium told her she wanted to go the way Burning was directing her.

A hot spot of intense heat from ultrasonics—the rain was too thick for lasers—turned a puddle blue with soniluminescence, then blew it up in a cloud of steam and mud. A burst of small-caliber tracers skewed across their path—brief orange hyphens that didn't miss by much.

"Hit the brakes; they're trying to kill us!" Lod yelled.

"No, they're not," Burning hollered back. "They're welcoming us."

He continued to steer for the closing gap in the fence, a ten-meter wall of graphite-epoxy snarewire. The last of it was paying off a roll mounted on the back of a tracked and waldo-equipped combat engineer vehicle. More engineering tracks were coming along behind to string additional layers of strand.

"Commissioner's envoy!" Lod proclaimed. "Renquald's envoy!" He sounded steadier than Burning would have expected.

Too late, Burning wondered if there was already a charge in the fencing. The strand was sealing from the ground up, but Artemis shot through the gap, scattering people and machines. There *was* some juice in the strand: power arced and crackled, but the annuloid insulated the cockpit and its riders from electrocution.

People in LAW exoarmor and other Periapt mufti dodged and yelled. The Weevil ran over and bent a trailer hitch, tilting a small coilgun and its tow motor. Something heavy grazed

Burning's helmet and rocked him but didn't penetrate—a crowd control bumpgun or nonlethal whapbag round. He saw bright spheres circling in front of his eyes for a few seconds but managed to hold on.

They rolled up and over a revetment. Burning spied the glowing egg mass that was the field HQ and cut a course for it. He felt his suit's sound-antiphasing gear tingling and knew it was canceling a sonics wave that had barely brushed past.

The next difficulty bore a crumpled Bastion Orman insignia: a tractor and water trailer rig crushed under the treads of a First Lander tank or field piece. The wreckage looked like a safer bet than swinging left toward the quad-mount autocannon or right in the direction of the tank traps. As the Weevil rotomoted onto and across the flattened water rig, Burning caught a glimpse of a pale, mangled hand hanging from the collapsed cab.

Then Artemis was suddenly in among the observation posts, gun pits, and weapons platoon nests, gutterballing between various obstacles the Weevil couldn't conveniently jump or circumvent. Spotlights quartered the area, sometimes stabbing directly at one another in mass confusion. Commo transmissions crackled, and loudhailers reverberated. Men and women shouted to each other, trying to make themselves heard in the rain.

The air blast of an oncoming surface-effect scout car came at the Weevil as the vehicle made straight for her. Artemis couldn't answer the primitive control system fast enough to dodge, so Burning goosed her with a stim impulse. She spun straight up the nose of the car, causing the vehicle commander to duck into his cupola and the blowcar to ground in the mud, jamming its fans. Down off the scout's stern—Burning howling in delight—the annuloid whirled on through the slop and swung onto a new heading.

Air spotters were aloft with high-candlepower spots that cut through the gloom and downpour. Troops that far back hadn't figured out what was going on, so most of them simply froze when they saw the Weevil churn through their midst, then got on the tactical and command pushes to add their voices to the welter. A big guy—Burning couldn't see what rank—tried to leap for the cockpit from a truck bed. Miscalculating, he bounced off Artemis's bony hide and flopped back to hit the mudguard of a self-propelled missile launcher.

Nobody was shooting anymore, not even warning rounds; a cease-fire order had to have come down the commo nets. More troops were arriving from one direction, so Burning took the other, even though it meant going down the side of a steep wooded ravine in near free fall. Trees were bent aside, and brush was flattened. It was deep and dark down there, with good upper-canopy cover.

Artemis's strength couldn't take her all the way up the opposite incline, and so Burning banked her downstream along the drainage, bouncing off rocks and deadfall. Nearing exhaustion, the Weevil was slowing. Burning knew that if he didn't end the ride soon, she'd "melt her tallow," as the paddock old-timers would have said.

When Artemis broke into the clear, he headed her directly for the mobile HQ. Seeing her vector, Periapt and turncoat spotter craft maintained their distance and followed the Wheelie in.

CHAPTER
SIX

Watching Burning's staunch but foolish Wheel Weevil charge through enemy lines in answer to her summons, Romola thought of something she had read back at Bastion Orman in one of his treasured utopian books.

It had been an Old Earth treatise by a man named Frank Mallel, who had made a sad but canny observation: Futurists, mystics, philosophers, and utopian schemers who set out to reason, to predict and recommend, all too often ended up *wishing*.

And Burning? He'd *set out* wishing the world were a better place. Small wonder that when the arrival of LAW disillusioned him and the war stripped him of virtually all he knew, he became a man who didn't care whether he lived or died.

She gazed down at the disorder the annuloid had created in the conquerors' lines. She had spotted the Weevil only once or twice after it had crashed the perimeter; the rest of the time she had followed Burning's progress by looking for strange attractors in the chaos.

The looks on the faces of the AlphaLAW leaders and Concordance quislings around her in the mobile HQ would have been hilarious if not for the setting—the charnel house battlefield where one more massacre was pending.

Romola was high up in an observation gallery outside a palatial situation room away from the functionary cogs, staffers, and support personnel with their equipment and their frenetic comings and goings. She was aware that some were stealing a glance at her now and again, but she was used to that.

A trim, fine-boned woman who struck men as both fragile and sensual, she looked like a sachem's beautiful young daughter, though in fact she was related to a bastion bloodline only via an older sister's marriage.

She had made the most of a nice figure by working hard on it, had acquired a patrician bearing through strict imposition of will, had cultivated social graces through self-discipline, and had developed a sense of classic chic that bastion dowagers praised as *avoir du chien*—style, in spades. During her mandatory active military duty she'd been tagged with the field name Tonguetide by squadmates but had shed it in civilian life by various showings of disapproval.

Hussar Plaits long gone, her amber hair fell in massed Pre-Raphaelite curls. She no longer even owned a battlesuit and currently wore a tastefully revealing, equestrian-skirted azure suit that made the most of her delicate looks and brought out the delft blue of her eyes.

She had accepted an arranged marriage with Burning because it had promised a bastion life in which she could pursue her flair for Old Earth–inspired jewelry design and raise children she could groom for better things. She wasn't smitten with him, but she appreciated his humility, his lack of interest in traditional Ext gambling and carousing, and the conscientiousness that gave him an aura of strength, to which he was largely oblivious.

All that had been prewar. Attached to the Gilead contingent that had accepted a cease-fire with LAW, she had made herself useful in interbastion coordination, then in peace talks, and lately in LAW oversight planning. By having served the survival and other interests of the Exts, she had advanced her status and discovered where her true gifts lay.

The display holos showed the Weevil emerging from a heavily wooded ravine and making straight for the field headquarters. Romola was certain that Burning's diminishing speed had as much to do with the animal's survival as with his having made his point.

Sharpshooters were posted inside and outside the HQ. Periapts in exoarmor had their steadiguns ready, and platoons of engeneered Manipulants—as big and inhuman-looking as storybook trolls—had been brought in. Even so, Romola saw with secret amusement that Tonne-Head was tense and distracted as Burning drew near.

Every so often the clan sachem of the Gileads would let out a whistling, unhappy breath through his nose. Taller than Burning, Tonne-Head was ferocious enough in unarmed Skillsfighting that the Allgrave wouldn't have had much of a chance against him. That didn't change the fact that Tonne-Head—fist clenching and unclenching near his sidearm—looked apprehensive.

While Romola watched, he reached up to resettle the jeweled, platinum-knobbed torque that encircled his bull neck; it was a magnificent piece, though its significance was likely to make Burning even more NoMan than he already was.

Soon it was nearly as easy to make out Burning and Lod through the gallery viewpane as it was to see them on the screens. As it entered a muddy area that fronted the HQ, the annuloid slowed like a runaway Ferris wheel, losing momentum and stability. At Burning's stim signal to her sensorium, the Weevil churned and backed oars in the slop until she came to a stop; then she unwound herself from the ring cockpit, lay down next to it contentedly, and evacuated her bowels. Romola let out a throb of laughter as she saw, through borrowed photo-enhancers, Lod's put-upon look as soldiers closed in around him and Burning.

A few among the VIP group joined her in chuckling, but not Renquald, and so the jollity died away quickly. The AlphaLAW commissioner was wearing his usual probing hard-to-read expression.

"We'll meet them in Receiving One," he announced to the observation gallery.

Romola had come to admire the understated way the Periapt gave orders that people leaped to obey and was beginning to get the hang of it herself. Time for roles to be acted out, she thought.

More urgent than possessive, Tonne-Head stepped forward

to take her arm after she had handed the enhancers back. But it was Renquald who led the way, paying her no further attention.

Renquald gazed out under the dome of Receiving One, a multiuse space that had served as everything from execution room to literary salon. The vaulted chamber was set in Periaptnoir, with massage-nap carpeting, varimorph conforming furniture, and a few magnificent pieces of Concordance art. A prodigious buffet had been laid out, and a string quartet from a First Lands military band was playing Vivaldi. The sharpshooters around and above were the only reminders that the place was a conquest command center.

Renquald had a lean, handsome face that was even more versatile than Receiving One. He was more comfortable in magisterial robes with brassards of rank and badges of office—as now—than in lounging clothes. Concordancers thought themselves fairly egalitarian, but in fact they were unconsciously intimidated by the trappings of eminence, and so, if only to further confound them, Renquald frequently confronted them with the aloofness and severity of a medieval Pope.

At Renquald's right hand stood Field Marshal Vukmirovic, ranking military officer of the AlphaLAW Concordance mission and now of the planet as well. A pile of muscle going to fat, he had salt-and-pepper eyebrows that looked as if he combed them the wrong way. The string quartet drew an unquiet sneer from him; a quartet of steadigunners, waiting in that exact spot to open up on Emmett Orman, would have made Vukmirovic far more festive.

Well, let him stew, Renquald decided. It would get Vukmirovic accustomed to the fact that the time of the military solution had drawn to a close and that Renquald had advanced to a new agenda.

In due course Burning was escorted into Receiving One. He entered on foot and was stripped of all equipment, his helmet included. The fact that he had been allowed inside was bonded proof that he was not armed—no hidey gun, no *fukumijutsu* spit needle hidden in his cheek, no explosives in his marrow.

But even Receiving One's excellent aircirc system and costly mood-aroma propagators were powerless against the stench of death and putrefaction on him and the stink of months in the field. He was like the war itself walking in.

Lod followed, moving with the energy and grace Burning had had drained from him. Burning's little kinsman had gotten rid of the trench coat, rinsed his face and hair of mud, mustered his savoir faire, and put his fine blond locks back in order. He was busy reading faces in the room and was ecstatic, Romola could see, to be back in the comfort and safety of the HQ. A fetching female junior officer in the Periapt liaison branch made especially warm eye contact with him.

Burning spotted Romola almost at once and did an imperceptible change step, as if he were going to throw his arms around her. Out of undue concern for safety, perhaps, he checked the impulse and instead looked around the room, not missing Tonne-Head. Romola was startled at his stare and considered what it must have taken to cauterize the wonky openness of the prewar Burning.

She understood that he still thought of her as his fiancée and as the secret heroine of Santeria Corners as well. She felt a pang for him but suppressed it. Either she steeled herself, or tonight would bring the Exts' annihilation and the Broken Country years more misery and affliction.

Burning continued to stand fast, searching the room for the assassin, sharpshooter, or armed remote who was to cut him down. There were guards but no headsman in evidence. Finally he cut his eyes back to her.

"Are you all right?" he asked.

It took no effort to make her answer sound wooden; indeed, it was Romola's easiest out. "Yes, I am, Burning," she told him. "And you?"

As Emmett Orman nodded, Renquald inspected the young man—just twenty-three baseline years old—who had become, by chance of birth and a degree of unassuming ableness, Allgrave of the Exts.

The intel-reported changes were quite apparent: every gram

of peacetime softness had been rendered down by campaigning and privation, his nose was crooked from a fracture, and the inner layers of his hair were braided with twists of aligned carbon-nitrite fibers to form Hussar Plaits. Even though the partially flattened nose had been sustained after he had tripped over an antenna guywire during a nighttime artillery barrage, the injury had qualified as a combat wound, entitling Orman to a Red Shield. Renquald had been interested to learn that Orman had refused the decoration in embarrassment at the ignominious way he'd been hurt.

Orman's ungainliness had been replaced by that body-aware sureness of movement common to those who had cultivated and gained a facility for those damnable Flowstate Skills. Some hint of animation had come into Orman's eyes at the sight of Romola and Tonne-Head, but the excitement was soon engulfed by the seared NoMan stare.

All in all, Renquald—who approved of the way hardship honed people—viewed the changes as an improvement. It was likely, however, that Orman did not see things the same way and might even become violent at the suggestion.

But no, Renquald decided a moment later. To preserve his sanity Emmett Orman probably had retreated to reveries of peacetime and what might have been: a comfortable life with his utopian monographs and an arranged marriage to the lower-born though striking Romola.

Orman's *old* future, at any rate. It was Renquald's intent that he salvage none of it. None.

Burning looked at Renquald. "What do you want with me?"

Lod tch-tched from where he was fixing himself a fragrant cup of kavajava fortified with a jigger of rumble, whipped cream, and a dash of green crème de menthe. "Don't be so curt!" The doffing of his trench coat had revealed a dashing dress uniform as splendidly tailored as a handmade tuxedo. "Take a load off your treads, Cousin. Have a bite." He motioned to where six kinds of meat had been barbecued and broiled Ext-style.

Burning shook his head and swallowed slowly. The smell

nauseated him, as the odor of scorched meat always did since he had walked among blackened, smoking corpses after the First Landers' incendiary attack at Four Fens.

His NoMan stare returned to Tonne-Head. "What're you doing here, Gilead? And wearing *that*?"

He indicated the torque with its glittering, faceted gryphon's eyes, ice moons, dawn stars, and lava nodes. Torques of rank were not uncommon among bastion office bearers, but the motifs and workmanship on the one Tonne-Head wore with such combined unease and arrogance were different. They drew on, though they did not duplicate, the look of the hereditary torque of the Allgrave. The real torque had been lost when Allgrave TomTom—Burning's great-uncle Thomas Orman—had spiked into the Boho River in a command VTOL.

Tonne-Head made a false start at an answer, but Lod supplied, "For one thing, he's hoping for news of his nephew, Burton."

Burning answered, "Dead."

He told himself that the word didn't say it all. How much would any non-Ext understand of that polar-cold night at Staging Point Crazy Quilt when an RPG round had blown Burtie to scraps and the Exts had begun calling dibs on his belongings? Burning himself had scavenged Burton's boots after the firefight; the left one had been lying out in the open, though it had taken some time to find the right one with the leg still inserted into it.

"Now that's a tragedy," Lod muttered. "But we're here to put an end to tragedies."

Abruptly, Lod's voice made Burning realize that everyone was staring at him—except Lod, who was refortifying his coffee, his back to the chamber.

"Take stock for a moment, Cousin," Lod went on, "and at least have a cuppa."

Lod turned suddenly and approached with a cup of tea Burning didn't want but reached for anyway, quickly discovering that Lod's hand held a tiny sliver pressed against the underside of the saucer. Burning accepted the saucer without losing the spit needle hidden under it. Flowstate kept his perplexity from distracting him.

He took a careful sip while palming the spit needle, mulling over just who in Receiving One he should toad-crank and when.

CHAPTER
SEVEN

The presence of the hulking LAW Manipulants in Receiving One made it a certainty that Burning would get only one chance to use the spit needle. The deadly neuter clones carried sidearms and huge Moplah-style chopper blades. The Manips weren't unbeatable supertroopers, but each was strong enough to tear Burning apart like boiled poultry. And because Periapts absolutely refused to deal for their own hostages—a rule that would apply even to Renquald—there would be no escape and no rescue of Romola.

He lifted his eyes from the tea to Renquald. "You still haven't explained why I'm here."

"Not to hear any more threats," Renquald surprised him by saying. "Only facts this time. There's a new policy gaining currency with the Periapt Hierarchate, or at least there was five years ago."

Burning understood that he was referring to speed-of-light delay. Policy changes in the Hierarchate, LAW's governing body, might have aged a good deal since word of their existence had been transmitted to Concordance.

"Nevertheless, as commissioner I am obliged to weigh carefully the portent of this new policy. After all, I'll be returning home someday, and in the meantime my own dynastic group could suffer should I misjudge the winds of change." He paused for a moment. "In short, Allgrave, you and your holdout Exts might be allowed to live. Or are you too set on that clichéd Wagnerian death you've poised yourselves for?"

Burning hadn't thought about the final stand in terms of

glory; no Ext had. They were too close to it. Glory and heroism were words in some other language, significant only to people with live nerve endings.

"New surrender terms, is that what you got me down here to hear?" Burning wondered how close he could ease to Renquald before anyone intervened; spit needles had a short range. "Or is it a matter of bigger, better slave implants?" He smiled for the first time, but only with his mouth, then reached to put the tea aside, palming the needle with a technique that was part of *ſukumijustso-do*. "You're underestimating us again, Commissioner."

Renquald shook his head. "You have my word that there'll be no implants, no slavewares. You won't even have to lay down your arms. Under this new policy you'll be spared to serve out an enlistment with LAW, under full amnesty. But not on Concordance," he was quick to add. "You'll be posted to another human-settled world. Your hitch, and that of your troops, will be six baseline years—*subjective* years, of course. I might add that the clock begins running the moment you agree. By tomorrow night it could be six years less one day."

Burning had waited until Tonne-Head was exchanging glances with Romola to transfer the spit needle to concealment between gum and cheek. Now he laughed. "Oh, so we can die fighting the Roke on behalf of Periapt? Or are the aliens nothing more than propaganda to ensure continued funding for LAW?"

Renquald's face remained imperturbable. "I assure you, Allgrave, the Roke not only are very real but pose a potential threat to *all* human-colonized worlds, your precious Concordance included."

"Real or not, the Exts would rather die fighting *you*."

"You should know that the prospect of your deaths under any circumstances does not entirely sadden me. But certain bleeding hearts both within the Periapt Hierarchate and outside it are pressing for interplanetary benevolence. Therefore, some pretense of forbearance and solidarity is needed."

"Or so said a transmission five years out of date," Burning thought to point out.

Renquald inclined his head in a curt bow. "As I said, I must be circumspect. Moreover, I'm wary of allowing several hundred Exts to martyr themselves on a forlorn mountaintop. Such incidents have a way of perpetuating vendettas and fueling troublemakers." He shrugged elaborately. "Besides, LAW doesn't necessarily want the Exts to fight *anyone*. Perhaps LAW will have you serve as peacekeepers or security forces."

"On some backwater world like Aquamarine, I presume."

Tonne-Head's patience finally broke. "Your refusal of amnesty won't restrict the suffering to the Exts, Burning. You asked about implants . . . Not for you, of course, you reeking, posturing Joan of Arc. But for kin and friends of everyone on the Tor!"

Burning winced. "They'll take the knife. LAW won't have any of them alive."

"Allgrave, LAW already has them." Renquald made it sound harsh. "LAW, along with the Concordance Defense Force: hostages, friends, and relations of every Ext. Surrendered into our custody, stripped of suicide options, available for implantation."

Burning shook his head. "For a lie like this you made me get an innocent Wheel Weevil all wet and shagged out? They'd never surrender. The bastions would never give them up."

"Not without their Allgrave's decree, perhaps," Renquald conceded mildly.

Burning couldn't make sense of it. "If you expect me—"

"The Allgrave pro tem," Renquald said, cutting him off and eyeing the torque around Tonne-Head's neck. "Chosen by special electors, as stipulated by Concordance doctrines."

Past anger, Burning lowered his voice. "What electors would choose a turncoat like you?"

"All," Romola said steadily. "We *all* did. *I* did."

Burning felt as if someone had e-tooled a fighting hole in his middle. "Without matrilineal ties to the bastions you've no claim to an electorship, Romola."

Tonne-Head moved to Romola's side, putting his weighty arm around her shoulders. "She does now that she's my wife."

A fiery flush turned the pale, dirty skin of Burning's face and throat vivid scarlet even through the screen of red stubble. His breath quickened, and he trembled in spite of the Skills. It was clear that he couldn't master himself enough to speak.

Renquald was fascinated. As Lod, Romola, and other sources had said, Orman had an intense, uncontrollable blush response to anger, embarrassment, or humiliation. But what mix of them was he feeling now?

Flicking a look at Tonne-Head, Renquald saw that the upstart Allgrave was watching the legitimate one nervously. Emmett Orman had become a daunting unknown despite the fact that the Exts had won only a few minor victories and a single significant one since his elevation. Renquald wondered if Orman realized how high he'd ridden in his troops' esteem. Probably he didn't; the man had some sort of compulsion against thinking well of himself.

When Romola would have gone to Burning, Tonne-Head held her back—an illogical show of caution in Renquald's opinion. Orman's red rage had already made the guards edgy. It would have been more strategic for the Gilead to conclude that if Orman lost his temper, he could be somewhat messily dispensed with. LAW could then approach Daddy D or some other successor with its proposal.

Lod spoke again, almost languidly. "Cousin, consider a moment. They have got several thousand hostages held ready for slave 'wares. All well and good for you to go down swinging, but the survivors are the ones who'll pay the price."

Burning cut his NoMan eyes to Romola and found his voice. "How could you sell us out?"

Romola didn't flinch from the answer. "To keep you alive. To keep us *all* alive."

She was pitching it straight from the shoulder, without apologies or tears. Renquald already had her slated for more important things as the annexation of the planet went forward.

For a woman with Romola's looks, inner strength, and political savvy to ally herself with a well-connected dullard like Tonne-Head . . . Renquald could only conclude that she really *did* put her obligations to her people before her own happiness.

"The old days are over," she was telling Orman. "The Exts will have to adjust to change, just like everyone else on Concordance. We have no choice but to make the best of things."

Burning flashed a quick glare to Tonne-Head. "This is the best of things?" Before she could answer, he moved toward her, his face still bright crimson, opening his arms for a last embrace. "Then good-bye."

Romola and Tonne-Head were Skills-trained, but Burning's sudden move took them off guard. He watched them waver as he shortened the range between himself and his fiancée.

Accepting his own death, Burning found himself entering a pure realm of the Flow, a more complete access to the Skills than he had ever achieved on a training field, in a dojo, or in a meditation chamber. The background tone that had buzzed in his head was silent.

Tonne-Head pushed Romola aside as Burning had intuited he would. Movement around him had slowed to a crawl, and he could see every detail, count the beads of sweat breaking out on his victim's upper lip. He felt buoyant, invincible. The fact that he could reliably summon up Flowstate in the middle of his imminent demise was the difference between the Skills and mere episodes of untutored peak experience.

He bit down hard on the spit needle to prime it while he made a deft grapple-parry of Tonne-Head's hands. The Gilead let his fear get the better of him, dispersing his Flow and impairing his Skills. Burning made a sliding transition to his attack hold. Tonne-Head recognized what was happening by then but was unable to stop it.

Burning's hold let him pluck the Gilead's lid away from his left eyeball, nearly tearing it loose. Then he got in close to avoid hitting his own hand and spit the needle, its tiny whisk tail expanding as it left his lips. The needle lodged in Tonne-Head's eye, drawing blood as the pneumosyringe discharged its poison.

CHAPTER EIGHT

Tonne-Head barely had time to grunt. Sliding out of Burning's grip, the sachem of Bastion Gilead went limp as a trickle of blood found its way down his cheek. Burning stepped back to admire his handiwork. Targeting dots lamped him from every direction. He assumed that Renquald's sharpshooters would cut him down, but he about-faced to the commissioner just the same.

"I'll convey your offer to Anvil Tor," Burning intoned regally. "My best guess is that most of the Exts will demand their amnesty here on Concordance or, at a minimum, insist on taking their dependents offworld with them."

All eyes were on Burning, but ears were cocked for the order to corpsify him. With Field Marshal Vukmirovic and Romola looking on, a medical corps colonel had moved to Tonne-Head's side, but the Allgrave pro tem was dead.

Renquald looked at Burning curiously. When he finally spoke, people flinched and one or two of the more anxious sharpshooters almost opened fire on Burning. "Absolutely nonnegotiable. Exts go; hostages remain behind. That's *my* insurance."

Burning narrowed his eyes. "How do we know you'll keep your word?"

Renquald made a frivolous gesture. "I could betray you, I suppose, but then, I could simply wipe you off Anvil Tor, too. Consider this: I'll allow you to retain your arms as well as take along any personal items that can reasonably be fetched to you. No home visits. Should the Exts accept, you'll leave aboard *Sword of Damocles* in very short order."

Burning felt nothing, neither triumph nor relief, but did not doubt Renquald. The commissioner had nothing to gain by lying about the bastions having reached a truce, and Romola, Tonne-Head, and Lod had corroborated the story. The only true Exts were the ones at firing pozzes on the Tor.

LAW would absorb the Broken Country no matter what. Continued resistance would bring down retribution on the hostages or cause them to be made less than human by implants.

"I can only convey your offer," he repeated.

"It's a beginning."

Renquald made a careless crook of a forefinger, and the beauty in the liaison uniform who had earlier made eyes at Lod marched over to Burning, proffering a compact communication device. The commo gadge was Periapt work: a camouflage-gray unit contoured for an easy one-hand grip.

"To keep me apprised," Renquald explained. "Field Marshal Vukmirovic will see you back to the lines."

He made no further signal, but all at once escorts were moving into position and someone was holding Vukmirovic's campaign cloak ready.

The liaison strode over to Lod, picked an imaginary piece of lint off his sleeve, and fluffed his ascot. He put his lips to her ear, murmuring. She nodded, then fondly lit the cigarette he had fitted into his golden holder.

Burning couldn't figure Lod out. Why the heavily toxed spit needle? A guilt-driven act of secret patriotism or some grudge against Tonne-Head? His future survival, like his past, lay in taking what personal advantage he could from events he could not oppose.

Tucking away the commo unit, Burning felt something in his pocket—the engagement bracelet.

Romola was on her feet, more weary and dispirited than grieving. He extended the bracelet to her, and she surprised him by taking it with a moment's tenderness.

"Oh, Emmett, *shit*! You've killed the only person in this whole sorry mess who was an even worse politician than you are."

Burning couldn't think of anything to say. Nothing fit recognizable patterns anymore. He kept waiting to feel something even as Vukmirovic was drawing him out under the HQ portico.

The rain was coming down more heavily than ever. Burning's helmet, weapon, and other gear were waiting in a big hover staff car that flew Vukmirovic's pennons. Driver and assistant were already in the cockpit, and the turret gun was manned. Burning ducked in and slid across a plush bench seat. The field marshal alone joined him, leaving his staffers behind. Several LAW infantrymen in exoarmor hopped on the running boards and grabbed handholds, steadiguns poised one-handed. Then the staff car rose, warning lights cycling and flashing, siren whooping.

Burning could only figure that the Periapts had to trust him a little. In the display-lit dimness of the passenger compartment there was nothing to keep him from conducting a .50-caliber cavitation experiment on Vukmirovic's head.

No, the hour for blind retaliation was gone—gone as Tonne-Head Gilead, as the glory of a last stand on Anvil Tor, as the engagement bracelet's symbolism.

Romola went off resignedly with Tonne-Head's corpse and the body detail. Lod's admirer made herself scarce when she saw that Renquald wanted to talk to him privately.

"I thought for just a moment that he might kill her," Renquald remarked.

"*Romola?* Never. I told you, I know Burning like my own hand." Lod managed to sound blasé but was vastly relieved that matters hadn't gone the other way. "Makes a nice, tidy package, doesn't it? Tonne-Head's thick-witted interference eliminated; reasonable Romola inherits wealth and influence, especially if she's pregnant; the murderer exits the scene, putting any bastion vendetta on hold indefinitely; and the Exts

are transformed from martyrs to inadvertent symbols of con-
ciliation—"

He stopped as Renquald showed him a look of mild displeasure. Lod's plan had worked, and gloating over success was a
waste of valuable time.

Summoning advisers, the commissioner left him. Lod tried
to blow a smoke ring, but it refused to take shape.

The staff car lifted slowly. Even though warnings were
being transmitted to the Exts that their Allgrave was return
ing under a flag of truce, the driver was proceeding with
caution.

Vukmirovic turned to Burning and said, "*Damocles* is due to
launch for Periapt in five days. We delayed departure so that
you'd be onboard." He quirked a smile. "Renquald didn't get
to be a commissioner by being a fool."

The AlphaLAW expedition had remained on station since its
arrival three years earlier. Concordance's first starship, *Dhul-
Faqar*, was being built in orbit under close LAW scrutiny
Damocles would be taking back the tangible and intangible
wealth of the Concordance system to enrich Periapt in general,
the Hierarchate in particular, and Renquald's dynastic group
especially. When completed, *Dhul-Faqar* would depart for the
planet Resurrection, 5.2 light-years farther out from Periapt, to
annex a world of vast natural resources whose inhabitants had
regressed to preatomic technology in the wake of the Cyberplagues. First Lands moguls were already competing with one
another to be dealt in on the next tier of LAW hegemony and
plunder.

"Your troops won't have much time for prep," Vukmirovic
continued. "Feasibility studies view the Exts as a self-sufficient,
rapid-deployment peacekeeper battalion. You'll draw organiza-
tional equipment on Periapt. But if there's anything special you
want—"

"Our own TO&E replacement equipment," Burning interrupted. "Weapons, ammo, spare parts. That sort of thing."

Vukmirovic laughed harshly. "Why limit yourselves to Ext

junk when you can have your pick of the First Land stuff—*mountains* of it? We're disarming your whole world!"

Burning glanced at him. "We're used to what we've got. Or maybe you didn't notice that it works for us."

Vukmirovic blew his lips out in derision. "After a fashion, Allgrave."

"I'll have to go before the bastion electors and surrender the Allgraveship," Burning said, mostly to himself.

"You can't," Vukmirovic contradicted him.

"I only inherited it as a field expedient, anyway."

"But you killed your pro tem rival, Burning. Which means you either retain the title until it's rescinded by referendum of all the Exts or you take the knife."

Technically, the field marshal was right. No second pro tem Allgrave could be selected until Tonne-Head's death was investigated and Burning's fate decided, because both would determine the balloting formulas. With Burning alive but unreachable in *Damocles*, there would simply be no Allgrave or any legal way of choosing a new one. All higher accords and fealties would theoretically be dissolved. The wrangling and angling over renewals and a replacement could go on for years, which would suit Renquald just fine as he helped his sympathizers in the Broken Country accrue power.

"So here," Vukmirovic said, putting something into Burning's hand. "I suppose this belongs to you." It was the gold and platinum torque Tonne-Head had worn.

"Congratulations," Burning said ruefully. "Even the counterfeit torque will be seen leaving Concordance." He stared at the rain beading the windshield and at Anvil Tor, which was ringed by the lights of LAW and turncoat armies.

"I'm willing to help you with key personnel problems as well," Vukmirovic added leadingly. "Powers of conscription and so forth. I can draft anybody you think might be useful on Periapt or wherever your unit's posted. That is, any Ext within reason . . ."

The staff car was already angling for the foot of the mountain and the Ext lines. Burning gazed at the besieging forces

and contemplated the Byzantine nature of Periapt politics and
LAW dynamics.

"There's one," he said.

CHAPTER
NINE

On Anvil Tor suspicion was at an even higher pitch than before, and now that Burning was back out in the raw cold and mud, he started to think that way himself. He therefore kept people at the LPs and outer perimeter, the lower heavy-weapons pozzes and fighting holes from which they could listen over the command push. That left a few hundred gathered in the darkness near the C&C bunker as the rain began to taper off.

He stood helmetless on the low dirt roof and spoke through a headset mike to amplifiers as well as those on the freq. He violated light discipline by standing illuminated by hand spots. First he told them about Tonne-Head. No one decried him, not even the few Gileads among the Exts. One of the first to roll over for LAW, Tonne-Head had condemned the Exts often and loudly. For the most part the Exts heard him out with a moribund silence.

Then Burning described Renquald's offer of amnesty and what would happen to the hostages if the Exts refused. Vukmirovic's parting word had been that if the holdouts wanted to watch via A/V links as friends and family members urged them to surrender while being measured for implants, it could be arranged. When they raged, he didn't try to rein them in.

The debate surged back and forth through the night with the smoldering violence of a brewing riot. Burning had to invoke an absolute pax or there would have been Skillsfights, stabbings, and worse. Some called for immediate surrender, others for a suicide charge directly into the LAW guns. Zone in particular was for that.

With the argument taken out of his hands, Burning went to Ghost and attempted to read the expression behind her newly made death scar. Behind her the Discards edged into the light, cradling their assault pistols and gutting knives. Most had closed their helmet breathers, and since they favored the type shaped like demon half masks, their blank eyes were even more dehumanized than usual.

"I thought you wanted to die here," Ghost said. "Death alleviates all pain and makes one so much stronger."

"I thought I was stronger for being willing to die," Burning confessed, "but now I don't know if I'm strong enough to live. Either way, it will be unforgivable to die in battle if it means LAW implanting hostages with slave 'wares."

"I've no *use* for anybody's forgiveness." She thought for a moment, tracing the angry zigzags of her facial markings. "What LAW does is LAW's responsibility, not yours. That's how people keep using you. But if you feel honor-bound to accept their bargain, I'll bind myself to it, too. Fiona would have, and you're my blood no less than you were hers."

She backed away from him a few steps, raising her voice so that others nearby could hear. "I say we accept the amnesty, if only to keep implants out of the Broken Country. If LAW goes back on its word, there'll be time to find oblivion later—killing Periapts, if it comes to that." She pointed behind her without looking to where the Discards knelt or sat in an unapproachable huddle. "They stand with me on this."

Burning already knew that the children would do virtually anything for her, as she would for them. Now the Discards took her at her literal word, rising to their feet silently to show that her decisions were their commandments. It didn't really conform to the time-honored Ext tradition of an independent voice for each fighter, but no one there, not even Zone, wanted to wring separate pronouncements out of the Discards.

"She makes sense," a voice in the dark said.

Others agreed; some disputed it. But Burning sensed that his sister had put momentum into the amnesty.

Then Daddy D took over as moderator. Leaving the debate to veer on, Burning retrieved Tonne-Head's pretender

Allgrave's torque, his to dispose of now by right of combat and Allgraveship. He handed the gleaming collar to Ghost.

"In token of your brother's gratitude."

Once Fiona would have been grateful beyond words to receive such a treasure. To Ghost, however, the torque brought only a faint smile to burgundy lips. "Largesse, Burning: another thing Tonne-Head lacked."

She went to the stump of a shorn-off tree, where she drew the soot-black dagger that had been one of Siri Mahfouz Orman's few bequeathals. The Discards saw what she was doing and crowded in close, faint excitement lighting their eyes. Ghost held the torque to the stump and brought the carbon-vapor deposition blade to bear on the soft gold, cleaving it easily.

Her scars bracketed with effort as she sliced up the collar like a length of sausage and tossed pieces to her little slayers. The youngest kids reached for the fragments eagerly, almost gleefully. Suddenly Ghost was their ring giver as well as their patroness, the bestower and withholder of favor.

The debate over the LAW amnesty wore on, though at a certain point it became clear that a consensus had been reached. Vote counts were passed up the chain of command. Burning suspected that Zone had altered some of the figures, but it didn't matter. It was still four hours to dawn when he stepped onto the bunker to declare aloud and over the freqs, "It's the amnesty."

There was a sudden silence so profound that they could hear activity at the enemy HQ.

Then, all at once, there were streams of orange-red tracers shooting high into the rainy blackness, slowing at the top of their arcs, drawing parabolas over the Scrims. Strung beads of fiery fully automatic bursts went lofting every which way; red star clusters and other signal flares went up; somebody started shooting illumination rounds out of a fireball mortar. People were throwing their helmets aside and starting to scream like lunatics.

Burning never found out who had fired first; maybe no one Ext had. In any event, there was no joy in the fireworks. No soldier who had fought a night battle under live rounds could feel much good from them. But there was release.

More and more Exts opened up, launching rockets and grenades, waving 'ballers around over their heads, and squeezing off .50-caliber rounds as fast as they could. Burning couldn't make out a single coherent word amid all the raving, shrieking, and howling. Caution had been flung to the winds.

Burning felt something hit his foot and saw that a spent slug had dropped there, grazing the boot shank's tough synthetic. An RPG swooshed by overhead, so low that it stirred his hair. Then he was tackled and realized that Daddy D had borne him over the side of the bunker.

They lay together beside it, watching as Zone staggered around in the light of flares and muzzle flashes, swigging hard from a squeezebag of jangle. He had a flamethrower on his back, and with his other hand he was sending tongues of fire into the air.

Burning spotted Ghost, wild-eyed, climbing up onto a boulder with a blazing magnesium flare in each hand. Her unbound hair and Hussar Plaits swung and snapped like black whips, while around the boulder capered and exulted the Discards, misshapen in their outsize boots, helmets, and battlesuits.

In the moment when the rest were at their most abandoned, Burning felt the weight of responsibility come down even harder. He grabbed Daddy D's shoulder. "Renquald'll think we want to fight it out!"

He fumbled out the little gray LAW commo unit, struggled with its unfamiliar controls, but ultimately got it working, all the while expecting an apocalyptic barrage from LAW.

"LAW, this is Anvil Tor. Hold your fire!" he screamed. "I say again: Hold your fire! Renquald, do you hear me? This is Burning! This is *not* an attack. I say again, this is *not* an attack!"

Shortly, the stylish little Periapt gadge carried the commissioner's amused voice. "Allgrave Orman, I quite understand. Welcome to the ranks of LAW and the cause of interstellar righteousness."

PERIAPT

CHAPTER
TEN

"Maripol—sweetie—I forbid you to go all snively on me at a time like this. I am *not* cross with you, though Sinnergy's going to wish she'd never showed her face here."

The au pair nodded, wiping her nose on the back of her hand. "You *sounded* mad."

Good instincts, child, Dextra Haven noted. After all, I've only got an interstellar war to resolve, and now you've gone and allowed my twit-wit ex-spouse to talk her way in here and make off with our baby.

Still, pretending not to be angry with Maripol was the most benign kind of lie after the whoppers she'd been trading with the Preservationist delegates all afternoon. Getting those lounge chair conquistadors to see how mucking insane it was for humanity and the Roke to wipe each other out over a measly few dozen habitable planets . . .

With little Honeysuckle suddenly at risk, even Hierarchate interparty mud wrestling would have to take a back seat. Dextra drew a deep breath, invoking an ersatz mantra she'd given herself for times of uncertainty and peril: How now, foul Tao?

Maripol added on her own behalf, "You gave explicit orders that you were not to be interrupted while you were closeted with the other Hierarchs. And Sinnergy has an adjudicator's court order for visitation rights—"

"Enough," Dextra warned the teenager. "Sinnergy isn't permitted on villa grounds or near Honey again unless I'm present, clear?"

While Maripol was gulping out "V-very clear, Madame

Hierarch," Dextra whirled to the small, well-knit man standing attentively a pace behind her. Since Dextra was sporting a semiformal peplos for the negotiating session with her Preservationist guests, Ben had chosen a businesslike beige livery and wore his long blue-dyed hair caught up in a clip carved from a single glitterwheel.

"Ben, convey my profoundest apologies and respects to those warmongering pinheads. And beg to extend the recess another fifteen minutes. Spread the usual joyjam. Hint that I'm call caucusing."

She gave her executive assistant's shoulder a quick offhanded pat. The all-competent Ben hastened for the solarium, where the three Preservationist Party Hierarchs were waiting.

Dextra looked back to Maripol. "Where'd Sinn go?"

"The lower garden gazebo, Madame Haven."

Dextra set off that way, bringing her plugphone on-line. She avoided using one of the house terminals in case any member of her company was snooping around. "Tonii?"

"Here, Dex," a throaty voice responded.

"Sinnergy's on the grounds, and she's got Hon. Lower gazebo, I think. I'm en route; come back me up. And try to appear casual. We can't have the opposition getting a look at my dirty laundry." She paused to add, "Of course, it'd be just like those underhanded gremlins to have arranged this intrusion."

"The perimeter's sealed," Tonii reported. "I'm on my way."

Dextra hurried her pace. At times like these she wished she were more the beanpole type and promised herself she would have her legs lengthened as soon as she could budget the recupe time.

Automatically she cut around a newly planted bed of Buddha's Crown. She was barely hanging on to her composure; while she looked young and curvy enough to pass for some other Hierarch's trophy spouse, she was old enough by decades to have known better than to permit Sinnergy to box her in.

Dextra had agreed to parent the baby back when it had been so nice to be in love, or at least in lust, again. At the time she had just ended an experimental interlude of chemical asexuality, and with her libido switched on, Sinnergy's carnal radar had been quick to pick up on Dextra's vulnerability—and to exploit it unerringly.

In retrospect she realized how foolish she had been to make a decision regarding childbirth during orgasm.

I should be a great-granny by now, not a mother. But oh, it's hard to say no when your back's arched, your toes are curled down, and somebody's sending you on a tour of the stars.

Dextra rounded her exquisite *ochaya* teahouse and forged downhill past a big white planter of gaff-grass, careful to keep the hem of her peplos from snagging on the wicked barbs. A timid little medusa from the villa's menagerie—all coiling, iridescent tentacles—slithered through the trees at her approach.

I ought to ease off the geron treatments and let nature take its course, that's what. I'd be white-haired and short on teeth, but at least I'd be done with sexual schlemielhood.

She let out her breath in relief when she spied Sinnergy in the gazebo, sitting in the wicker rocker with her back to the entrance. Dextra entered with bomb squad calm. Getting a better look at her ex-spouse, however, she almost guffawed out loud.

Sinn's hostile-looking road flare haircut with its stinger extensions was gone in favor of a mass of banana curls; the transparent-skin body illusion had been replaced by a chastely high-collared Victorian gown and high-button shoes. The last time Dextra had seen Sinn's feet, they had been long and prehensile.

She sat holding the bundled Honeysuckle, crooning some sort of lullaby. Dextra stepped around the rocker to stand facing her, relieved to find the baby unhurt.

"Sinn, they should keep the historical disks and sob operas locked away from people like you," she barked, releasing some of her cautious restraint. "You look ridiculous."

Still humming, Sinnergy looked up with a beatific smile, held one forefinger to her lips, then whispered, "Our little gift from heaven is asleep."

Dextra set her hands on her hips, thumbs forward. "I think I liked you better when you were the siren of the DepArtures movement. You may have been popping cortexalin hourly, but at least you were honest. Now, give me Hon and decamp your artificially pert posterior from these premises." When Sinnergy's wanton-vestal smile didn't slip, Dextra wondered if she was on something, after all.

"Darling Dex, we care for each other and our daughter *so* much," Sinn said after a moment, "it's our duty to give her a loving, traditional two-parent family. You'd see that if you were thinking clearly."

"That's not what you said when *I* carried her and delivered her solo because you were in the midst of your neo-Dadaist auto-da-fé phase, remember?"

"Nonsense. You were elated to have a second child—and a daughter at that."

With Sinnergy off on her neo-Dadaist gigs, Dextra had decided within days that full-time motherhood wasn't for her anymore. She had brought in a wet nurse, au pairs, and support 'wares before turning all available energies back to seeking tolerance for the populations of annexed worlds and some solution to the Roke Conflict.

When Sinnergy *was* around HauteFlash—typically with her entourage—mere child-care arrangements weren't enough. She was already being eclipsed by the young sylphs of the AberRational craze, and her mood swings kept the villa in a constant state of upheaval. And since she was equally bored with parenthood, her demands had become more unrealistic: a share of the credit and royalties for Dextra's literary output, justified by Sinnergy's "key creative input and inspirational *prajna*"; a place on the Rationalist Party's steering committee; backing for a seat in the Hierarchate Lyceum . . .

Refused on all counts, Sinnergy had threatened to take sole custody of Honeysuckle or drown her in HauteFlash's fishpond. She'd been rash enough to say as much at a gallery opening, and Dextra had forbidden her to set foot on the grounds again. Tonii and Ben had been directed to arm themselves with thumpguns loaded with nonlethal nettle shot, prod the remaining moochers off the property, and reprogram all the locks.

That had been two months earlier. Now Sinnergy kissed Honeysuckle's pink head and fluttered her eyebrows. "She needs us both, Dex. Let me put her back in her crib, then I'll take you to bed and devour you. We'll forget about all this."

Dextra was beyond regret or consolation. "I'm too old for these dramas. Give me my daughter."

Honeysuckle stirred, waking, and Sinnergy came to her feet. "If I can't have you, you can't have her!"

Faced with the bright glassiness in her eyes, Dextra went cold.

"Say you love me!" Sinnergy screamed, abruptly holding a styrette near the baby's fat cheek as she struggled weakly and began to cry.

"Baby, you *know* I love you," Dextra said, eyes fixed on the trembling styrette. "Why would I be trying so hard to drive you away if I didn't love you?"

Melodramatic dialogue came easily to someone who had been selling fiction since she was a teenager and had been elected Hierarch three times now, and melodramatic dialogue was precisely what her violent ex wanted to hear. Sill, Dextra recognized her own limitations and remained motionless.

She had been born and reared in Crapshoot, the Periapt system's oldest and biggest O'Neill, where the essence of space colony survival was coexistence, equable conflict resolution, and nonviolence. Martial arts were neither condoned nor taught to average citizens; mere possession of a firearm meant years of punitive labor or even the termination of life and the recycling of all biomass.

Raised to be self-reliant and socially responsible—educated, like her mother and grandmother, at a women's academy—Dextra saw weapons and violence as more likely to be the problem than the solution. On Periapt, confronting a less disciplined society, she had had to adapt to survive, though she had never overcome her aversion to mayhem. Someone else was going to have to handle that rough stuff; she'd known that even before she'd reached the gazebo.

Now she let confusion and misgiving show on her face.

"But you wouldn't hurt Honey, would you?" She leaned toward Sinnergy slightly, squinting at the styrette. "I don't even see a dose in that hypo."

"You nearsighted old cow!" Sinnergy, brandishing the injector, startled the baby into crying louder. "You need an ophthalmic tuck—"

It was Sinnergy's turn to be startled. A golden right hand had reached over her shoulder to snatch the styrette away. The left slipped around her throat, forearm locking in a choke hold that lifted her off her feet and made her loosen her grip on the infant. Dextra rushed in to grab Honeysuckle; Sinnergy didn't resist, understanding what might happen to her neck.

Tonii, Dextra's all-around troubleshooter, chicken-winged and immobilized Sinnergy. The hands holding her were sinewy but had a longish grace.

Tonii was wearing archery whites, as if fresh from some rec time on the villa's range. Power swelled the V of the torso, but there was also a flare to the hips. Fibrous muscle mass showed a graceful suppleness. The breasts that mounded against the archery shirt were small but nicely curved. Tonii's face could have been an exotic woman's or that of an imperfectly beautiful man, and the cropped tow hair had been combed into a unisex gutterglam cut.

The style was fitting only for an engeneered gynander, a hermaphrodite with two functioning sets of genitalia and mixed secondary sexual characteristics. Optimization had endowed the gynanders with reflexes, physical strength, and coordination in the lead corner of the human performance envelope. Like the Manipulants, they were living artifacts of Byron Sarz's early LAW biogenetic research.

Tonii looked to Dextra for instructions just as Ben came on-line to say that the Preservationist guests were getting impatient.

"You broke the rules," Dextra told Sinnergy while she patted Honeysuckle's back. "The adjudicator's order gave you visiting rights under *my* supervision. My attorneys will be petitioning the court within minutes to sever all contact between you and Hon. Counterfile if you wish, but surveillance cams have recorded this whole scuffle." She paused to press the child to her chest. "In the meantime, if you try another stunt like this, Tonii'll book you on a one-way flight in an ambulance."

Sinnergy could barely grunt, let alone answer. Dextra departed, looking to deliver the baby into Maripol's care, while Tonii half carried, half pain-marched Sinnergy off in the opposite direction.

The gynander took Sinnergy down past the motor stables and opened the personnel hatch of the villa's trade entrance. Sinnergy understood that the most faithful vassal in Dextra's little fiefdom was not susceptible to bribes or seduction, even though she had bedded Tonii once and troised with Dextra and the gynander several times.

Opening the hatch let in a rush of noise and aromas from the nacre, trillion-faceted city just outside. On Dextra's idyllic hilltop, with its high walls and sound cancellation system, this might have been a quiet rural afternoon, but Abraxas—the unsleeping capital of Periapt and LAW—was going full-bore.

Tonii took her through the surveillance and security vestibule and out to the springy green energy-return sidewalk nap beyond, where 'e released her. "Put Honey out of your mind and find your bearings, Sinn. Stay away from HauteFlash and from everyone who resides here. Don't make me hurt you."

Rubbing her arm where bruises would appear, Sinnergy giggled eerily, then spit at Tonii's face. Tonii dodged the spittle by tilting 'ers head aside just enough. Something that was part grin, part storm warning moue crooked 'ers full lips.

"*Keep* Hon, that little misconception!" Sinnergy rasped. "I didn't want a baby, I wanted *Dex*, you dumb-ass she-male *synthia*!"

Tonii studied her stonily. "Many people want Dextra Haven one way or another. That's precisely why her defenses are so good."

Sinnergy sniffed and wiped her mouth like a neurodyne addict in need of a wheeze. "Take me back inside, Tonii. I won't make trouble."

"Trouble's all you can be for Dextra, Sinn." Something viridescent came into the gynander's expression. "And please keep in mind that I'm one of her principal defenses."

Tonii went back through the vestibule and the personnel hatch. The heavy valve closed, leaving Sinnergy dazed and bereft on the Abraxas pedway.

CHAPTER
ELEVEN

Dextra had chosen the solarium to engage the Preservationists because of its atmosphere of openness and light. They wielded tremendous influence and prerogative, like Dextra herself, which was why it had seemed a good idea to pry them away from the Lyceum. There was a kind of natural law that made Hierarchs more reasonable as their distance from the Lyceum's pomp and grandeur increased. Today that effect was not helping as much as she had hoped it would.

Returning from the confrontation with her ex, she was received with chilly stares and frozen smiles. Nevertheless, she gave them back warm for cold while rearranging her peplos and letting her varimorph executive chair recontour itself to suit her thin frame. The conference table was there simply to provide everyone with psychological space. Twirling autoservers circled, offering tea cakes, sushi, cold beer, and more, but nobody was indulging.

The data mosaics were continuing to flash the *Scepter* survey team's findings regarding the planet Aquamarine. Opticals of sundry Aquamarine throwback cultures ran on-screen with analysts' comments on the nature of the inscrutable Oceanic and cost projections for mounting a second LAW mission to the Eyewash star system.

Most LAW bureaucrats felt otherwise, but Dextra had a growing certainty that Aquamarine could play a role in resolving the Roke conflict. Somewhere on or in that water balloon of a world was the key to accord or even victory. But Lyceum approval of an AlphaLAW mission to Aquamarine

71

was going to require a host of Preservationist votes, and Dextra meant to have them.

"I apologize for the delay," she began. "But since we've covered just about all points of disagreement, I think we can start cutting a deal here that'll make everybody happy."

She showed confidence and charisma by political second nature, but she had a feeling she'd lost any chance of swaying them in the short time it had taken to rescue Honeysuckle.

How now, *foul* Tao? she asked herself.

Old Albert P'ing, noble-looking and innovative as a treadmill, thumped the table with a hand more beautifully manicured than Dextra's own. "Dextra, the Hierarchate will *not* squander a full-scale Alpha mission to a planet with little usable surface area, medieval cultures, and no unique resources. Most assuredly, we've nothing to learn from people who live in terror of some soggy, overgrown cell mass!"

"But the Roke seem to fear the Oceanic, too," she reminded him. "Or at least *something* about the place has made them keep their distance; we know that much. The *Scepter* survey team found debris consistent with Roke design elsewhere in the Eyewash system but no evidence of Roke presence on or near Aquamarine. Am I the only one here who sees the possible significance of that? If nothing else, Aquamarine could serve as a safe harbor for LAW forces."

She did not mention peace because peace was not something the Human Preservationist Party had much interest in pursuing.

Doll Van Houten, two years older than Dextra but as sleekly soignée as a fashion database icon, went *"Phui!"* dismissively. "It's as simple as this: The Roke don't consider Aquamarine as any more strategic than we do. Darling Dex, planet Hierophant is out there for the taking, a few light-years beyond Aquamarine but an industrial and technological powerhouse."

Dextra frowned at her. "You're not intrigued by the thought of uncovering the technological wonders left behind by the Optimants' civilization?"

"Archaeology?" Doll asked. "Please, Dex. Save your

enthusiasm for two-hundred-year-old relics for the curators of the Museum of Interplanetary Studies."

Albert P'ing sniffed, "Technology Assessment Bureau has reason to suspect that Hierophant antivirus research might allow us to return to neural interface cybernetting—pre-Plague style—in due course."

Dextra shot him an arch look. "I'll believe that when I see it."

Calvin Lightner, majority leader of the Lyceum and kingpin of the Preservationists, eyed her from across the table, showing only a polite disregard for her lack of faith. Now that he'd gone neutant—embracing the most ascetic manifestation of the asexual movement—his ageless face put Dextra in mind of a machine shop blank waiting to be stamped with humanity.

In addition to courses of libido-deadening treatments, Lightner had undergone surgical excision of his genitalia. But since no right-thinking Preservationist would undergo permanent asexualization, his reproductive organs had been deposited in cryo-sequester. Intense population growth was considered sacred to the war effort, and party leaders had to at least give the appearance of standing ready to help carry on the human race if called upon. Power players who showed distaste for or even renounced sex at the same time legislated for larger families.

"The point remains," Doll chimed in, "that we must move to annex Hierophant now, before they acquire military technologies and consolidate defenses that close our window of opportunity. Think lead time, Dex!"

Lead time—a LAW preoccupation. Periapt had come through the Cyberplagues relatively unscathed, but it was a planet short on strategic resources such as metals and petrochemicals. Periapt's partially intact infrastructure had helped it climb out of post-Plague debility faster than had any other world, but a number of stellar systems were closing the gap. If Periapt's once-only edge in lead time were frittered away, if more resource-rich worlds achieved parity in military, industrial, and space technology, LAW's expansion and the new wealth of Periapt would be over. To perpetuate itself, LAW had to go on as a kind of virus—as opportunistic a one as possible.

"At the very least Hierophant could be producing a new starship per year for us, and the same holds true for Zion and Shabash." Doll made the words sound like a serenade. "The Hierarchate hasn't the time or wherewithal to waste on Aquamarine."

Dextra nodded as if considering those words, though secretly she was certain there was more to it than that. The *Scepter* team had not been sequestered simply because LAW was fretting about the allocation of assets. Everything pointed to the conclusion that Aquamarine's Oceanic was a rather powerful intelligent being. If the single inhabitant of the planet's only sea *was* intelligent, it would be only the second sophant life-form on record, after the Roke—or the third, if one counted the pre-Cyberplague AIs.

The Preservationists were running scared, Dextra surmised, from the danger of the existence of an organism that might be more evolved than *Homo sapiens*. Revelations about the Oceanic could well alter the public's attitude about the Roke or quite possibly erode support for LAW hegemony.

Dextra didn't want to be sidetracked, either. "Wouldn't we do better by considering all the facts? If Aquamarine has nothing to offer us, then the survey team is being quarantined for no good reason. I propose that LAW trot them in from the outback to attest to Aquamarine's worthlessness."

Cal Lightner stirred at last. "I'm given to understand that the *Scepter* team will have all it can do answering charges of dereliction of duty. It's likely that the acting commander—this Claude Mason person—stands to be court-martialed."

"For bringing back news that doesn't square with this year's fifty-year plan?"

Lightner said, "No. For possible complicity in the deaths of the *Scepter*'s original commander and the other personnel."

Dextra simpered instead of grimacing. "From what I heard, Captain Marlon died in a misadventure of his own planning.

Claude Mason and his people at least carried out a cursory reconnaissance and amassed data on the Oceanic."

Doll flicked beringed fingers. "Those smatterings of data are disjointed and inconclusive."

Dextra gazed back disingenuously. "Except as they prove *your* assertions?"

It went on like that for another hour, with Dextra pressing hard but making no headway. She brought to bear what leverage she could, threatening to tie up or help defeat legislation and appointments they wanted, but they were adamant. The missions to Zion, Shabash, and Hierophant would enrich the dynastic groups to which Doll, Lightner, and even P'ing belonged. The building of those stupendous fortunes and the political careers that protected them were what LAW and the Roke Conflict were really about.

When she holoed up proof that monies for an Aquamarine AlphaLAW mission could be shifted from other, overfattened budget lines, Lightner unbent enough to show some anger. "Kindly keep your hand out of *my* pocket, Madame Haven," he advised.

She tried hard to resist but couldn't. "Why, Cal? Since the operation, what's down there to loot or damage?"

In no time she was seeing them to their airlimo and watching them lift off into the traffic over Abraxas. She had never even gotten to broach the subject of the *Sword of Damocles*, now in orbit around Periapt, and the Concordance forces onboard it.

Claude Mason, recently returned from Aquamarine, looked out on the Blades, the most forlorn of Periapt's high deserts.

I never wished for this, he told himself. No, not for this.

That wasn't to say that he had not looked forward to the glory and reward that he expected would greet his return. But uncertainty over the fate of his Aquam wife and child had plunged him into wretched sorrow earlier on. Then had come LAW's shocking condemnation of his survey team's conduct and results.

It had become clear when LAW reassumed control of

the starship that the higher-ups were not pleased with what Mason and the rest had to say about Aquamarine, the Oceanic, or the planet's regressed populations—the only legacy of Old Earth's techno-elite Optimants. No one cared that Aquamarine seemed to be anathema to the Roke or that the Oceanic was a being of unprecedented capabilities and importance.

So here he was in the Blades, a stone-finned sweep of mauve wasteland, wild and raw and intimidatingly beautiful. Blades Station was his prison, and its sole saving grace was that it was far from ocean water.

To finish off his will to endure, Mason had received news of death and financial ruin in his blood family and abandonment by his espoused several—his marital group. Verushka, Chen, and Monty had annulled Mason from the relationship in absentia and had signed on with the AlphaLAW mission to Tintaginel. The cosmic joke had a double punch line: The three embryos that had been his share of the settlement were among the tens of thousands destroyed in the ghastly Cybervirus slaughter of the Providence Clinic in Abraxas.

Nowadays when Claude Mason wished, he did so in a vague and fatalistic way for divine intervention. He knew that wishing couldn't make it so, yet he was powerless to stop himself. He felt marooned in that final night on Aquamarine, on the walkway of the monumental lighthouse at New Alexandria. Mason and Incandessa side by side as the waves of Amnion crashed against the rocks and the Oceanic put on its overawing, unknowable show.

He yearned beyond words to be back there, to hold Incandessa once more, to helo himself and her into hiding until the *Scepter* was departed on her preprogrammed voyage home, to see his wife safely through childbirth and raise their son or daughter to be kinder and stronger than Claude Mason had been.

For all he knew, the child had been born an Anathemite—an outcast—affected by one of Aquamarine's countless mutagens and left exposed on a hillside for the jackjaws and rakefangs.

Countless times each day he thought that Boon would have been able to straighten him out, tell him what to do and how to proceed. Boon with his candor, steadfastness, and penetrating mind. But Boon was dead, horribly unmade by the Oceanic in the sea swells off Execution Dock that final night on Aquamarine.

He had not related the incident to the debriefing panels or quarantine authorities, had not even told everyone in the *Scepter* crew. There was enough peril from LAW's scrutiny as it was. He had absolved himself of blame for Boon's death but had yet to stop it from gnawing at him. What if the Oceanic could just . . . *curse* a man?

An air cushion turbofanning made Mason look downslope: a helipod was coming his way, out of Blades Station. He'd switched off his plugphone, beacon and receiver both, so whoever it was had to have followed his bootprints in the mauve sand. He came to his feet, dusting off the seat of his wearwithal. As the helo began to descend, he could make out two individuals in the canlike airframe, one of them piloting with controls built into the armpit high rests. The turbine whistle fell as the 'pod approached, grounding in a fierce fan blast of desert grit.

Mason wasn't surprised to see that the woman was a LAW officer. She walked up the hill to him and put her hands on the waist of her flightsuit, thumbs to the rear. "Thanks for taking your phone off-line, Mason. I really needed to waste an hour tracking you down." She pushed a strand of shiny black hair from her face. "I'm Deitz. I've been assigned to represent you at the inquest."

Mason nodded knowingly. "No wonder you're in such a rush. I'm sure that LAW's eager to get on with the court-martial."

She frowned at him. "No one has said anything about a court-martial, Administrator. This is only an inquest." She glanced back at the helo. "But I do have several hundred questions for you, and I'm going to need the answers by tomorrow A.M. if I'm to be any help to your case."

"I've no expectations, Ms. Deitz."

She nodded. "Then the sooner we get started, the better." Her pointed chin indicated the helo. "It'll be a tight fit for three, but it's the fastest route back to Blades Station."

Mason swept his hand in a gentlemanly gesture. "After you, Ms. Deitz."

CHAPTER
TWELVE

In A.D. 2103 the first colonial expedition to leave Sol had fled for Aquamarine, cynosure of the Eyewash system, bearing with it the agencies of its own destruction and the obliteration of its grandiose, even megalomaniacal dream.

A breakaway conspiracy of self-styled techno-utopian *Übermenschen*, they had dubbed their new order the Optimacy—with a nod to the Romans—and themselves Optimants. Their regressed Aquam descendants called them the Beforetimers, and some LAW sources referred to them as the First Colonists.

The Optimants envisioned the seeding of nearby star systems, then the galaxy, and in due course all galaxies with its progeny and concept of a scientopian Eden. Contact with the Roke was still generations off, and there was no hint of the existence of the Oceanic.

The Optimant's grand scheme dated back nearly two centuries at that point, and some of the technology remained to be devised. Even at greatly subluminal speeds, replicating seedships could carry forth humans in cachesleep, plasm, and/or dormant fetuses to propagate *Homo sapiens* throughout the Milky Way. The 45,000-odd Optimants meant to have a critical head start on any such competing effort from the Earthbound masses, whom they called the Mundanes. Most Optimants were of Caucasian stock, and for many there was an unapologetic element of racism in the destiny they were charting.

The linchpin of their original plan was that all resided in or had access to the L5 colony *Thomas Edison*, a multiconglomerate-built O'Neill that was a research facility, factory complex, resort, and experimental living arkology. The zero-point-energy and spacedrive application research being carried forward there was central to their enterprise.

The Optimants would have preferred to covertly mount their departure from the solar system. That hope was dashed when the nearly nineteen billion have-not voters on Earth swept the Stewardship coalition into power. The Stewardship's agenda of deprivatization and enforced egalitarianism threatened to bring *Edison* and similar offworld resources under the direct command of central government overseers.

The Optimants' fallback plan called for a complete break with the Mundanes. The tens of thousands who were onboard the O'Neill constituted over eighty percent of the Optimacy's core membership. Their many dupes were left behind almost without exception.

Thomas Edison fired up a zero-point-energy drive that authorities had thought to be a crude prototype. Sympathizers who had rendered secret aid to the Optimants abetted their flight as well. The three-kilometer-long O'Neill accelerated ponderously out of orbit, easily destroying the first pursuit sent after it, and eventually outran the rest. Those who weren't loyal Optimants were dispensed with, their remains recycled in one fashion or another.

Rechristened *Atlas Shrugged*, their starship tapped the limitless quantum foam for its power and accelerated into the trackless darkness.

With them went all the resources and technological break-throughs that were theirs by right of genius or at least possession. All remaining data concerning zero-point energy as well as bioengineering discoveries, radical AI/AL cybernetic advances, and other *Edison* innovations were spurious or had been wiped from Solarian records.

The Optimants coldly calculated that Earth would require a minimum of two generations to mount a punitive expedition.

Only a small watch was required to run the hijacked O'Neill, although R&D would be carried on in shifts throughout the centuries-long crawl to Aquamarine, over sixty-five light-years from Earth. To conserve consumables, abate crowding, and allow them to live to see their destination, the Optimants set up a cachesleep apparatus and a rota of long suspended animation between waking duty tours.

The fugitives' data had indicated abundant water on Aquamarine. Their preliminary survey of the planet made them exultant. Granted, it was vexingly short on landmass, but Aquamarine offered everything needed to carry forward their high destiny.

No communications or other artificial electromagnetic signatures were being detected from Earth. Whether that was due to some catastrophe or to the difficulty of reception across the light-years, the Optimants could not be sure. As time and Terra's silence wore on, the fugitives became convinced that some planetary breakdown had overwhelmed its wretched masses. There was even talk of an eventual return to assume dominion.

In dealing with the Oceanic, they understood from the outset that they were confronting an unguessably powerful entity with absolutely no tolerance for contact. The limited observations convinced even the Optimants of the wisdom of live and let live. The inscrutable Oceanic showed no objection to their presence so long as they quarantined themselves to land and sky. While the marine resources of the planet were clearly vast, they were not indispensable to the high destiny; the humans adopted a policy of total avoidance and painstaking nonprovocation.

The staggeringly beautiful water world and the rest of its system provided all the raw materials for the next step in their high crusade. Many felt they owed it to themselves, after their long confinement, to savor fresh air, elbowroom, and natural sunlight as a reward for their hardships and successes. They erected structures of grandeur and whimsy and road systems that were more aesthetic than practical. They indulged themselves in fanciful and even bizarre cultural trappings. The preeminent among them proved their status by building flying pavilions that migrated through the sky on endless circuits of revelry. Others carried out engineering projects on an imposing scale: riverine rechanneling, dams, bridges, monuments of overweening scale. Much of it was a sop to the Optimant ego, supposed proof that while the Oceanic controlled the sea utterly, the Optimants were masters of the high ground.

The Optimants wanted a large workforce a lot sooner than conventional childbearing could give it to them. Highly automated GeStations and child-rearing complexes were established. Seedship research was readily applicable. Aquamarine's biosphere harbored countless mutagens, but genetic stabilization was basic science for the First Colonists.

Even more than their signal progress in robotics and bio-engineering, their vast leaps in artificial intelligence and biocybernetic interfaces allowed them to create, manufacture, and construct at an unprecedented rate. Subdural cybernetic shunts, quantum chip technology, and omninetworking made each individual a protean task force—an enhanced intellect—at need.

Accordingly, with the raw materials of Aquamarine's surface areas at their command, as well as those of the planet's moons, the immigrants spent much of the next seven baseline decades populating their new world, indoctrinating their new populations, forging a techno-industrial power base, and playing demiurge.

But impediments came from unexpected quarters. R&D conducted in transit and after arrival was pointing to dramatic improvements in the zero-point-energy drive. What was the point of launching a slower starship when another few years of work would yield a vessel that could complete the voyage in a fraction of the time? Adding to the complication, research promised even greater leaps in speed. It made no sense to begin a craft that would have to undergo reclamation before it was half-finished.

A more divisive debate centered on just what kind of ship's complement the Optimants should send forth. The majority still favored the proliferation of natural and/or cloned Optimant offspring, but a vocal and influential minority pushed for bioengineered *Meta sapiens* or even the bodies inhabited by godlike AIs drawn from Optimant matrices. There was also bitter disagreement about which of Earth's traditions and values to immortalize. Contentious meetings ended more and more often with nothing resolved.

Earth was a low priority, to be looked into at some future date. Confirmation arrived that other Terran expeditions with relativistic drives faster than that of *Atlas Shrugged* were still inferior to those in the Optimacy's CAD/CAM banks. The Optimants' giant head start made them contemptuous of any threat from planets such as Periapt, Concordance, and the rest. They were increasingly absorbed with a new facet of their high destiny: personal immortality. In the meantime there were the delights of their planetary empire to enjoy.

Until the Cyberplagues came to Aquamarine.

Early analyses suggested that the initial vector was the long-range surveillance arrays trained on Earth, but further investigation was not to be. Perhaps because they had evolved the most pervasive computational ecology humans had ever devised, the Optimants and their offspring suffered the worst devastation.

The havoc wrought by a worldwide infrastructure gone berserk was horrific enough, but even ghastlier were the monsters suddenly sprung to life within the Optimants themselves. The kamikaze crash of an automated OTV and the *berserker-gang* of foundry lasers were less terrifying than the rebellion of physioimplants and cyber-shunted AIs.

The fortunate ones were killed quickly by a simple cortex burn or an OD from a pharmaceutical bleb. Others battered their bones to jelly in imposed seizures or thrashed in agony while subminiaturized automatons savaged their bodies from within.

There were indications that the Oceanic took measures against what it considered aggression, but those measures ceased early on, possibly because the Cyberplague apocalypse carried no danger to Amnion, Aquamarine's single sea. Some speculated that the Oceanic was intimidated by the orgasm of destruction playing out across ground, sky, and space.

Only in the aftermath of the first cataclysmic day did the Optimacy's true vulnerability become clear. Their power had lain not in their artifacts and wealth but in information, and that was suddenly gone as a result of suiciding AIs and ALs. Because they had had the utmost confidence in their cybernetic edifice, hardcopy and other backup formats scarcely existed. The few bound books on the planet were mostly literary and historical works of no practical value.

People were helpless without their smart apparatuses and/or AI collaborators. There were virtually no manual tools with which to fashion higher tools to repair their complex world and no data on how to proceed. Engineers who could do CAD/CAM miracles in a single work shift were suddenly at a loss about how to build a fire. Weeping doctors, impotent and lost, squatted before dying patients in the burning ruins. Even when crude surgical instruments were improvised, there were no AI dopplegangers at their ear to diagnose, guide, and oversee. Aristocrats of the High Destiny were digging through garbage for food scraps, cowering from wild predators, tying rags around their feet. The irreplaceable underpinnings of their intricate, interdependent civilization had simply vanished.

When the initial fury of the Cyberplagues was past, the Optimants discovered that they had a vulnerability far beyond that of their computers: they weren't really a homogeneous society, after all. Rather than a cohesive and unified world-nation, they were nothing more than an alliance of egocentrics kept from fundamental conflict by their immense assets.

Though the majority were from essentially the same racial stock and broad cultural background, they found abundant excuses for hatred and hostility. There was no shortage of proximate motives for violence. The GeStation-bred labor forces found rationales for establishing agendas as well, including the extermination of the Optimants.

Ironically, it was the onset of survivor wars that reformed

tight and circumscribed communities. Scraps of knowledge were slowly regained. But there was no way back to Optimacy or anything like it. The age of the Beforetimers was over.

CHAPTER THIRTEEN

"The court is particularly interested in the incidents that led to the death of Captain—" Deitz ran a manicured finger down the screen of her electronic assistant.

"Marlon," Mason supplied.

Deitz nodded and tapped the screen. "Yes, here he is." She gazed at Mason. "I've read your report, Administrator, but I'm afraid I'm going to have to ask you to run through it again." She shook her head. "There is so much I don't understand . . ."

Mason snorted a laugh. "You're in good company, Ms. Deitz."

She smiled. "I'm sure I am, Administrator."

She brought her gaze back to the screen for a moment as the wind howled outside the tinted window wall of Blades Station. The view encompassed miles and miles of Periapt wasteland.

"Suppose we get right to that day at—Gapshot, is it?"

"Styx Strait," Mason corrected her. "Gapshot is the town overlooking the strait that separates Scorpia—Aquamarine's principal landmass—from the Trans-Bourne, an island to the south. It earns most of its profit from tariffs levied on Jut-hoppers."

"Jut-hoppers?"

"Traders crazy enough to dare crossing the Styx Strait when the tide is out." Mason laughed, mostly to himself. "When the Oceanic's out."

Mason took a breath. "Gapshot was ruled by an Aquam named Majestica; she was the hereditary autarch of the place back then. As shrewd and relentless a woman as I've ever met. Marlon was synapshit over her. He was older, at least in somatic years, and should have had the upper hand, but she played him brilliantly, offering herself like a prize Marlon couldn't have unless he met her price."

"And what price was that?"

"A permanent land link between southern Scorpia and the Trans-Bourne that Gapshot—Majestica—would control."

"A bridge, you mean."

"Yes and no. Marlon understood the risk from LAW for enhancing the lot of a single ruler. Leaving behind a big-ticket construction project would let the indigs make their own progress in LAW's absence. It was such a fundamental violation of doctrine that Marlon refused to give in—no matter how much he wanted her.

"But Captain Marlon was a man whose ego and visions of personal glory responded to stroking, and a lot of members of the *Scepter*'s crew were eager to please." Mason motioned to Deitz's machine. "Check your data banks for the psych profiles on a kiss-ass named Nick Musto."

"Planetological Sciences," the lawyer said after a moment.

"Musto suggested a solution to Marlon's dilemma. Why not simply raise the juts to serve as a permanent causeway, well above any high-tide line? That way the whole thing could be explained to LAW as a planet morphing experiment of sorts.

"Marlon loved the idea, of course. He persuaded himself that the land link could be rationalized as the co-opting of a solidly loyal indig sovereign. There was talk that he was thinking of taking Majestica back to Periapt or even remaining behind after the *Scepter* departed." Mason gave his head a rueful shake.

"Go on, Administrator," Dietz told him.

"Musto's plan called for the use of a prototype plasma drilling rig that would punch through the littoral on the Trans-Bourne side of the strait and penetrate all the way to a magma bleb several thousand meters down. The engineers were confident that the upwelling would plug the Styx Strait for good. Any excess magma could simply be diverted into Amnion by means of judicious lateral enlargements of the original drill hole. Naturally, the drilling would be done at low tide, so there'd be no contact between machinery and sea."

"So this creature, the Oceanic, wouldn't mind."

"Unfortunately, it did mind. The moment the plasma drill penetrated the superficial rock and hit pockets of salt water underlying the juts, the whole damned planet started shaking."

Dietz's eyebrows beetled. "You can attest to this personally?"

"I was right there in Gapshot, though on the sidelines, you might say. Majestica, Marlon, and his staff were inside a command and control VTOL. There were also two linesman helos on the lookout for any devout Aquam addled enough to try to interfere, plus half a dozen hoverpods serving as spotters for the op."

"Did anyone attempt to interfere?"

"No. Marlon and Majestica had managed to convince everyone that here at last was a human empowerment that could defy the Oceanic."

"The Oceanic caused a quake, I take it."

"A quake?" Mason said. "A quake could have been dealt with. No, Ms. Dietz, the Oceanic produced a manifestation none of us had ever seen, something the Aquam call a Skyskein."

Dietz glanced at the screen. "I read something about these manifestations . . ."

"You won't find much in there," Mason said. "Manifestations are just one of the Oceanic's inexplicable activities. They can be observed all across the planet." He paused, then grinned. "Think of them as living geysers."

"Living?"

Mason nodded. "The Skyskein reached up, following the line of the drill rig, and took hold of the flying crane that was holding it. It grabbed the thing like a fist and yanked it back into the strait. Then about two million cubic meters of seawater just mounded up and moved over onto the beach at the Gapshot side of the juts, covering the LAW tech support field station we'd set up. The seawater covered everything."

Mason swallowed hard. "I remember the temperature falling about fifteen degrees and the wind kicking up. Farther out I could see a huge bowl in the surface of the ocean where the water had been displaced into the sky and onto dry land.

"The water kept rising until I couldn't even see the sky. It swallowed the lifter and Captain Marlon's VTOL, and streams of it—like flycatcher tongues—nailed the spotter craft and the linesman helos." Mason wiped sweat from his upper lip. "I could see bits of the craft swirling in the turbulence of the uplifted water. I thought for sure it was going to come down right on me."

Dietz studied him in quiet concern. "What did you do?"

"What did I do? I dropped to my goddamn knees, flung my arms over my head, and waited for the end."

She put a hand atop his, as if to calm him, but he continued to quiver.

"We lost half the survey team to that creature, and the entire shoreline of the juts was changed. As the senior survivor, I became the de facto commander of the *Scepter*."

Dietz waited a moment before saying. "The crew accepted you?"

Mason blew out his breath. "They recognized my authority. I tried to be more than a figurehead, but we were a disillusioned lot from that day on."

"Is it true that you married an Aquam woman, Administrator?"

He nodded. "Incandessa. Of the family Rhodes."

"And your second in command—"

"Boon."

Her finger touched the screen. "Eisley Boon. He's listed as killed in action. Obviously, if he was your second, he didn't die at the Styx Strait."

"That's correct."

Dietz sat back in her chair. "Then when and how did he die?"

Mason averted his eyes. "On our last night onworld."

"Yes, there are several things about your hasty departure that remain unclear." Dietz leaned forward. "Tell me about that final night on Aquamarine."

Dextra took a roundabout route through the grounds to her study. She brought her plugphone on-line but avoided the household holo terminals, preferring to hear her backlog one item at a time rather than see it all in hyperparsed mosaic.

Ben had left a short items-waiting list.

Her first husband was suing because she had withheld his support payment pending court reappraisal of his earning power.

The High Periapt Repertory Company wanted to kick off its next season with a revival of Dextra's best known play, *And on the Way, We Dropped It* provided that she would grant permission to contemporize it somehow. The cordial, witty inquiry came from the troupe's new artistic director, Nike Lightner, daughter and favorite of Hierarch Cal.

Her publisher was again begging permission to issue a collection of her letters, since she had refused to write an autobiography or cooperate with a biographer.

Appended to Lyceum public information was a schedule of available seats for Hierarchs and senior staff wishing to conduct media-op and fact-finding tours of near-orbit LAW facilities, including the currently debarking interstellar vessel *Sword of Damocles*.

And Sinnergy had filed for sole custody of Honeysuckle.

But all those things were secondary. Foremost in her mind was the need to rally support to spring the members of the *Scepter* survey team from administrative detention and get public support for an AlphaLAW mission to Aquamarine.

Once in the study, she cranked up the aircirc and lit a swizzle-stick-thin cigarillo of Trinity tobakkum. The varimorph lounger had just reshaped itself to her body when a chirp from Ben interrupted her thinking.

"Please accept my apologies for bothering you while you're working," Ben said, "but we've just received an anonymous burst transmission. Audio without visual."

"Originating from?"

"Undetermined. It seems to have simply *arisen* out of the municipal grid," he answered.

"Put it through."

"Madame Hierarch Haven," the caller began. "Please be advised that an inner circle of Preservationists and their LAW partisans are planning to discredit and incriminate the subjugated forces from Concordance while they're still onboard the starship *Sword of Damocles*." The voice was flat and artificial, obviously processed to prevent ID and stress analysis.

"The Exts?" Dextra said in guarded surprise. "Why on Periapt—"

"Chiefly to discredit you, Madame Hierarch."

Dextra understood. Over a decade earlier she had been a prime mover in the Rationalist Party's drive to change LAW policy regarding the treatment of former belligerents. The treaty that had wrung an oath of enlistment from the Exts had been one of the more high-profile fruits of her labors.

Unfortunately for Dextra and the Exts alike, Periapt had become addicted to its periodic economic rushes from starships crammed with resources and technological plunder. Hostilities with the Roke had slowly gained momentum as a consequence of the obliteration of two human planetary populations, resulting in a political climate very different from the one that had prevailed when AlphaLAW Commissioner Renquald had been told to be magnanimous in victory. In the current climate there was much less compassion for defeated annexed-worlders, especially ones like the Exts.

"Our analysis of the Preservationists' plan," the voice continued, "suggests that your combination of entry, high visibility, Rationalist credentials, and Hierarchate authority makes you the optimal choice to intervene on behalf of the Concordance forces."

"Me?" Dextra said in genuine confusion. "What can I do?"

"Consider, Madame Hierarch, that you possess an open invitation to conduct media-op tours of near-orbit LAW facilities, including the *Sword of Damocles*. Properly finessed, media exposure could permit the Exts to reach Periapt with at least the appearance of cooperation and goodwill all around."

Dextra mulled it over briefly. "Your answer doesn't exactly speak to my question, but I'm willing to ignore that for the moment. I do, however, demand to know to whom I'm speaking and just why you have an interest in what happens to a couple of hundred Concordancers."

The voice took several seconds to respond. "Let us say for
the time being that our interest in the Exts has a direct bearing
on your interest in the planet Aquamarine. We who make this
contact speak for the Quantum College, Hierarch Haven. You
need only agree to enroll and all will be revealed."

Open-mouthed, Dextra leaned back in the lounger. Well,
how now, foul Tao? she wondered.

CHAPTER
FOURTEEN

Maybe LAW understands war and the Exts never really did, Burning brooded as he stepped through a hatch at Frame 104. On the other side of the hatch a half-frightened, half-furious LAW Aerospace Forces lieutenant waited with a half dozen or so Aero Police armed with neuroprods, bumpguns, and waround tubes.

Burning was wearing a 'baller, and so were his staffers and senior cadre. Ghost and Daddy D, bringing up the rear, stopped when Burning did. The enlisted rating who had guided the three forward into that part of *Sword of Damocles* saluted and made herself scarce.

"They're in there," the Aerospace Forces officer told Burning. He gestured toward a flag-status suite, its hatch decorated with the insignia of Vice Field Marshal Ufak—Vukmirovic's right hand—who was returning to Periapt for promotion and reassignment.

"I want *all* you growlers back in your own part of the ship in plus-five minutes," the lieutenant warned. "And counting."

Burning held himself in check. He hadn't been able to track down where or when some Periapt on *Damocles* had hung that nickname on the Exts, though he had gotten better at not letting his anger show. He looked at the lieutenant mildly.

"*Your* OD is the one who wants them ejected. If you've got such warm rads for the job, fine. Delta-V. We'll observe."

The Periapt gritted his teeth. Instead of saying anything, he pointedly held up his wrist UNEX and glared at the lapsed-time function.

Burning reminded himself that he had almost five and a half

subjective years left in the traces with people like the AP.
"Forget I said that, Lieutenant. We'll take care of this."

There had already been enough friction between Exts and
Periapts; for that matter, there had been too much between Exts
and Exts. Big as it was, the starship was confining, especially
for Exts, who were for the most part restricted to a few specific
internal spaces. A few more months of travel, and there would
have been a mutiny. He led Ghost and Daddy D to the stateroom door, then stepped into the foyer of Ufak's sumptuous
quarters.

LAW moguls saw no virtue in spartan living. What with its
soft lighting, thick draperies, and plush bulkhead upholstery,
those quarters struck Burning as something more on the order
of a Costa Hedonia love-hotel suite than a warcraft stateroom.
The muted music and pretentious and obvious works of art had
been plundered from Concordance First Lands nations.

The place was strewn with minor luxury items that had to
belong to Ufak: gewgaws, tech novelties, and toys no Ext
owned. Burning noticed one headset in particular, a slim black
data-linked visor that gleamed like a crescent of polished
tektite.

He sniffed the musky aromatics and wondered suddenly if
he was breathing some aerosol drug. Too late to double back
for a mask, he realized.

"Just another upper-caste flesh mill," Ghost said with
chilling atonality.

Burning couldn't afford to stop and ask what she meant
by that, and it ate at him, but she was right in specifying
caste. Most LAW overlords saw personal luxury as their
birthright even as they called for stoicism and sacrifice from
subordinates.

He pressed through a curtain of feathery, drifting stuff into
an opulent compartment carpeted in bright colors. There were
varimorph couches, cushiony platforms, and strangely config-
ured furniture that looked more like padded gym equipment or
prettified torture devices.

"Makes me think of past encounters with a speculum,"
Ghost commented dryly.

Daddy D snorted. Burning couldn't tell whether the general was amused or pissed.

In the center of the room was a satiny little valley. A slowly shifting pile of five or six languorous bodies lay in it. There were all the sounds, smells, and cycling body kinetics of diversiform sex. Burning took a step toward them and kicked something with the toe of his soft ship boot—a small gas cartridge, color-coded for the psychotropic drug the Perries called Bong. LAW regs forbade it on the starship, but the Exts had long since tumbled to the fact that regs did not always square with reality, especially forward of Frame 104.

He gave Daddy D a hand signal, and the general grated out of the side of his mouth, "Ten . . . SHHUT!"

They watched with clinical interest as bodies sprang up like a basket of jack-in-the-boxes in flesh-pink, flesh-brown, and gold. The general stood with fists on hips, garrison cap pulled low. Burning's hot flush of embarrassment was plain even in the soft light.

The group sex had included two LAW liaison people, a male and a female, whom Burning ignored for the moment, having no authority over them. That left three Ext men and a woman, all from Zone's several—the sexual menage of which he was the principal.

Two of the Exts were built like Zone—lean below the rib cage with powerful sloping trapezius muscles and shoulders and veined, heavily sinewed arms. The third was burlier, with a pocked and battered face. Shaken by Daddy D's roar, Zone's severalmates were all at attention, erections wilting, nipples subsiding.

Burning glanced at Wetbar, one of the Zone look-alikes and something of a second in command. "Where is he? Sound off; I don't have time to waste on you!"

"He's in the Theater of Dreams, Allgrave," Kino, the Ext woman piped up. She was shapely and delicate-looking, bones prominent beneath her porcelain skin. She indicated an inner doorway with a jerk of her head. "The computer-assisted imagery studio."

She seemed a rather petite creature to be with Zone's circle of roughtraders. Severals were a Periapt and First Lander institution—there weren't many among the Exts—and women tended to cycle through Zone's rather quickly. Kino, a demolitions expert, had been with Zone since Santeria Corners.

"Repair to quarters!" Daddy D ordered the braced quartet. "Consider yourselves under confinement." When they began picking up their uniforms resentfully, he bellowed, "Put 'em on walking! I'd boot you up your asses if I didn't want to ruin my spit shine."

They hobbled and hopped for the suite's main hatch, pulling on what clothing they could as they went. The LAW liaison couple saw the better part of valor, excused themselves tersely, and left.

Burning crossed to the hatch Kino had singled out, with Ghost and Daddy D close behind. The general sounded abashed at having to say "I'd remind the Allgrave that even with push coming to shove, Zone's one of us. Stood with us at Anvil Tor, took the oath to serve out a LAW hitch alongside us."

"And he has his uses," Ghost added in a curiously neutral voice so that Burning couldn't tell if she was agreeing or deriding.

He opened the beautifully flocked hatch to the so-called Theater of Dreams. It seemed to be a smaller space, but it was difficult to tell because of the sound FX, the music and subsonics, and the flickering and flaring light effects. The room contained only two living people but swelled with a kaleidoscope of images.

The glare spilling in derezzed some of the lighting and holo illusions, so that for a moment Burning could see the couple through the mirages clothing them. It was Zone and the other woman currently in his several, an eel-thin and long-shanked gunner whose field name was Strop. Both were naked. He was standing with his knees bent, cupping her buttocks; her legs were wrapped around him. Both wore protective eyecups to avoid having their retinas burned out by the holo lasers.

The room's systemry compensated for the light spill, and the fantasy auras came up again. Walls and ceiling displayed montages of images. Burning, teeth locked, about-faced to order his sister out of the compartment, but she had already slipped past him.

Zone was a skeletal vision of death, here bleached bone and there mummified but muscular, and impossibly endowed. Strop, bucking against him in abandon, was wrapped in a shimmery overlay that gave her the body, face, and scars of Ghost. Strop's scalp was shaven and tattooed, but the compartment's computer-driven hallucinations gave her Ghost's unbound hair, Hussar Plaits and all.

Burning reached for his pistol without any clear idea of what he was going to do. One sequence of events would have him tried by LAW, he supposed, or even by his own Exts. But at least killing Zone would put Ghost beyond the reach of his dark, insidious tidal radius.

Burning's hand got to the holster only to find that it and the 'baller's grip were covered by Daddy D's big, knobby brown one. Burning was trying to decide what to say when he felt the peripheral tingle of the general's sonics shot sweeping the bulkhead opposite with a sustained burst.

The handgun's sonics feature was effective only against animal tissue, but the computer-assisted imaging components in the Theater of Dreams were extremely sensitive and fragile. A string of glassy cracking noises, crystalline tinklings, pops, and sizzling sounds filled the cabin space. Large sections of the holo-illusions vanished, and emergency lights came up to reveal bare bulkhead, projector mounts, sensors, and aroma emitters.

Strop half warbled, half tittered, but Zone showed utter calm, lifting her free of him and setting her feet down in the ankle-high nap. Overrides shot down the imaging system, and the conventional lighting came up.

Most Exts had lost the NoMan stare during the six subjective months of the voyage from Concordance, but Zone had yet to relinquish it. The unblinking protruding eyes saw that it was Daddy D who had shot up the components and also noticed

Burning's hand coming down from his unused handgun; then they went on to lock with Ghost's.

"No oath ever gave the Allgrave any say over a bit of consensual slurp-'n-slide, Burning," Zone said with a leer. "Or aren't we Exts anymore, since you bought us a tour of duty with LAW?"

Burning knew that the misrepresentation was supposed to get him too angry to think. Certainly no military superior or Allgrave had any right of command over a subordinate's personal relations so long as coercion wasn't involved and unit effectiveness wasn't impaired. But there were strong points of common law dealing with provocation and insult as well as recognized matters of honor and personal and family pride. Therefore, Burning was on unsure legal footing. Wishing that he could lash out, he felt heat and color in his face.

Daddy D took up the slack. "Colonel, you're in a restricted area. The Periapt OD wants you out, so move."

Strop made a derisive sound but didn't quite have the nerve to say anything.

Zone wasn't at a loss, however. "If the OD'd bothered to check with Vice Field Marshal Ufak, he'd know that we were *invited* to use this place. In fact, Ufak's planning on joining us later. Besides, we're off duty."

Delecado's glare never wavered. "Nobody's off duty till we de-ass from this crate. LOGCOM's moved up our debarkation time. Y' got two hours to get your battalion strac, Colonel."

Zone had left his utility suit on the carpet but made no move to get dressed, waiting for them to leave. They could have either his compliance or his loss of face but not both, Burning realized. He motioned to his sister and the general.

"We've got other things to do." No salutes were exchanged as they left.

The outer compartment was empty. Burning noticed, as he passed through, that the wraparound data-link visor was gone. He hoped the LAWs had taken it; he had enough problems without having to root out petty thieves.

His thoughts shifted back to Zone. A million gold ducats worth of soldier and about a tin half pip's worth of human being. He remembered the man's almost insane heroism at the sinkhole raid and in a dozen other actions, most of all Santeria Corners.

If ever anyone had found his life's central event, it had been Zone at Santeria Corners: point-blank firefights, bloody knife-work on night infiltrations, sapper assaults, and ambushes. Twice he had called down fire support on his own position. The Exts weren't blind to his flaws and hazards, but they also appreciated his great value in specific venues, as only combat veterans could.

"You'd better see to the Discards personally about our upped debarkation," Burning told Ghost. "We don't want them trying to shove another LOGCOM sergeant's head into a med-specimen sorter."

She saw through him, nodding back toward Zone and showing the faintest amusement. "Afraid I'll linger for a closer look?"

"No, it's just that—"

"Stand easy, Brother. The things Zone demands I don't give up."

Stepping off down the passageway, Burning kept his eyes straight ahead to seal his thoughts. If he wound up having to kill Zone, he wouldn't have to worry anymore about letting people down as Allgrave. After a moment he realized that Ghost was still talking.

"Ufak must be monumentally bored to decide to make it with vile-smelling subhuman Exts."

"Passin' strange, isn't it?" Daddy D weighed in, the tone of his voice letting them know he was thinking more than he was saying.

Despite LAW directives against fraternization, there had been isolated cases of organ grinding between Exts and LAWs, but only among the lower ranks. The general's comment started Burning wondering what it meant that a LAW vice field marshal was suddenly looking to swap body fluids with a bunch of lowly parolees. Perhaps Ufak wanted to get them into a locale with excellent tech surveillance, possibly loosen their

tongues with drink, eros, or aerosol psychotropics to find out
how morale stood or even plant a few ideas.

AlphaLAW Commissioner Renquald had given Burning all
kinds of handlube about how the Exts would remain together,
how they were guaranteed unit cohesion and ethnic identity.
Just maybe the suspect friendliness from Ufak was another
page from Renquald's book of strategy.

When Burning didn't answer Daddy D, Ghost did. "Who
can say how some jaded LAW oligarch gets his wrinkles
steamed?"

Burning shook his head. "Not I. But I don't like our debark
being moved up, either." He, too, stopped short of saying anything more.

When they got back to Ext territory, Daddy D made an
excuse to draw Burning away from his sister. Ghost pretended
to have no interest in the matter and went her way. In the con-
nected locker-size spaces that served as regimental HQ, the
general secured the hatch.

"One more thing about Zone," he began. "Before you
decide to toad-crank him, talk to me."

Burning tried his best to show no reaction but could feel the
heat in his cheeks. "I'm *not* planning on killing him."

"Sure you are—someplace in the back of your head,
anyway. He's an asset, but a time may come when you'll either
have to mow him or watch this whole lash-up come apart. So
all I'm saying is, come see me first. He'll be damn near impossible to take single-handed and head-on."

Before Burning could confirm or deny, Delecado went on.
"Now, what about these games LAW's playing with us? I'd
like to hear your thoughts on their plans for us when we're
transferred down the well. What d' you think they're gonna do
with us?"

Burning was grateful to switch topics. "They mean to boon-
dock us someplace while they puzzle out how to use us. Some
remote subarctic base, say, or a desert outpost."

Daddy D nodded. "No surprise there and not much we can
do about it—at least they're not quarantining us in orbit. But

suppose the plans have changed since they offered parole. Maybe the Hierarchate feels differently these days."

"That's occurred to me, too. Too late to turn back, though."

"Has been since we came down off Anvil Tor. Though there is one variable we can still fiddlefuck with . . ."

Burning grinned. "General, kindly get the company commanders together and let them know we'll be sharing out live ammunition."

"That's roughly eight, ten rounds apiece. But it could make a world of difference."

Burning nodded. Maybe he didn't have what it took to be a wise leader or even a decent, feeling man, but he knew the minimum the Exts expected of him, and that was the chance to live and die as Exts.

Astern in *Sword of Damocles* was a reconstituted short regiment of Broken Country fighters without an implant or pain collar in sight. Burning was confident that if push came to shove, he could arm his people in a formidable fashion, take hostages, and seize control of a great portion of the immense spacecraft, if not all of it, by a coup de main. He likewise knew that it would never happen.

The last days before *Sword of Damocles* had left Concordance had been a royal bunglefest. The scramble to requisition the weapons, equipment, and other supplies to see the Exts through their indenture to LAW had been so frantic that it had even made Burning set aside his self-reproach over the Exts' defeat and the loss of Romola.

He had been escorted to a sprawling depot where First Lander fighting vehicles and aircraft had been impounded, but nobody had been able to find him a single maintenance and repair disk or operating manual. It had been like that over and over in spite of Field Marshal Vukmirovic's promises that night below Anvil Tor.

In the end the Exts had taken mostly what Ext stuff they could beg or commandeer. They had departed underequipped with a grab bag of hardware that had given the supply and maint people shivering nightmares. Nor had they been allotted much time to gather personal items. By Burning's order, the baggage allowance had been shared equally: one light duffel apiece.

When Burning had understood Vukmirovic's heavy-handed hint that Commissioner Renquald wanted Lod out of the way, the advantages to the notion had rapidly become clear. There was some retaliation for Lod's siding with the First Landers–LAW coalition, but getting the little schemer offworld would also very likely save the fellow's life. More important, the Exts would need him; he was the nearest thing they could get to an informed adviser on LAW intrigues. Lod might make a much bigger difference than some outmoded fifty-ton blowtanks.

Haunted by his failure to lead the Exts to victory, Burning had withdrawn into himself as much as possible during the voyage from Concordance, poring over military data and trying to find his mistakes. From Caesar's diaries to the strategist AI Earthmover to the campaigns of LAW itself, nothing had quite prepared him for the subtle ways in which he and his fighters had been manipulated and co-opted.

Commissioner Renquald's devious brain, that's what I should've studied in transit, it occurred to him late in the trip. Dope out exactly how the AlphaLAW had marshaled the First Landers against the Broken Country and undercut the bastions' militancy.

Like that planting ceremony presided over by the new Orman sachem. A hermit-fruit sapling from Periapt had been planted, the act accompanied by a lot of high-flown talk about how by the time its first yield was ready to be harvested, Burning and the Exts would be home to taste them.

Brilliant agitprop, like so many of Renquald's stratagems, but Burning wouldn't get to find out how the commissioner pulled them off because Renquald was far astern, making Concordance dance to his tune. It had gradually dawned on the Exts that there was really no way home even if LAW kept its word and got them back to the Broken Country someday.

News from Concordance had trickled in, current events turning into irrevocable history right before the Exts' eyes. The planet and the system had become a thriving LAW war factory.

The Broken Country had been cemented into the new military-industrial supereconomy, its population tripled by forced immigration. Exts had been assimilated like everybody else into the larger new culture.

Renquald had married Romola.

Almost every Ext had received news along similar lines. As Renquald must have known they would, those tidings thinned and frayed the exiles' emotional connections to a Broken Country that was no more and reinforced the inescapable fact that their most solid tie and lifeline now was to LAW, much as they might detest it.

CHAPTER
FIFTEEN

Cal Lightner gazed on Periapt from his castle in the air and found it good. There was much that needed doing. Any smugness would be unworthy, any complacency dangerous.

"It must look credible," Lightner was telling his small group of conspirators. "More importantly, it must appall. And it must *define* those whom it exterminates."

A bare thirty baseline years after the last major outbreak of Cyberviruses, it had pleased Cal's great-grandmother, Perelandra, to demonstrate the eminence of the Lightners by building the new family citadel. An admirer of Old Earth art, she had decreed that the citadel be modeled on Magritte's painting *La Condition Humaine*. Thus, Periapt technologies had given the project every appearance of a huge gray boulder or small asteroid with a modest keep on its summit.

Its magnetic field powered by a cleverly concealed superconducting array, *La Condition Humaine* hung suspended and stationary. Being hollow composite, the monolith was light and had far more living, working, and systems space than its aspect suggested.

Deft insider exploitation of Periapt's economy in the post-Cyberplague age had made the Lightner dynastic group the wealthiest and most influential of any in the era of LAW, and so, from the citadel spread invisible lines of influence, some few of which Cal Lightner had stroked like a harpist to bring about this morning's council of war.

His cohorts were on the castle's eastern wall, watching Medusa, Periapt's primary, climb higher over the gilded sea. Cal was framed against a champagne sky and the gray battlements.

"We're not just orchestrating some gratuitous little scandal to embarrass a rival here. We need to inflame people across the spectrum, especially those who've supported Dextra Haven and the Rationalists. We must make this a warning trumpet to all those good right-thinking voters who need their politics glandular and uncomplicated."

Doll Van Houten, wrapped in a shawl of neoduchesse wasp lace, nodded once.

Two other senior Hierarchs were present: Predicant Shackleford of the Body Teleological and Lepskaya, the Human Preservationist Party whip, who chaired the armed forces appropriations subcommittee. Also present were Lieutenant Wix Uniday of LAW Political Security and the former Hierarch Buchanan Starkweather. The latter two men had refused refreshments from the buffet dumbots and stood with eyes fixed on Lightner.

" 'Glandular and uncomplicated,' " Wix Uniday repeated. "What my contacts have in mind will fill the bill ideally." He flip-flopped a color-coded gas cartridge across his knuckles from one finger to the next, an ancient trick gamblers still called the steeplechase. "Some of the Exts have already sampled Bong and drugs of that sort. Relatively harmless. But we made certain that a good quantity of Bong was laced with inactive trace markers of hecatomb—enough to be detectable after the crash."

Blond and raffishly handsome, Uniday wasn't wearing his PolSec branch uniform or any sign of his lieutenant colonelcy. His morning suit showed that he could afford to be dressed by a superb tailor.

"And the tethership, too, will be salted with hecatomb?" Lepskaya asked.

"Yes, but the Exts' going berserk or not doesn't matter," Uniday assured everyone. "The explosion will make it look like they went synapshit, and so will the telemetry and commo trail we're creating. The markers should be detectable in debris and are already in place in the Ext berthing spaces onboard *Sword of Damocles*."

"And if autopsies are conducted?" Lightner asked.

Uniday flashed an easygoing grin. "There won't be enough left of the Exts or their tethercraft for autopsies. But there'll be hecatomb film on berthing space bulkheads from breath and perspiration and in urine residue in the head holding tanks." He paused for a moment. "LAW's forensic teams have elaborate and exacting means of detecting the stuff, which is precisely why it wouldn't have sufficed to simply plant the Exts' follow-on baggage with the drug, though we've seen to that as well. Independent investigators, including those tiresome saints at the Lyceum General Inquiries Bureau, will want proof that the Exts have metabolized it."

Buchanan Starkweather had been listening unhappily. Pale, dun-haired, somatically older than Uniday though chronologically younger, he had had a brief career in the military as well as the Hierarchate, though he had not done particularly well in either. Having all the right loyalties and ties to established power, however, he was in line to be nobly rewarded for unswerving mediocrity.

"I still think we should do this some other way," he commented. When the others' eyes converged on him, he realized that he had only seconds to salvage himself. "That is, rather than sacrifice a tethercraft and crew. After all, the war effort needs everyone and everything . . ."

Cal Lightner bristled at having Preservationist dogma quoted at him, but the lowered expectations that attended Starkweather saved him. "Buck, this *is* part of the war effort," he said calmly as the winds ruffled the silvered locks of his patrician feathercut. "And it has to be big—a meltdown. All of us here have sanctioned enough covert operations to know that painful sacrifices are sometimes unavoidable. It's one tethercraft and crew offered up now to avoid polluting Periapt with a mob of partisan terrorists and losing control over LAW to hordes of intractable war wogs.

"Let them serve and die on the frontiers; it's far more than their lives amounted to when we found them. But start bringing them here, enfranchising them, parading them around as coequals? The Rationalists will hand LAW over to them in a generation. Subhumans who haven't the brains, the backbone, or the racial vision to defeat the Roke. But after today there'll be no more of this cobelligerent drool Dextra Haven and her lot have been trying to peddle for a decade. Only LAW can defeat the Roke, and only Periapt can make LAW work."

Wix Uniday heard him out with a carefully cultivated expression of attention and approval. "That's exactly the way we see it at Political Security. In the wake of this Ext op, no one's going to object when we come down hard on resistance, be it on Hierophant, Tintaginel . . . or Periapt."

"Public reaction will support major legal reforms," Lepskaya put in. "Better press censorship, loyalty oaths, emergency detention powers. We can put all the defeatists on the run and root out these Quantum College pranksters while we're at it. They can run their paranoia games on each other in the Miseria Isle detention camps."

"Annexed worlds are the engine of LAW," Doll Van Houten said, getting back to the point. "Periapt is the pilot. And when the Roke are eliminated, an unchallenged and unadulterated Periapt *must* shoulder the burden of guiding the destiny of our species. That's our holy destiny. That's what the teleological energies have chosen us to do."

"It's clean, taking care of this in orbit," Lepskaya said dreamily. "That way, no wog-worlders set foot here. Besides, the aftermath of the disaster will be the ideal time to start pushing openly for universal conscription. Mandatory service will be the answer to LAW's growing personnel problems, and authority over policy, assignments, and exemptions will give the Hierarchate stupendous new influence and fund-raising opportunities." He glanced at Lightner, only to find him moving toward the small corner tower at the end of the parapet walk. "Cal? Something wrong?"

"Not at all," Lightner threw over his shoulder. "Minor detail. Please carry on."

The tower was appointed as an ornate sitting room, but like most places in the floating citadel, it was well wired for quick communications. A few voice commands and Lightner had sealed the chamber from intrusion and eavesdropping; then he brought up his family calendar file on the central holofield to reference Nike's schedule.

She had said something about visiting one of LAW's assets in near orbit in the company of that freak show of arts and theater vagabonds that had latched on to her. Something about staging a production in the Eden orbital. Even so, Lightner experienced a sudden and uncharacteristic sense of apprehension, an urge to make certain that his daughter wasn't planning to be anywhere in the vicinity of *Sword of Damocles*.

He abhorred wasting time double-checking on Nike but decided to put in a call to her nonetheless. A commo glitch somewhere along the line, however, delayed what should have been instant communication.

He wavered for a moment but reassured himself that *La Condition Humaine* systems were virus-free and immune to tampering. Leaving the retry function to persist in trying to reach Nike, Lightner returned to his guests and fellow patriots.

CHAPTER
SIXTEEN

Burning's company was in place outside *Damocles*'s air lock a half hour in advance of the scheduled disembarkation time. The big shuttle could have descended without being unspooled, but it had become necessary to transfer angular momentum to the starship because *Damocles*'s orbit had decayed somewhat. As the tether's burden was lowered away, the mother ship would receive a minute boost; in that sense the Exts were just so much ballast, Burning had been informed.

The difference in mass between the tethercraft and the colossal starship was such that it would take a day of tether ops of various lengths and masses to adjust the interstellar vessel's orbit. *Damocles* could have achieved the same thing with its secondary drives, but LAW engineers felt that the tether ops personnel could use the practice, and the frugality of the solution appealed to the skipper.

Exts in battlesuits were lined up along either side of the outboard passageway. Many of the mustered troops were trying to recoup some of the sleep they'd been denied by the moved-up debarkation hour; others were making final adjustments to gear or lethargically bullshitting. Some were reading or watching visor vids, and as always with Exts, there was a good deal of gambling going on, with cards, dice, *gan-jan-po*, and two-ups predominating.

Zone and his leadership were off sharing out live rounds. There were only enough bullets to equip the senior officers and NCOs with a few apiece, and Zone was getting the ammo into the right hands quickly and inconspicuously. Despite their talk about toad-cranking him, Daddy D had maintained to Burning

that Zone was the man for the job because, when on duty, he
cut no slack and got things done.

It had struck Burning as reassuringly true to form that the
Exts didn't rate a comfy ride in a conventional passenger
shuttle. There had been enough snafus and disorganization
since the starship's insertion around Periapt to prove that LAW
could trip over its own dong just as any other big outfit could.
Burning conceded that hints of LAW betrayal might be in his
imagination. He hoped another few hours would find him quietly re-collecting the ammo and sneaking it back into the transport cases before anyone found out it was missing.

A Logistics Command petty officer reported that the drop
countdown had resumed and that the tethercraft was at the air
lock. LOGCOM had said the same thing two orbits earlier.
Burning decided to wait until he heard the lock cycling before
he passed the word to move out.

Ghost was monitoring drop operations on a nearby PA holo
terminal. Burning was on his way to join her when a voice
spoke behind him, thick with distaste. "Preferable, in my
opinion, to dispense with this flycast ride and simply march out
an air lock, sparing ourselves a great deal of pointless delay
and vain hope."

Lod, who had spent the subjective months of the voyage
brooding, was pulling ineffectually at the adjustment tabs and
keepers of his battlesuit. He had gotten it to fit perfectly but
was never going to get it to look stylish. It didn't help his natti-
ness quotient any that he had neatly graffitoed the suit's back
"RANDOM EXECUTIONS WILL CONTINUE UNTIL
MORALE IMPROVES."

"You have a mission critique, Cousin?" Burning inquired
politely.

Lod's small chin jutted out. "I'm trillions of klicks from my
favorite chef, I keep hearing ominous jabber about field
maneuvers, and it smarts when I urinate. Plus, you didn't even
have the decency to draft my tailor when you shanghaied me."

"The supply sergeant's your tailor now, Cuz," Ghost commented as she approached them. "And I for one think you look
dashing." She squared away the shoulders of Lod's battlesuit.

Its pouches and loops were empty; he refused to carry so much as a spit needle. With his unlined face and profuse golden hair, he resembled one of Ghost's taller killer children.

Lod was as fond of Ghost as she was of him in her own unfathomable way but at that moment was doing his best to conceal it.

"I told you both, I'll never forgive you." He toed his bulging duffel. "The least you could've done was get someone to fetch my luggage."

"It improves your posture," Burning said.

The hull boomed as the tethercraft and onboard locks equalized pressure, then undogged. The PA began nagging the Exts to stand by, but everyone pointedly continued his or her lounging, awaiting the Allgrave's order by way of company commanders and platoon leaders.

Commotion was a given in the passageways, but the one suddenly moving in Burning's direction caught his ear because it sounded so civilian.

"—exactly right, Nike, my sweet! The interior of a starship is the *perfect* set for a reinterpretation because, after all, the central metaphor of *And on the Way, We Dropped It* is human beings trapped in surreal surroundings and cut off from their natural environment—"

At the same time some nameless liaison geartooth was yelling, "Hit the walls! Make a hole! Hierarch Dextra Haven coming through!" Whoever was yelling it was shouldering up through the tour group's rear guard.

Burning eyed what had to be Dextra Haven, a voluptuous, self-possessed woman who stood about collarbone-high to him, wearing a civilian fieldsuit that looked couturier-made but very serviceable and *tabi*-toed deck boots with gripsoles. Point to a pack of young adults, she was coming his way with breezy elegance and an aura of royalty that had lolling Exts impressed enough to retract their feet. She had mounds of ink-black hair and sloe-lavender eyes that put him in mind of Egyptian wall paintings. Her mouth was a lush recurve, mobile and cunning.

"I ask you, Nike," Haven was saying to the young woman

beside her, "what are the Exts but today's counterparts to my play's All-Fodder Chorus?"

The half dozen others in the entourage didn't resemble any Periapts Burning had encountered and didn't look like LAWs at all. They were an even mix of men and women of assorted shapes and sizes. The variety and flamboyance of their clothes made him wonder if somebody was throwing a costume party forward of Frame 104. An Elizabethan ruff, high-top Romanesque sandals, tasseled chechia caps, ballet skinsheaths, slippers . . . The hairstyles were hayricks, alleychics, boetians, and the like.

The one named Nike was a pretty ingenue in dance tights and a beautifully embroidered doublet, her auburn hair in a bowl cut. She carried an instrumented monocle that she held to her eye and panned around every few seconds.

Only one of the pack stood out as not being part of the ambient fabulousness: a midsize woman with tow hair done in a combed retro look. Or was she a he? Burning couldn't tell because of the loose-fitting civilian shipsuit. But whatever it was, it had a striking Slavic face and moved with the kind of tightly knit grace and certainty of body placement that marked good martial artists.

While Burning was trying to make up his mind about the towhead's gender, Lod slipped past him to make a limber kowtow to Dextra Haven.

"Madame Hierarch, light of the Lyceum! Greetings, radiant lady!" He had one hand out to her palm up, the other over his heart.

Haven appeared charmed by the blandishment. She showed Lod an arch smile, though Burning thought she seemed distracted.

Lod's smooth uptake made Burning appreciate all the more the fact that he'd brought his clever little cousin along. He himself had no idea what the protocol should be, and nobody had mentioned anything about a top-echelon VIP party onboard *Damocles*.

Lod was still shoveling it on. "I speak for the exalted Allgrave of the Exts and the rest of our unit when I declare the honor you do us by your gracious visit, Madame Hierarch!" He introduced Burning and Ghost before adding, "I'm Major Lod of the clan Orman, battalion liaison and protocol officer—your admiring servant!"

It was the first Burning had heard of such a job slot in the provisional battalion's TO&E, much less of Lod's occupying it. He decided to head off the sycophancy.

But he was beaten to it by Commander Rampling, the LOGCOM coordinator, who had been yelling from the back and now came rushing up, looking apoplectic. "Madame Hierarch, this part of the vessel is off-limits to civilians. We cannot have you and your entourage in an operational embarkation area."

The Exts on the sidelines were so interested in the goings-on that the gambling had stopped. Lod was about to insinuate himself again when Burning pulled him out of the cross fire. The androgynous one in the civvie shipsuit had moved up wordlessly to stand within striking range of the commander, silently watching.

"Commander Rampling, is it?" Haven said. "Between now and the time your disciplinary board's convened, I suggest that you review your facts." She motioned to Nike. "Citizen Lightner and her distinguished guests are scouting locations by the arrangement of her father, Hierarch Calvin Lightner, for a revival of a play of which *I* am the author. I am here as part of a prescheduled Lyceum inspection junket, but as a Hierarch and especially as chair of the general oversight committee, it's my prerogative to visit government facilities and vessels." Dextra Haven's face had gone cold and hard. "Now go inform your superiors that I intend to block the military pay hike bill, if only to demonstrate how I dislike being pestered by a brass hat rack like you."

Bled the air right out of his helmet, Burning mused as Rampling withdrew in apologetic disorder.

CHAPTER
SEVENTEEN

Dextra let go a mental sigh of relief as the LOGCOM officer retreated, leaving her momentarily unhindered. Maybe she could rescue the Exts, after all, and rescue Aquamarine while she was at it, if the voice of the Quantum College was to be believed.

The very idea seemed insane now that she stood before them at last, one nonviolent and recently soft-living politician out to save hundreds of flinty-eyed, battlesuited combat vets. But the anonymous message from the QC had been definite on the point, and what facts she had been able to root out with her own discreet inquiries seemed to support it. LAW had paid lip service to the recruited Exts, but the actual preparations—refurbishing quarters and facilities, shiftings funds and equipment, transportation and other resources—hadn't gone anywhere.

Then there was the secret transferral of hecatomb from a police evidence depository, just as she had been told. None of Dextra's sources had been able to provide hard evidence or verifiable data on what was to be done with it.

To denounce LAW's termination scheme on the floor of the Lyceum with no more proof than a blind message from the officially proscribed QC underground would have been political suicide. The Preservationists would have howled for a recall election, and some Rationalists probably would have gone along with it rather than suffer the blowback a fight would have entailed.

In the meantime, LAW might simply put the tethercraft massacre on hold and expunge the Exts at a later date. What Dextra had to do was get them alive to Abraxas, where she could build media awareness of them. Public fancy would forestall PolSec from any extreme wetwork for the time being.

The only method of ensuring that was to make use of Nike Lightner's coterie both as a political shield and as a spotlight of public attention. Nike had been thrilled to hear that Dextra was amenable to shooting a revival of *And on the Way, We Dropped It* and positively delighted with the idea of staging it onboard a starship.

Tonii had argued against the plan, then had insisted on going along when Dextra wouldn't be dissuaded. With the LOGCOM officer hurrying off and the members of Nike's retinue trying to outdo one another in their enthusiasm, the gynander now retreated into the background. The tethercraft operation would soon be a matter of independent public record. Dextra hoped that the exposure would be all the weapon she needed, because it was about all she'd been able to come up with on short notice.

"What a *figmental* place to stage the play!" Nike said suddenly, throwing an arm around her. "I've never seen Lazlo-Lazlo so inspired!"

She indicated the fatigued-looking young guy in pseudo-Victorian dress.

"If that's inspiration, what's his boredom like," Dextra asked under her breath, "cachesleep?"

"Fiction and drama are dead," Lazlo-Lazlo pronounced, stifling a yawn. "The vicarious reality of electronic reportage and documentary has eclipsed them. Still, this setting has an undeniable absurdist legitimacy."

Dextra patted Nike's arm. "Sweetie, I want you to meet Emmett Orman, Allgrave of the Exts; his sister, um, Ghost; and their cousin, Major Lod." She studied the trio for a moment, then added, "Lady and gentlemen, would you do me the honor of accompanying me and my party down the well to Periapt? Moving into a bay farther aft, I've got a passenger shuttle that should be able to accommodate the entire Ext contingent."

A few members of Nike's troupe complained that they

hadn't absorbed enough of *Damocles*'s aesthetic auras yet, but Dextra wasn't in the mood to linger longer than necessary.

Lod tugged at the Allgrave's elbow. "Cousin, we thank the Hierarch for her gracious invitation, don't we?"

"Uh, yes, of course," the Allgrave answered somewhat mechanically. When General Delecado approached, Orman spoke briskly: "We're leaving with Madame Haven, here, from lock number—"

"Eight-sigma," Tonii supplied for Dextra.

"Send one runner forward to tell Zone," the Allgrave resumed, "and post a rear guard here in case the runner doesn't connect." He swung to Dextra. "Will that be all right, ma'am?"

"'Ma'am,' how debonair," she remarked casually. "But warn them that I'll be forced to leave them behind if they're not at the shuttle directly. You *know* how it is."

Nike gathered her little artbeat flock and headed off. Major Lod proffered his arm, but Dextra pretended not to notice. Orman gave a hand signal, and the Exts fell in along either bulkhead.

Dextra heard him add a watchword for them to pass back. *"Zanshin."*

As she led the way, Dextra steeled her nerve. It helped to have Tonii there, a silent step behind her.

To her relief, the Exts hadn't balked, although Emmett Orman was wearing a wary expression. They made their way aft with a kind of focused ease, a calm attentiveness to the details around them.

The shuttle was in place, fueled and replenished to take planetside a cargo of Concordance artifacts Commissioner Renquald had sent home to his dynastic group, though the actual loading hadn't commenced. The pilot and copilot were having a confab with some LOGCOM people when Dextra, Nike's troupe, and the Exts arrived.

Dextra gave the two men no time to mull over their options. "Flight crew aboard, please. I'm preempting payload space on a Lyceum priority."

In her war correspondent days she had sneaked a wounded

Reformist—a local who had acted as her interpreter—past Fundamentalist pogrom units to safety. Her heart hadn't whomped in her throat in quite the same way until this moment.

The shuttle crew chief stalled, "But—but we yanked the seating modules for cargo space."

Dextra tugged at the integral fast-roping harness built into the Allgrave's battlesuit. There were also carabiners and assorted short lines and straps, neatly rolled and secured. "The deck couplings will do nicely for tie-downs, Orman," she suggested. "If you're game, that is."

Orman shrugged. "Delta-V, Hierarch Haven. That way there'll be no squabbling over aisle seats."

Burning's reflex was to stand fast until Dextra Haven told him what was really happening, but his instinct was to get everyone off *Damocles* by any means possible. Why, after all, should a Hierarch display such nervousness aboard one of LAW's most powerful spacecraft? Lod, too, seemed all in favor of abandoning ship, and he had a sixth sense about which way to jump in the murk of guile and counterguile. As for the rest, they were deep in *zanshin*.

One of the core disciplines of the Skills, "remaining mind" was a concept borrowed from Old Earth's *bujutsu* fighting arts. It was the state of unfailing alertness, constant preparedness to react or take action, a primary tool for harnessing Flowstate to Skills applications. A good Skillsfighter was in or near *zanshin* most of the time, but it hadn't hurt to remind the Exts when they'd moved out.

Burning made a low back-and-forth hand signal to Wetbar, Zone's XO, who had been left in charge of B Company. "Get aboard and secure the spacecraft."

Wetbar added his own signals, and his first platoon double-timed into the ship by fire teams. Nike Lightner's followers looked poleaxed by the realization that they had all at once become bit players in what seemed a very grave drama.

Burning heard Haven urge Nike toward the air lock: "You dears had better get to the jumpseats before they're taken."

For all her effervescence, Cal Lightner's daughter was no naif; aware now that she'd been used, she gave Haven a furious glance. Burning moved to block her path of escape; whatever was going down, this was no time to lose the added insurance she'd provide. Nike made a quick decision and led her nervous flock down the boarding well in the wake of the B Company Exts.

The shuttle crew remained rooted, however, the pilot making uncooperative grunting noises. Dextra glanced to Burning, and Burning glanced to Daddy D. The general held up his giant old hawkbill knife, flicked it open, and began cleaning his nails with it while exchanging stares with the pilot.

The aero officer quieted, and the flight crew was herded onto the shuttle. The LOGCOMs backed away as the passageway grew crowded with Exts filing into the shuttle's boarding well.

Zone finally appeared with Kino and Strop from his several, along with the runner Burning had dispatched and the man he had posted at the tethercraft's air lock. All were cross-slung with bandoliers packed with cassettes of caseless ammunition.

"They doped the ammo somehow," Zone told Burning on the sly, giving a thumbs-down. "Even the stuff the cadre hung on to. I tried to let off a round—nothing. And the LOGs claim they can't find the power packs for the sonics."

Burning looked to the transshipping Exts. B company was already onboard and A Company was half gone, but movement had stopped, backed up. To make matters worse, the Discards were nearby and acting edgy. Getting their ammo away from them might have led to a firefight if not for Ghost. The kids were fingering their empty weapons, bunching up for the only comfort they trusted—one another.

The thud of lug-soled boots brought Burning around in time to see a LAW Special Troops colonel, flanked by a pair of Manipulants, hastening his way. Burning gave a low, curt whistle that was relayed into the shuttle and back along C Company, while Dextra Haven stepped forward to motion the colonel to stay back.

The colonel gargled a quick command to his engeneered soldiers in the privy battle-*gullah* they shared, and the two ogres paused a step behind him. As an officer of Manipulants, he wore a uniform different from regular LAW ground force issue. He was armed with a stun baton, beltknife, and pepperfoam shooter but no firearm—not onboard a spacecraft. The Manipulants were equipped the same way, their gear scaled to their size.

"Madame Hierarch, you can't seriously be thinking of escorting these troops downside," he risked after a moment. "Perhaps you and Hierarch Lightner 's daughter should accompany us."

"I'm as serious as a pallbearer," Haven answered, careful to keep out of his reach. "Be so good as to finish boarding," she threw over her shoulder to Burning. "We are, as they say, winging it."

Advancing on Dextra, the Special Troops officer put his thumb to a small belt unit and pressed. Abruptly, compartment hatches slid open along the passageway. At the same time, the two gargoyles who had been flanking him went for Burning and Ghost. Out from the interconnected engineering and maintenance spaces to either side charged platoons of Manipulants bent on closing with the Exts hand to hand.

CHAPTER EIGHTEEN

Tell me about that final night on Aquamarine, the court-appointed lawyer, Deitz, had said to him. Memory had risen up before Claude Mason's eyes, almost as if the years had been wiped away.

He and Incandessa, who was heavy with their child, were standing on the lighthouse's uppermost promenade when Hippo Nolan, the survey team's engineer, came pounding into sight around the broad curve of the tower.

Boon's gone synapshit, Hippo shouted. *He's trying to stop the suicides!*

Is Boon drunk? Mason wondered. But no, not Saint Boon. It was just that a group of Conscious Voices were threatening to take their own lives in a last-ditch attempt to hoodoo the survey team—the Visitants—into remaining onworld and sharing power with the Aquam. Boon had decided to throw in with them.

Mason had had little patience with Aquamarine's innumerable cults and creeds, but the enmity of the Conscious Voices had come as a painful shift in relationships.

When the *Scepter* first arrived, there were Voices in many parts of Scorpia as well as on many smaller landmasses and outlying islands. The Voices had never been successful in curbing the Aquam penchant for bloodshed, but they wielded formidable leverage by dint of their rallies, sit-ins, civil disobedience, and protest fasts. And they revered the Oceanic.

However, even the most resentful local honcho or headwoman would think hard before using force to silence them. The order's voodoo was very effective among superstitious

Aquam, particularly when helped along by purgatives slipped into drinks or vomitics dusted onto food.

The women of the order had greeted the *Scepter* with hosannas, but when LAW's expansionist Roke Conflict–oriented intentions emerged, the Voices mounted a campaign to drive the Visitants back to the stars.

Scepter's crew members were too insulated by their technology for the order to hunger-strike on their doorstep, and in any case, Captain Marlon had absolutely no qualms about letting them starve to death en masse. Marlon used bribery and threats to keep Aquam laity from becoming involved, and civic disobedience failed because there was nothing LAW wanted or needed in the way of Conscious Voice cooperation.

After failing to discourage the Visitants, the Voices lost their protective aura of inviolability; they learned that nonviolence could prevail only if some countervailing force imposed restraint on the opposition. Many secular Aquams were only too delighted to purge the Voices who had constrained their actions for years. Adherents deserted in droves, and lay supporters ran for cover; Voices who remained steadfast wound up as sling-gun practice targets, slaves, atrocity victims, and fresh meat.

The deaths of Marlon and his command staff came far too late to save the sect, yet a few Conscious Voice members managed to go underground.

With unease and resentment rising among the Aquam, owing to *Scepter*'s imminent departure, rumors circulated that several Voices had resurfaced and formed a suicide pact as a final gesture of denunciation.

Mason tried to ignore word of the impending deaths and concentrate on the return to Periapt, distracting himself with images of loved ones, prestige, and the tranquil living that awaited him. But not Boon, who Incandessa thought an exemplary Periapt, with a more acute moral sense than Mason.

Even so, there was nothing Boon or the Voices could do to stop the departure of the *Scepter* or block the full-scale annexation mission by LAW. All that aside, Boon was Mason's chief supporter and closest friend, and he had suddenly blundered into a volatile situation that would possibly draw the wrath of a LAW mission review board.

So Mason hastened off after Hippo, while behind him Incandessa wept openly for his safety as much as for his imminent leavetaking.

Mason tried to use his plugphone to communicate with the team's groundside complex, but the COMSAT relay was down. Hippo had had other news to relate: He and Farley Swope had discovered four caches of pilfered LAW equipment, including Optimant and LAW weapons, telecom gear, and biochemical modules.

The Aquam aren't as resigned to postponing progress as you think, Hippo had said.

Mason nearly stumbled headlong over one of Hippo's toy-like gizmos—a mollywood cart no bigger than a child's wagon self-propelled by rocker arms. The rocker arms were worked by the same system that cocked and fired the Aquam's sling-guns: lengths of transplanted freshwater mussel contractive tissue made to flex by means of Scourland galvani stones matched against contractive straps of treated plant-sap rubber. Hippo had dubbed his invention a muscle car.

Then Farley Swope and her young Aquam lover, Sunbeard, were beside them. Sunbeard's namesake tow whiskers were tied off in a dozen gold-beaded braids. They had located the Voices and Boon.

"Where?" Mason demanded.

"On Execution Dock," Sunbeard said.

Mason did not even try to stifle his moan. Execution Dock wasn't on the shore but stood alone on the other side of seven meters of churning, lethal ocean.

Why the hell hadn't he tasked someone with monitoring Boon? He had seen his friend grow disillusioned with LAW service, just as Mason and the others had. But Boon's idealism was the most fervent of all. The truth was that no one could have been spared to baby-sit Boon. With *Scepter*'s team cut by more than half, the survivors had been forced to take on a double workload just to complete a cursory survey before the preprogrammed voyage home.

Execution Dock was a microatoll that stood some two meters higher than the overhang on shore and boasted a fairly level area to either side. There were no stocks, manacles, or pillories attached to the dock because the Oceanic would have obliterated them when it covered Execution Dock at high tide.

As he approached, Mason heard Boon's voice raised in fury above the dirge wails of the Voices. Intent on plucking Boon from the rock if necessary, he ordered Hippo and Farley to bring in one of the helos. On the open area to the right, twenty-five square meters or so, four Conscious Voices knelt in a circle, gazing into a crystal lamp. They were wearing their traditional black shroud robes and ritual aspect: heads shaved; scalps, faces, and exposed necks heavily coated with white claylike makeup; eye sockets kholed black; lips, gums, and teeth stained the same color.

To one side of them stood Boon, hands dangling uselessly at his sides, wearing a look of desolation and madness.

Mason ran forward, searching in vain for the whamboo gangway that was used to conduct the condemned to their place of death.

"Boon! Boon, where's the gangway?" he shouted.

In their time together—in LAW fundamentals training, through subjective months onboard the *Scepter*, and for nearly three baseline years on Aquamarine—Mason had seen the man in many moods, often somber and even dispirited, but never the way Boon looked then.

"Don't . . . dunno, Claude; some of their followers took it away after I forced 'em to let me cross. Claude, go back to the lighthouse. There's nothing you can do here, and seeing you's liable to set the Voices off."

Muttering to one another, the women had pointed to Mason—readily identifiable to many Aquam because of his intricate auburn queue and biosculpted comeliness. In contrast, Boon was absolutely unenhanced—strong but compact build, receding dishwater-blond hair, a nose too thin, long, and upturned. What made him stand out in a crowd was the glitter of intellect and fervor in his eyes. But that glitter had become unnerving, giving him the air of a man who had been pushed beyond some crucial limit.

"Just stay put and keep your eye on them," Mason called as calmly as he could. "The evac helo'll be here straightaway."

Boon only took an unsteady step toward Mason and the crashing, lethal moat between them, putting his back to the death's-head women.

"We've caused enough loss of life on this miserable water-ball, Claude. I'm going to talk these four out of it if it takes till high tide. Bad enough we're going to fly off without offering one iota of real progress so that when LAW gets back this way in twenty or thirty years, it'll have that much less trouble taking over. But I'm salvaging *something* before I go!"

"Boon, stay away from the edge!" Mason warned.

The Oceanic could kill in ways beyond counting, and the uncertainty of its actions had always been for Mason one of the greatest terrors of Aquamarine's dominant life-form.

A howling came from the dock.

At first Mason was not able to tell whether Boon had grabbed one or more of the Voices to prevent a jump or if they had pounced on him while he was distracted. What was certain was that Boon and the women were suddenly in a thrashing, strug-gling moil, so close together and changing positions so rapidly that Mason couldn't risk a shot even if he had the presence of mind to unholster his gun. His hoarse screams for them to stop went unanswered.

Although Boon did not want any more Conscious Voices to die, neither did he intend to die himself, but trying to get free of them looked impossible. Raised in a low-tech culture in which great physical hardship and arduous manual labor were the norm, an adult female on Aquamarine commonly had more endurance and a higher strength-weight ratio than did the average male Periapt workstation-chair drone.

Yet somehow Boon shoved and beat his way free of their grasp and retreated up the low crag at the middle of the rock. Mason thought he would have an opening in which to draw his sidearm and hold the women off, until Boon's heel slipped out from under him and he tumbled out of sight.

Thinking his friend had fallen into the waves, Mason shrieked, but it was clear from the way the women swarmed after Boon that the struggle was not over. When the flailing, grappling human knot appeared to the left of the crag on the lower, smaller flat area, Boon's face and hair were red with blood. One of the Voices carried a bloodstained rock.

Boon's movements had grown faltering and uncoordinated. With exultant cries, the Conscious Voices dragged him down, seizing his arms and legs, then hoisted him up again. Mason had drawn the superconducting pistol, the laser aimspot as much on Boon as on any of the women. But even at that moment he found a rationale for not squeezing the trigger.

The Voices yelled in a harsh, discordant chorus as they broke Boon's feeble grip on them and flung their victim up and out—not far, but far enough to clear Execution Dock and splash into the Amnion. The women instinctively threw themselves back to avoid any wetting.

I should've killed him, Mason told himself all those years later. I should've had the guts to do that at least, to spare him—

All around the point of Boon's impact, moving phosphorescent strands converged, and the water itself seemed to coalesce, to take on a semisolidity. Boon's drifting body was visible as a silhouette inside a pool of blue-green turbulence. His form shifted, lost in the murky swirls; then, just as suddenly, it became more distinct. Mason saw that he was naked as a fetus, though there was no hint of where his wearwithal suit, field belt, or other accoutrements had gone.

The Conscious Voices had scrambled out of sight behind the crag, perhaps fearing Mason's gunfire. Their dirge had resumed, louder, a weaving of broken wails and ululations.

All at once, the heaped Amnion gathered itself around the body trapped within. Mason howled Boon's name as the body jerked, whirled around by the irresistible power of the water, and began . . . everting.

All that was inside erupted from him, turned inside out: palate and tongue, epiglottis, and pharynx disgorging; teeth drifting loose from the extruded jaws; eardrums and auditory ossicles set afloat; nasal membrane and conchas burgeoning forth from nostrils; rectum coming forth, and pleated sigmoid colon following; urethra feeding out the urinary meatus like unspooling string . . . The body shrank in on itself as its contents were warped out; blood clouded around him but dissipated again and disassembled even more quickly than it had appeared.

It was all the more appalling to know that the ghastly things the Oceanic was doing to Boon were impersonal, dispassionate—indeed, some of the little data the survey team had managed to garner about it suggested that the organism could not truly comprehend anything that was not itself. Uncounted humans had met their end at the touch of the Oceanic—no two, it was said, in precisely the same way.

Miniature versions of some of the more common manifestations of the Oceanic—Farfeelers, Locobrates, and Tendrils—took form in the shape-shifting water. Boon had lost any resemblance to a man, though not quickly enough.

And Mason turned his eyes away . . .

Sometime later Hippo Nolan, Farley Swope, and Sunbeard found him sitting in the sand, gazing at Execution Dock. The waves had quieted, and the Oceanic manifestations had dispersed, along with any sign of Boon. The dirge of the Conscious Voices had dropped to a low, crooning elegy. When Mason emerged from shock sufficiently to tell his teammates what had happened, Hippo wanted to kill the women, but Farley stopped him. They had wasted too much time already, she said. There was the shuttle run and a preprogrammed departure to make. She was sorry about Boon, but their responsibility was to the living, not the dead.

Mason went along not because they were right but because it hurt so much to gaze at the Amnion. He thought at the time that the pain would abate once he got back up to cool, clean, quiet *Scepter*.

Outside the rearing, dilapidated Optimant lighthouse a small contingent of locals had gathered—leaders of the Rhodes clan and a crew of armed fighters.

Despite the rancor and violence of the evening, the mood of Skipjack Rhodes, Incandessa's father, was almost light. Rhodes's cousin HazeHoller, grandee of the high dam stronghold of Wall Water on Lake Ea, far upriver to the west, had died without issue or close kin aside from his wife. The widow had asked Skipjack, who had a reputation as a war leader and diplomat, to come assume joint rule and help her hold the place against the land-grabby grandees of the region.

None of it made any difference to Mason, save that Incandessa and their child would be that much more secure. Skipjack was shrewd and fond enough of her to arrange a good political marriage. Incandessa herself was absent, and Skipjack blocked the way when Mason started off to find her.

"She'll see you no more, Claude," he said. "You'll never return here, and you say you cannot take her with you, so she's declared you dead. She mourns your passing tonight and will hereafter accompany me to Wall Water."

Skipjack had seen LAW guns work, and he knew the Visitants could get into the lighthouse if they wanted to. But Skipjack also knew that the Visitants wouldn't shoot. Haunted-eyed and numb, still seeing Boon's gory face as the Voices took him down, Mason allowed Hippo to pull him away.

Barely three shipdays out of Aquamarine orbit Skipjack made voice contact with the *Scepter* by means of the shitsimple commo unit Mason had left behind, uplinked via one of the long-term survey SATs the team had left in orbit.

Rhodes came on long enough to say only that Incandessa had gone into difficult and premature labor but had successfully birthed their child. Rhodes terminated the link without mentioning the newborn's gender or whether it was Anathemite.

Mason's distraught efforts to reestablish contact were scrubbed permanently when the SAT glitches reappeared in epidemic strength and all six birds went off-line. Hippo had wondered aloud if it was some vestige Cybervirus at work.

Mason's distress at not knowing the fate of his wife and child hit him with a force that amazed him. His agitation grew until Hippo had to restrain him bodily from tampering with the starship's navigation suite in an attempt to return to Aquamarine—a foolhardy if not suicidal idea given the team's lack of experienced deep-space hands.

He remained on meds for some time. When the meds wore off, he discovered that the pain of loss wasn't at all assuaged by distance and vacuum. With time dilating as the *Scepter* climbed toward relativistic speeds, Claude Mason wept long.

Light-years worth.

The better part of a decade.

The previous day, when he had finished relating the story to Deitz, she had studied him for a moment before speaking.

"I'm reasonably certain that the inquest won't go to trial," she had said at last. "I only wish there was something I could do about the prison you've already sentenced yourself to."

CHAPTER NINETEEN

What made the onslaught of the Manipulants doubly bewildering was that so many had been mustered so quickly and without the Exts' being aware of it. *Damocles* was stupendous, its layout labyrinthine, but infiltrating the Periapt shocktroops by back routes wouldn't have been possible unless someone in LAW had had them more or less prepositioned.

The attack wasn't a sudden reaction to the Exts' decision to forego the tethership drop, Dextra reasoned; the engeneered Specials had been somewhere nearby as insurance of some kind, a contingency force.

The Exts' ammunition had apparently been rendered incrt, and the Manipulants carried no firearms, probably because the Aero Forces quailed at the mere idea of bullets flying onboard their starship. But sonics, irritant foams, electroshock batons, and whapbag rounds were useless against Exts in battlesuits, who could seal their breathers against riot gas, too. Thus, the Manipulants simply charged, wielding their huge, cleaverlike fighting blades.

Shock and confusion would have paralyzed other troops, but the Exts were in *zanshin* vigilance. With no avenue of retreat and no alternative but surrender, they met the Manips head-on without hesitation.

The utter horror of the attack had Dextra frozen in place, appalled, unable to believe what was happening before her eyes. She seemed to be experiencing it all through a shifting prism. She reasoned that she had lost her balance, though no one had bumped into her and she had not misstepped. The deck felt as if it were tilting under her, threatening to throw her headlong.

Directly in front of her a Manipulant was trying to eviscerate an Ext fighter. The Ext half pivoted, leaned aside, and avoided the Manipulant's upswept chopper blade with only a glancing parry; then he began to bore in, using his gauntleted free hand for a blocking blow to the Manipulant's wrist. The offworlder held his carbon-black quillon dagger in a kind of fencing grip. The Manipulant was wearing a vest of woven armor, but the vest left a lot of the Special Trooper exposed. The Ext levered his head out of a powerful one-handed choke hold that could have broken his neck like a peppermint stick and got inside his foe's guard. The lusterless black point of the vapor-deposition blade stabbed deep and tried to rip sideways but was stopped by armorply. Manipulant blood spurted, as red as any unreformatted human's.

The Manipulant should have been mortally wounded but didn't act like it; perhaps it simply didn't care. Jaws yawning wide like an animal trap, it tried to hold the Ext still long enough to gut him. But the Ext held off the enemy's knife arm with his raised elbow, released his grip on the Special Trooper, and slithered clear by way of a momentary gap between the Manip's right arm and its side.

The so-called Skills, however, weren't a magical charm of invulnerability, Dextra saw; another Manipulant appeared behind the first to strike at the Ext before he spotted it. The Ext went down, chest hacked open and collarbone cleaved in half. Two more Exts closed in on the Manipulant who'd gotten their buddy, one spearing it with her bayonet and the other going for its knife hand with a long, black bowie.

Another Manipulant went stumbling by, the undersides of its wrists cut nearly through, as if it had attempted suicide with a power tool. The remaining muscles had contracted, pulling its meaty hands back as far as they could go, fingertips angled back and down, almost touching its own upper forearms.

A sudden realization gave Dextra the willpower to tear her eyes away from the butchery. Where was Tonii? The gynander had been only a few steps away when the Manipulants had burst forth, but Tonii hadn't tried to shield her or pull her from harm's way.

Then Dextra saw what had diverted 'erm. The gynander had engaged one of the Manipulants, probably because it had been coming Dextra's way. The thing had failed to gut or get by Tonii, who had managed to get the stun baton out of the creature's belt loop.

Dextra had the presence of mind not to yell out. Compared with the eerily composed and unerring Skillsfighting of the Exts, Tonii's moves appeared plagued with split-second false starts, hesitations, and flinches.

The Manipulant put its oxlike shoulder and arm into a downward stroke that suddenly doglegged to the right. Tonii evaded it and darted in to jam the charged tip of the baton over the top of the vest, a hard tonfa strike into the hollow of the throat. Even without an electrical discharge the impact would have put any normal human out of the fight, but the Special Trooper was only staggered. Tonii gave it more of the same to nose, teeth, and temple, leaving it rocked but still on its feet, then turned to look for Dextra.

By then, however, Dextra was being carried toward the shuttle's boarding well by Emmett Orman—Burning, as she'd heard him called. She clung to his arm and called for the gynander to follow.

The blood on Burning's ka-bar was witness to the fact that he had fought alongside his Exts, though he'd given most of his attention to rallying defense and organizing the withdrawal. Exts were moving in to run interference, Lod and the almost anorectically slender Ghost among them.

The soldier named Zone was part no-motion-wasted war machine, part silent hollow-eyed berserker. His implement of choice was an entrenching tool modified for grip and with what looked to be an enhanced edge on its bush knife feature.

The jam-up at the boarding well had kept the Exts who already were in the shuttle from returning to render help. But the confined space and limited number of doors connecting the engineering areas to the passageway had similarly made it impossible for the Manipulants to bring their numbers to bear on a wide front.

With Burning bellowing orders over the bedlam and combatants fighting furiously, the rear body of the Exts closed on the boarding well meter by meter. The decks were treacherous with spilled blood, and screams and roars filled the passageway.

Ghost, in the thick of it, was rammed into a bulkhead and momentarily stunned. Dextra shrieked warnings no one heard. The human officer of Manipulants who had importuned Dextra raised his own chopper, plainly meaning to take Ghost's head.

But a group of gnomish-looking Exts intervened. When one of them lost a helmet, Dextra realized that the Ext was nothing more than a kid. As fearless as the Manipulants, they swarmed over the colonel, hamstringing and half disemboweling him. One was slicing the colonel's jugular when Ghost hissed an order, and in a moment they were all falling back in good order.

Zone cleared the blockage in the boarding well by clambering over people and laying about him with the flat of his e-tool. Burning got into the well, followed closely by Ghost. Somewhere behind them the two sides were breaking off contact, the din abating as the Exts yielded the field but won their freedom.

In the middle of being trundled down the ladder well, Dextra gritted her teeth and threw everything she had into regaining her composure. What happened in the next few minutes would decide the fate of hundreds of people and make or break her chance to influence the outcome of the Roke Conflict.

She shut her mind to the slaughter and shouted for Burning to put her down.

He ignored her as he continued to pick his way through the forward boarding lock and into the shuttle. The Exts' training and discipline had kept the featureless deck space from becoming complete chaos, but the cavernous cargo bay was filled with uncertain milling, queries, and overlapping calls for assistance.

Dextra pried at Burning's fingers. "Quit mauling me, for God's sake!"

The stridency of her tone got his attention, but it was something else that gave him pause. Tonii seized the crook of Burning's free elbow and without making any show of strength halted him in his tracks.

"Allgrave, I'll take her now," Tonii proclaimed.

Burning gave the gynander a reappraising stare. Dextra could see that he still hadn't figured Tonii out, but he understood that Tonii was a presence to be reckoned with. He glanced to make sure the lock was well guarded, then complied.

The last of the casualties were being carried aboard, as well as the Ext dead. Led by Zone, the rear guard reported that the Manipulants were withdrawing. While Dextra combed her hair back out of her face with her fingers and took a few yogic breaths, Burning blew a signal whistle for quiet.

"Company commanders or their execs report to me. Get all casualties moved to the aft bulkhead. Everybody else stand fast."

General Delecado emerged from the cockpit. "We're in control for now," he told Burning. "All locks secure and guarded. No unfriendlies encountered."

Burning nodded approval. Dextra decided that the Exts had to have run endless tactical simulations and training problems during the months-long voyage from Concordance, including familiarization sessions and enter-and-clear drills in assorted LAW craft.

Zone appeared, wiping scarlet off his e-tool with his sleeve. Someone from his outfit laughed. "Your eeter got some good eatin' today, huh, Colonel?" Zone didn't lower himself to acknowledge it.

"What's down, Allgrave?" General Delecado wanted to know.

"The whistle blew, and the shit flew—" Burning began.

"You two, get everybody strapped in," Dextra said, cutting him off. "And get someone to the boarding lock who knows how to operate the manual releases. Prep your people for free fall, maneuver forces, and possible micro-g nausea."

The sighs and sounds of the bloodbath were still with her, but anyone who had been raised in an orbital habitat knew how to thrust aside all distractions and turn to what needed to be done in a life and death emergency. "If we stay up here, we're finished. But if we can make planetfall, I can get us out of this."

Burning and his sister exchanged dubious looks.

"I say we trust her," Ghost said at last. "All that's certain is that there's no way back."

Half into a bottle of vodka he had discovered in one of the station's storage rooms, Mason watched through the window wall as a helipod touched down on the pad outside. The fair Ms. Deitz with more questions, he decided. Instead, however, it was Farley Swope who climbed out of the 'pod.

Where LAW's injustices had drained the fight out of most of the survey crew, they had only made Farley more stubborn. If leaving Sunbeard had bereaved her, she refused to let it show. She was still the stocky, dynamic, frizzy-locked woman Mason had met in LAW mission fundamentals training, maybe because she'd had more practice than most at forging her way through life's embitterments.

She walked briskly to the station, peeling off her flight gloves as she came through the door. Mason didn't even try to rise from the chair the vodka had glued him to. She took one look at him and shook her head in a gesture that managed to mix disapproval and sympathy.

"Claude," she said, approaching him, "the time's come to bring you in on something important. From the sorry look of you, you won't last much longer without hearing me out."

"Have a drink with me," he slurred, blinking in her general direction.

Farley squatted down in front of him. "Claude, listen to me. There might be a way for us to go back."

Mason's sluggish confusion must have shown on his face: thoughts of his parents' estate, now sold off; of his ex-several now light-years away; of former family friends who had distanced themselves from him because he had blundered his way onto the political gallows.

Farley clicked her tongue in exasperation. "Not back to

Abraxas. I mean back to Aquamarine. Where you and I both know we belong."

He stared at her, not trusting his ears.

"We can put our lives back on track, Claude. But you've got to want it badly enough, because we're only going to get one crack at it."

Mason gazed at the torturous, windblown Blades and tried to make sense of what she was telling him. "Farley, it's impossible. LAW will never allow us to go back."

Farley, who'd seemed about to chew him out, softened unexpectedly, coming closer to touch his face. "So fabulous-looking and dutiful to boot. Your family made damn sure of both, didn't they?" She glanced briefly at the vodka bottle beside him. "Claude, there's something getting into motion onboard the *Sword of Damocles*, something involving the conscriptees from Concordance."

"The Exts," Mason said.

Farley nodded. "This incident, Claude; it's going to grab a lot of media attention, and we can make use of it."

"To do what?"

"To bring Aquamarine into the light. I'd do it myself if I could, but like it or not, you're the *Scepter*'s public face."

Mason sniggered drunkenly. "Claude Mason, momentary hero—preinquest, of course."

"This involves Dextra Haven, Claude."

"The Hierarch?" he asked, showing a hint of interest.

"No, Dextra Haven the plumbing supply spokesmodel." Farley let go of her frown. "She's pushing for an Alpha-LAW mission to Aquamarine, but she's being hemmed in by Lightner and a lot of other Preservationists. The thing is, we can change that. Or you can, anyway."

Mason's pretended scorn was lost on Farley, who had always been able to see through the handsome facade the bio-cosmeds and subdermal sculptors had given him. Even so, he said, "You're staking our lives on a bunch of old-guard progressives?"

" 'The enemy of our enemy,' " Farley told him.

Mason reached for the bottle but didn't drink from it.

"Who've you been talking to, Farley? I mean, just how reliable's your information?"

She hesitated, then said, "I have contacts in the Quantum College."

Mason blinked once, then laughed long and hard.

The Quantum College. He associated the phrase with everything from stale party jokes to ominous questions and warnings in security oath documents. It was invoked by would-be mystics trying to get laid, paranoids in locked wards, blood-chilling modern myths that said the QC was the mask and mantle worn by certain surviving Cyberviruses.

There were abundant ways to enroll. An applicant often wound up supplying complaint data to consumer fraud investigators or experiencing a much less auspicious interface with internal security investigators.

At its low end the Quantum College was lumped in with cybergeist trickster fables such as Obetron, fAIries, and Hackey Puck. At the high end Mason knew of at least two independent studies—LAW and Lyceum—that had investigated allegations that the QC was a vehicle for Roke incursion into the Periapt computational and communications TechPlex.

Farley clamped a hand on his upper arm. "After the things we witnessed on Aquamarine, you're going to doubt me?"

She had his attention now and began to fill him in while she walked him through sobering circles in the station's communal room. She explained how Dextra Haven fit into the plan, how the Exts did, and how Mason would. As she ran it down for him, one part of his mind veered off onto the tormenting need to know whether his wife and child were alive on Aquamarine.

But Mason was yanked back when she got to the part about the Exts' landing on Periapt—and about the ocean.

"Farley, I can't," he interrupted. "You weren't at Styx Strait when the Oceanic got Marlon and the rest. You didn't see it kill Boon. You don't know what you're asking of me!"

She nodded once more, all sympathy and understanding. "You're right; I didn't see it get Boon. But I do know that the Oceanic's six light-years from here, Claude. And here's another calculation for you: Let's say Haven manages to get an A-LAW mission launched in a year. Using the second-generation zero-point-energy drive, that's still seven years objective in transit."

Mason ran the figures automatically; by that point he could do it in his sleep. "Almost nineteen years old, baseline." Merely saying the words hurt him.

"By the time you get there," Farley agreed. "You can't raise your child—if he or she survived—but you could be there for a marriage or maybe even the birth of a grandchild. Make what you can of your fatherhood that way. As for what we're asking of you regarding Periapt's ocean and all—"

"Don't say it," Mason cut her off. "I'll cross that when I come to it."

CHAPTER TWENTY

The proverb etched into a white and blue marble wall of the Periapt Naval Museum read GRANDE NAO, GRAN CUIDADO. Chaz Quant, executive officer of the SWATHship *Matsya*, did not know much Spanish, but he knew this one by heart and could vouch for it personally: "Great ship, great anxiety."

Even so, a certain measure of anxiety aboard the *Matsya* would have been preferable to the decline and moribundity that had taken hold of her. It was a terrible thing when a vessel came to an ignominious finish, especially a vessel of distinction.

Now the mighty *Mats*, from flight deck to trimaran keels, was a caretaker operation, a glorified test barge with a skeleton crew and dozens of embarked second-rate science types. He found himself increasingly inclined to hold guilty just about anything or anybody else who presented a target. Better, then, to pay his respects to the naval museum, an institution whose days were also numbered.

He rose from the bench to drift among displays he'd first seen in his boyhood, decades earlier. The weather being hot and clear, the place was almost empty. Quant followed a route he knew well to look upon what he regarded as sacred objects.

He passed the mangled and bashed-open submersible, once superstrong, from the epic PN *Solaris* submarine rescue, and lingered at a plaque that had come from Old Earth itself:

> *Sea captain:* Upon his first popping up, the lieutenants sheer off to the other side, as if he were a ghost indeed; for 'tis impudence for any to approach him within the length of a boathook.

138

The quote dated back to 1707 baseline and Plain Ned Ward's *The Wooden World*; it brought a smile to Quant's lips, his first in days.

The smile faded as he gazed at the flat photo taken on the boatwell deck of the marifortress *McMurdo Sound*, a group shot of the young, hard-bitten skippers from her amphib assault force. Six men and two women in salt-silvered fabric body armor, all staring directly into the camera, leaning against one another or with an arm propped on a comrade's shoulder. In the thirty-odd hours after the taking of the still, they had carried out a series of riverine raids and amphibious attacks that had stunned the world and virtually ended the Turnback War, in effect eliminating any need for the use of strategic weapons. The squadron commander was a man with a teak-dark somber face and wiry, short-cropped, graying black hair. He stood 180 centimeters tall and looked as if he could bench-press a capital ship's anchor.

Quant confronted his younger self. He had been nine kilos lighter in those days, twenty years younger, and he would go on to a kind of heroic infamy commanding the frigate *Hornet*. But nobody could take the *McMurdo Sound* away from him.

A sea captain, by God.

He gazed at the face and the nonreflective captain's insignia on the body armor collar for as long as he could bear to, then strode off quickly for the museum's huge main doors.

"Commander Quant."

Quant looked back the way he'd come, recognizing the gravelly voice and wondering why Valentin Maksheyeva was being so formal. Quant had precious few friends, but the curator was one of long standing. Then he saw that a stranger was slouching along lackadaisically in the wake of the old man. The stranger wore a uniform Quant couldn't place, an ill-fitting one that would have looked a good deal worse if it had not been wrinkle- and stain-resistant. Then he recognized it as some kind of Hierarchate civil service flunky getup.

Maksheyeva's ugly old puss composed itself into a grin. Quant approved of the curator's unaugmented looks, having nothing but scorn for cosmetic treatments and enhancements.

Changes that counted couldn't be bought. "This young man has been sent with an air diligence to return you ASAP to the *Matsya*, Commander," Maksheyeva said.

Quant beetled his eyebrows. "A limo?" He had figured to hitch a lift back aboard a harbor patrol craft if the *Matsya*'s captain's gig and surface-effect whaleboat were unavailable.

"Central Liaison has been trying to reach you without success," the young driver explained.

Quant grunted and showed him the plugphone he had removed from his ear.

"So some kind soul at Central Liaison has sent this fine young fellow to fetch you aboard." Maksheyeva touched the driver's arm. "I trust there's nothing amiss," he added.

Quant squared away his white-visored cap and smoothed his beard. "As do I. We'll have that drink another time, Admiral."

Maksheyeva nodded, beaming a bit at the driver's surprised, reassessing look. Valentin claimed to prefer not to be addressed by his retired rank, but he liked hearing it from Quant. "I'll be here. But you'd better make your good-byes to my two doormen there."

He meant the exhibits flanking the entrance: two naval gun turrets, monolithic and sharply sloped. To the left was the turret *Musashi*, rescued when the heavy cruiser *Yamamoto* went to salvage; to the right was *Lord Nelson*, off the *McMurdo Sound*. Special circumstances had brought back the day of the naval big gun during the Turnback War, but only fleetingly. *Musashi*, with its two 240-mm rifles, and *Lord Nelson*, with three monster 635s, were the last of their breed.

"The reclamation yard so soon?" Quant said.

Maksheyeva's shrug said volumes. "Cost-reduction requirements from the War Board. The museum is obliged to yield three-quarters of its physical space and most of its budget to other operations. *Musashi* and *Lord Nelson* are headed for the recycling yard, where they'll earn back something on the order of one three-thousandth of what it cost to build them."

In similar fashion, the museum's piers had been emptied of storied warships, and the Naval Academy had been consoli-

dated with other maritime and oceanographic-atmospheric
schools. All to feed the needs of LAW.

Quant tugged his visor lower. "Wish I could help, Admiral."
He hated the sound of it even as it came out of him.

Quant gave *Lord Nelson*'s turret facing a slap as he went
by—an armored incline nearly seven hundred millimeters
thick. It was like hitting a naked cliff face, no sound or feeling
of hollowness at all. Then he made his farewells to Mak-
shcyeva at the top of the proscenium steps and moved quickly
toward the swank air diligence.

Sensing their approach, the limo's cockpit and passenger
compartment doors opened. Quant didn't look aside as he
barked. "Driver, you're supposed to be wearing a name tag.
Where is it?"

The kid had been covertly staring at Quant and was taken off
guard.

"Central transportation pool driver Kurt Elide, sir," he
labored a moment to bring forth.

"Don't call me sir, Elide. You're a civilian." Quant slid into
a passenger compartment that had the understated elegance
of a VIP lounge. "I won't report you, but if you're going to
wear a uniform, show some self-esteem."

Kurt Elide assumed the driver's seat, a lot more curious than
worried. Kurt's second cousin's severalmate was deputy chief
of staff to Hierarch Dextra Haven, which was how Kurt
had gotten his job. And Kurt's boss, the pool superintendent,
wouldn't care a fart's worth about a name-tag complaint from
some wet navy has-been.

Yet there was something about Quant that kept Kurt from
laughing in the black man's face, something about the impec-
cable dress whites and decorations, the impression that in
Quant's world things were expected to work right and that
attention to detail was a matter of pride.

Once Kurt had lifted off, Quant asked, "You have any idea
what the flap's about, Driver Elide?" He had his plugphone
back in his ear but wasn't having any luck with it. There was a

complete commo setup in the passenger compartment, but Quant apparently wasn't familiar with it.

"Something's got Abraxas jumpin' through its asshole upside-down, Commander. The Public Safety people're crapping doilies. I'd've been grounded if this wasn't a priority hop. Saw flying squads of Peace Warrantors headed for the aeroport, and the army's being mobilized, but it's all being done on the QT."

"I presume you have emergency lights and directional sirens, Driver Elide."

"I do. But we don't have authoriza—"

"*I'm* your authorization, Elide. Let's have it all."

Kurt showed the rearview mirror a grin. "My pleasure, Commander."

In no time the *Matsya* hove into view. Quant, on the edge of his seat despite the safety harness, swore softly. Elide got a good look at what was going on and pronounced softly, "A-fucking-mazing!"

The SWATHship was making knots all right, but it was towing along a bobbing, swinging array of work booms, pontoon rafts, floats, and small barges that were being bashed through the swells as the ship gathered speed.

"Kinda sloppy way to go cruising, isn't it, Commander?" Kurt observed.

"Shut your gob and do your job," Quant growled. He shifted closer to the window while punching up long-range optical displays. "Of all the times to be flying in some wallowing civvie *scheissewagon*," he muttered. "Elide, maybe you'd better lay to . . ."

Kurt ignored the recommendation and banked so sharply for the PNS *Matsya* that Quant was thrown against his safety webbing.

Farley had said that Mason's break from Blades Station would have to be by helipod because 'pods were the only craft accessible to the *Scepter* detainees, and that was only because the station authorities deemed escape by helipod impossible.

No sooner had Farley sobered him up than she got him

safely to an outlying motor pool. The station was between training cycles in high desert warfare and survival, and many of the cadre were away on furloughs, medical travel, or inter-cycle transfer.

They found Hippo Nolan doing a most unauthorized field modification on a government gray helipod like Farley's.

"Five-finger requisition," Hippo explained cheerfully when Mason asked about it. He'd fitted it with a heavy-duty power pack and raised the floor plate. "It'll either get you where you're going or blow you apart absolutely painlessly, guaranteed."

Mason looked Hippo over. The engineer had let his weight sine-curve on Aquamarine, where corpulence was in many places a sign of status. But appetite suppressants and dietetically engineered cuisine had trimmed him down by forty kilos or more.

"Are you also a student body at the Quantum College, Nolan?" Mason asked sourly, resenting the notion that Hippo, too, had been holding out on him.

Hippo looked surprised. "Don't be a yankwang, Claude. What it is, is that Farley's got some Rationalist pipeline among the station cadre but doesn't want to cop to it. Which is fine by me. But I don't think she should be insulting the rest of us with this QC anal gas. What counts more is that I believe the info itself. So give this caper your best lick, pretty boy."

Mason accepted a helping hand aboard the modified helipod. Farley passed him some dupes of survey data and overview briefing materials that the team members had man-aged to hang on to. A few others—Franco Luong, Lewis Pine-tree, Hilario Abrego—looked on.

"Don't tell me they want to go back to Aquamarine," Mason muttered to Farley as he belted in. He had to half squat to settle his armpits onto the rests; his quadriceps were going to feel a lot worse before they felt better.

"Half and half," she estimated. "But they know that you want back, and this is their way of saying thanks for getting them home."

She checked his helmet and pressed something into the palm of his right hand.

Mason knew before looking what it was: a pair of Holy Rollers she'd nabbed on Aquamarine. An artifact of the planet's pre-Cyberplague times, the Optimant-made dice—one translucent with red pips and the other red-tinted with clear pips— were used more for purposes of divination than for games of chance.

"For luck," Farley told him.

As Mason carefully tucked the dice into his breast pocket, Farley reboarded her 'pod and buckled in. Hippo gave a last wave, but nobody else had anything to add. Mason and Farley throttled up, rose from the ground, leaned their weight, ascended, and accelerated into the air.

High desert winds gusted and played with them as they raced out past the erosion-carved stone fins, vanes, and natural flying buttresses of the Blades, rolling up kilometers at a power-hungry rate. Mason's microflier with its heavier power pack was less responsive, and the steering duct fans were working harder to compensate. He and Farley were coming through a wide bank, bearing southwest, when Farley's voice sawed in his plugphone.

"This is the point of no return for me. We're counting on you, Claude." She peeled off for a thin, bowed formation from which she would keep watch for and decoy, if possible, any pursuers.

Mason kicked in more speed. Swinging and tilting the flying crow's nest among the eternal monoliths helped him keep his mind off what lay at land's end. He tried to shift his position to ease the strain on his thighs but couldn't move too far and still work the armrest controls. He also had to keep weight on his feet to lean and steer safely.

The helipod's just-adequate nav system projected guidance displays onto Mason's helmet visor. In thirty-four minutes of flying time he passed from the military reservation onto the public parklands sector of the Blades.

Park system beacons began to show on his visor. He had no difficulty picking up the correct pass and swinging south for the coast. The well-marked recreational flight path brought him down to a low traffic corridor that paralleled a surface multiway. He stayed out of centrally monitored lanes; the self-drive corridor was almost empty, and he cranked along at nearly 150 kph with no hitches. Still, he waited for the shadow of an intercept craft to fall over him.

Traffic thickened, passing down from the highlands. The helipod was the smallest thing in that low airspace, making for some uncomfortable moments with hovertrucks, air cushion buses, and such. Then, ahead, gleamed the sea.

Mason saw its pitted burnish and felt his stomach twist. He broke out in a sweat but kept himself from grounding the 'pod on the breakdown margin. Where the glacial flow of the multiway forked, he tilted away from Abraxas's lofty starscrapers along the coastal route. There was heavy midaltitude traffic; he wished he could trade places with anybody flying above, no matter who, no matter what that person's dilemma.

He forced himself to descend to surface-effect height and take the beach road but then passed up exit after exit. At last he faced the fact that he wasn't picking his entry point—he was *avoiding* it. He slowed, shifted his weight to bank, grunted at the fire in his upper legs, then eased out onto a firm, pale lavender strand forty meters wide.

The sandy stretch posted for public sex was back toward Abraxas; here it was for sports enthusiasts. There were people occupied with wave wings, surface-effect SErfboards, and such. Many were simply splashing around or lying in the sun.

Mason grounded the helipod and raised his visor. Taking note of his pale face and anxious stare, several bystanders gave him curious looks. He moaned, stretching his legs, transfixed by the dark and malevolent waters, feeling the paralyzing horror he'd carried since that day at the Styx Strait.

Don't tell *me* that Beast didn't fuck with my neurowares! he screamed to himself.

It was what he hadn't been able to confront back at the Blades, and here at last there was no avoiding it. He closed his eyes, bit down hard on his lip, and thought about his wife and child.

He brought up the throttle, lifted off, and leaned forward to put the 'pod on a course straight for the breaking surf. He gathered speed little by little, then hit the throttle and whooshed out over the sea with a yell—

No. He hadn't, he discovered. He had instead reversed course, slewing around and nearly crashing the almost idiot-proof helipod. Some of the beach buffs stopped what they were doing to gaze at the man in the institutional gray microflier, draped on the 'pit rests, weeping as though his heart would burst.

CHAPTER
TWENTY-ONE

Quant looked down at his ship and heard echoes of Spanish in his head: *Grande nao, gran cuidado,* indeed.

The *Matsya* was dragging behind her a flotilla of rafts and barges. Rigged for stationary use by the ship's nonmilitary technical and research contingent—called by all hands the Science Side—the towed craft were hampering the *Matsya* and imperiling her and one another like a bevy of drunken powerboaters. Along with her usual navigational and landing deck lights, she was flashing and strobing emergency beacons, flying warning flags, and Quant had no doubt, sounding Klaxons and other alarms to proclaim a hazardous landing situation. Crash equipment and personnel were deploying on her vest-pocket ocean-going runway.

The tows had always vexed Quant: The SWATHship was merely serving as a test-bed tugboat for 'wares, configurations, and equipment that would go aboard bona fide research vessels.

Yet Quant's heart leapt to see how cleanly she cut the waves. SWATH/SST was an acronym for Small Waterplane-Area, Tri-hulled, SemiSubmerged Trimaran. By design, shock waves created by its bulbous bow were damped by funneling wave trains at opposite angles between the main hull and the two outrigger sponsons hulls, canceling hydrodynamic energy that otherwise would have buffeted the vessel, increased drag, and cut into the efficiency of the actuator disk propellers.

"Whatever they're expecting, it's not us," Kurt Elide murmured as he brought the airlimo around for an approach on the flight deck's round-down aft end.

Quant hollered into the intercom. "Damn you, Elide, shear off! She's declared aircraft emergency. We can't foul her flight deck!" At the same time he scanned the sky wildly for the imperiled and imperiling inbound plane. Setting aside the question of why an aircraft in trouble hadn't been routed to one of the far-better-equipped military or civilian runways in the greater Abraxas area, he tried to get the passenger compartment commo to switch to *Matsya*'s air ops freq.

Kurt Elide shook his head without taking his eyes off the SWATHship. "My pool super just relayed a twix from your captain, Commander. He wants you back on board *right now*, so I'll try to ease us in through that big open door at the back. No problem with this sled."

The door he was talking about was in reality the hangar deck rocket–jet engine test area at the stern, under the round-down. Captain Hall, currently manning the conn, was evidently so rattled that he was pumping ship in his skivvies, authorizing a landing like that. It meant that Quant *had* to get aboard ASAP.

He considered telling Elide to try for the aircraft elevator doorway in the portside sponson, but the crosswind would have made that approach even more risky. "Very well, but take it slowly and mind the pitch and roll of the deck" he advised. There were no engines currently in the test area, and a vehicle with the dexterity of the aircar should have been able to negotiate it handily. "And patch the air control push back here, Elide!"

All at once Kurt's smooth, confident approach became rocky as he decelerated urgently. Quant felt the limo shudder as if it, not the driver, were debating breaking off the run.

Kurt called back, "Something blocking that stern doorway!"

Quant was getting passenger compartment feeds of pilot instrumentation, including an optical of the engine test opening. Someone from Science Side had parked an external helo package there. It poked into the test area opening somewhat but left nearly as much room as the limo would have had anyway.

"Gotta abort," Kurt announced shakily.

"Steady on, boy," Quant bade him with kindly reassurance. "You're doing fine."

"There isn't enough leeway—"

"You committed yourself to something, Elide. Now you see it through or I'll punch your yellow heart out the back of your rib cage and play handball with it."

The level, declarative way in which Quant stated it jarred Elide into action. Bucking the crosswind and finessing through air turbulence stirred by the *Matsya*, he adjusted the speed and angle of descent with a skill Quant found surprising. Elide, matching the pitch and roll of the vessel, slipped through the engine test opening and into the hangar deck with room to spare on all sides.

"Soft as a mother's kiss," Quant commented.

While filling in Burning and the others on what lay ahead, Dextra had a private moment of self-congratulation for having worn a fashionable fieldsuit that was crisis-worthy. Because it vented moisture vapor but was liquid H_2O–impermeable, it kept the Exts from seeing that her bladder had let her down during the bloodshed in the passageway.

It made her consider in passing what secrets the battlesuits around her might be protecting.

General Delecado—Daddy D—had the flight crew thoroughly persuaded to cooperate. The *Sword of Damocles*'s captain and the Aero Forces authorities knew how dangerous it was to risk violence in and around a docked shuttle. Moreover, a Hierarch and another Hierarch's daughter were hostage's or at least at risk. For the time being everyone aboard was on the same side.

Lock details released the docking tackle manually as LAWs stood by and let it happen. The shuttle cast off from *Damocles* and applied power.

There weren't enough deck rings for the hundreds of Exts in the cargo bay. Some were hooked up to others who were snapped down. Cargo webbing and safety lines had been used improvisationally: the space looked like a sea vine–tangled school of dark, warlike merpeople. With Flowstate deftness, most coped with micro-g. Parameds tending the wounded had missed some of the floating globules of blood with their aerogel wads, and a fine pink mist had begun to propagate.

Nike Lightner and her troupe sat silently, taking up most of the few jumpseats and watching the events in something of a daze. Lazlo-Lazlo was weeping openly. His camera had been smashed in the fighting, and he had no way to record what was to come.

When Daddy D returned to the cockpit, Dextra allowed Burning to lead her into the semiprivacy of an engineering station cubby, where he took his mike off-line and whispered, "Why did you do this?"

She gave him an abbreviated version of the anonymous warning, withholding the fact that the message had purportedly come from the Quantum College. She explained her sense of responsibility as a Rationalist for the Exts' predicament but kept to herself the fact that Nike Lightner's father probably was involved in the plot to eliminate them and thereby bring political ruination down on her.

Burning grew impatient with the story. "We have to land soon. What then?"

"We set down in a place where we can present your group to the media and through them to Periapt—in a favorable light, of course."

"So the Periapt public'll forgive us for feeding those Manips some silverware?"

"No. No!" Dextra said. "If we don't mention the violence, the opposition isn't likely to, either. An independent investigation could blow up in their faces. If we succeed in spinning you a positive image, you'll be ten times harder to move against. You'll have the protection of the spotlight."

He looked skeptical. "This shuttle can't just set down anywhere, no matter *how* many knives we hold to the pilot's neck."

Dextra smiled inwardly. The Allgrave had some quick neural 'wares under that battle helmet. For all its size, the shuttle could land STOL, but the hitch was that it required sophisticated on-site guidance equipment and telemetry. While there were a few facilities on Periapt that could handle that, the Preservationist faction, along with LAW, would be moving quickly to seal off the aerospace fields, bar the press, and try to dispose of the Exts, hostages or no.

"That's been taken into account," she said after a moment, giving him a campaign portrait smile. "Will you trust me for now?"

"Why should we?"

"Because I trusted you when you tucked me under your arm like a stuffed bunny. You impress me as a man who usually asks before he takes any real liberties, Burning."

She watched him swallow and lower his eyes, and in one surge his face went red. When she brushed back one of the Hussar Plaits that had floated free of his helmet, she felt the heat of his cheek on the back of her hand.

"*Ecce!* There's a quite fascinating aspect to this phenomenon, Allgrave. Did you know blushes can't be faked? Except perhaps by virtuoso actors or with behavioral programming or drugs. I find this unfeigned color rather attractive. It's honest, at least."

Angered by the teasing, he turned his face away from her touch. "Honesty's not much use in dealing with LAW, though, is it? Not much to impress a Periapt."

She tried but couldn't resist. "Impress? Why, Allgrave, that would depend on just how far the blush *extends*."

CHAPTER
TWENTY-TWO

The hangar deck was small and cramped by the standards of a fleet carrier but still was an impressive space for shipboard. Just then *Matsya*'s flight operations were almost nonexistent, and so it held oddments of containerized stores and equipment shifted from other venues.

The airlimo had not even touched down when a chief petty officer trotted up to it holding a heavy-duty command headset with a heads-up-display visor. It was marked "XO" in raised letters.

"Good job, Elide. Knew you had it in you," Quant said as he handed his white saucer cap to the CPO. Then, without giving Elide another glance, he departed at a run, pulling on the headset as he went.

Captain Hall's voice was already in Quant's ears over the command channel. "Ah, Chaz! C-capital!" Hall disdained formal commo procedure, just as he excused himself from so much that was navy custom. The relief in his voice, however, came through loud and clear. "We're in something of a slippery patch here."

"On my way, sir," Quant told him. "Suggest we meet on the port wing of the bridge."

"Yes, fine, Chaz; just hurry."

The port wing was actually just a wide spot on the observation deck overlooking the flight deck on the ship's bridge level portside. The flight deck itself covered the *Matsya*'s portside sponson and rested on part of the main. Quant arrived to find it disturbingly unoccupied. With navy personnel in short supply, every hand who could be spared had turned to. Regis T. "Hallowed" Hall was watching the preparations on the flight deck with uncharacteristic gravity. The stiff breeze ruffled Quant's beard as he reached his captain's side.

"How say you, Chaz?"

Quant had gotten updates via headphone along the way; now he chinned his visor's display switch. "An aerospace shuttle? Trying a deck landing here?" he asked in disbelief. "Skipper, wave them off, no matter what it takes. If you don't—"

"Not don't, Chaz—can't. " For once Hall did not sound amused by life's little follies. "I've been given my marching orders from on high. We *will* retrieve this shuttle and will *not* fail or we'll all be falling on our swords before the day is out. I direct you to take the deck."

Quant had been a seafaring man most of his life, while Hall's background was a university cadet program and a string of political appointments on dry land. In fact, Hall was on *Matsya*, like others before him, only to officially log a sea command, while Chaz Quant pretty much ran the boat.

At least Hall was smart enough to know his limitations. Aware that those on watch inside the bridge could see him, Quant backed up a pace, keyed his mike, and saluted exactingly. "I relieve you, sir."

Hallowed Hall's salute was for once passable. "I stand relieved. Watch section, Mr. Quant has the deck. Pass the word."

Not just the conn but the deck. Complete responsibility for and authority over PNS *Matsya*, except as Hall might— unthinkable as it was—countermand.

A pale, undernourished-looking petty officer second class moved up behind Quant to handle the telephone traffic, leaving Quant free to concentrate. An odd mix of geek and romantic poet type, Roiyarbeaux looked very grateful for the transfer of operational control.

Quant reduced speed, got *Matsya* turned into the wind, and, via Roiyarbeaux, called away a special sea detail to sever the lines that had been made fast to the various booms and floats.

Quant got on the channel personally to add, "Don't waste time untying or uncoupling. Chop 'em away or saw them through with emergency tools."

"Chaz, Doctor Zinsser's out there," Hall blurted, "and he expressly told me not to do that. Some of his paraphernalia's lost buoyancy . . ." Seeing the flash of Quant's eyes behind the HUD visor's racing imagery and readouts, he let his words trail off. The wrath of *Matsya*'s senior scientist was Quant's problem now.

With his ship disencumbered, Quant resumed Hall's previous course for open water, edging around the shallows that had made the captain drag Zinsser's water-skiing floats through a crosswind. In the meantime, Quant was getting the particulars from his air boss, Germaine Bohdi.

"Book says we're rated for this retrieval, XO," she reported tightly. "But the book was written before the navy went on starvation rations. The cross-deck pendants have me worried."

The newest of the three five-centimeter-thick arresting cables used to halt a landing aircraft by means of its tailhook had already logged over two hundred traps, where under normal circumstances a cable would be consigned to the deep after logging half that number of retrievals. The problem was that *Matsya* was far back in line for refurbishment and replacement parts, twelve years overdue in some cases.

"We make the trap anyway," Quant told her. "Let's have the barriers. Get your people set for a rough one."

Bohdi had been anticipating it. The words were barely out of Quant's mouth when a double fence of thick, woven composite netting sprang up on retractable hydraulic supports. The barriers were positioned up toward the bow end of the flight deck, which was angled up at twelve degrees, like a ski jump, for takeoffs. The shuttle would have only one shot at a landing: If it took out the barriers without stopping, it would lose too much speed to power-climb back into the air for another go-round.

Barriers and arresting wires weren't Quant's only concern. The scanty flight data gave the shuttle a total weight of sixty

tons. The SWATHship was an extremely stable platform—
her three hulls joined by a prodigiously strong box-girder
structure—but a too-hard landing might crumple the flight
deck, heel her over, and even damage the frame.

Around the headland, *Matsya* hit the violent offshore cur-
rents that presided there, her bows slicing two-meter swells.
Quant called for twenty-five-knot actuator turns and took her
into the teeth of the wind. Even with the shuttle's ducted-thrust
STOL capability, the landing was going to be a lot more like a
controlled crash than a soft touchdown.

The SWATHship surged forward, cutting the swells and
throwing foam spray over the bows. There was a whoop from
the bridge—Lieutenant Giaraszekh, OOD of the watch, who
was apparently monitoring the waterline cams. "*Mother Mats*
is carryin' a bone in her teeth!" It was the old expression for a
ship cutting the swells and throwing foam and spray up from
the bows; in *Matsya*'s case, it was three bones.

There were new feeds on Quant's HUD visor: particulars on
the shuttle's unauthorized departure from starship *Sword of
Damocles*, a possible mutiny by armed parolees, VIP hostages
and orders from on high that no hostile action be undertaken.
Quant did not pay the updates much mind. Landing telemetry
signals said the shuttle had opened its stubby double-delta,
variable-geometry wings for maximum surface area and
flareout and minimum sweep. It had just completed an energy-
shedding S turn, had banked at the designated break, and was
coming downwind, homing in on the flight deck's centerline.
Quant took a look at it via telescopic cam feed, a monster
flechette of exotic alloys and composites pulsating silently and
growing very quickly.

Six separate landing guidance systems—optical, illuminated, voice, two radar, and autopilot backup—were on-line,
and none struck Quant as an adequate safeguard. He instructed
the crash crews to get the towbots ready, make certain the crane
operator was wearing a fireproof suit, and have the washdown
systems primed to pump anticomfire suppression foam and
deck flush.

"If this landing goes bad," Quant told Hall, "I want what's left of the shuttle pushed over the side immediately."

Hallowed Hall cleared his throat melodically. "Chaz, the Hierarchate—"

Quant covered his lip mike with his hand and glared at Hall. "Relieve me or stand clear, Captain."

Both ideas terrified Hall, but the Lyceum was far away, while the plummeting shuttle was near. "Carry on, Mr. Quant," he said.

The shuttle had dirtied up, deploying landing gear and tailhook, lowering flaps, and angling its thrust downward through vectoring ducts to keep it airborne at what otherwise would have been substalling speed.

Quant thought for a moment that the shuttle was coming in too low and would make a catastrophic ramp strike against the round-down at the stern end of the flight deck, but Germaine Bohdi's calm voice got the pilot up just high enough to avoid it yet low enough to try for a cross-deck pendant. Even at greatly diminished speed the pilot would pass all three wires in less than a second.

The shuttle's shadow flickered across the deck, seeming to pounce at the spaceplane itself. The pilot missed the first wire but snagged the second, only to have it pull taut and part with a crack like a high-powered rifle shot. People dived for cover or hurled themselves into the permanently rigged safety netting. With deep metallic noises from the severed halves, the pieces of cable flailed the air like huge bullwhips. The starboard one flayed the superstructure twenty meters below the bridge wing, indenting the plating there with loops and curves of impact grooving.

Then, miraculously, the shuttle's tailhook caught the third wire, and the craft hit the deck with smashing impact, its landing gear striking clouds of friction smoke from the nonskid surfacing. Fed belowdecks through sheaves to electromagnetic arresting gear, the wire brought the shuttle to a smooth halt in less than forty meters as the added weight gave *Matsya* a perceptible list to portside. The shuttle's nose came to rest a mere five meters short of the barrier nets.

"We've got them!" Hall exclaimed, so relieved that he seemed about to weep.

Quant, mindful of who was aboard the shuttle and just how lightly armed *Matsya* was, asked himself, Who's got whom?

CHAPTER
TWENTY-THREE

The rave of the shuttle's engines died as the pilot shut them down. Quant directed Lieutenant Gairaszekh to reduce speed and come about for a slow and cautious return to *Matsya*'s previous anchorage. Quant wanted to be as close as possible to shore-based airborne and seagoing assets, medevac facilities, and the rest. Besides, there were the Science Side's rafts and rummage to recover.

Deck dogs and Science Siders alike emerged from cover to gawk at the smoking aerospace craft. Blueshirts and yellows rushed forward with their equipment. When Quant roared at them to stay back, they moved smartly to obey. Those crewing the hoses and playpipes that would sluice high-pressure jets of water across the flight deck were ordered to stand ready.

Hall was no more eager to play hostage negotiator than he had been to captain his ship. Quant relinquished the conn to Gairaszekh and headed for the descended shuttle. His chief master-at-arms, leading a security detail, offered him a pistol—one of only twelve small arms aboard—but Quant brushed it aside without slowing.

As he stepped out onto the vast and windy openness of the flight deck, he saw a puzzlingly familiar face. "What the fore-'n-aft are you doing here?"

Pool airlimo driver Kurt Elide turned his gaze from the silent shuttle to Quant. "Public Safety's grounded everything in the region. I couldn't leave."

Quant fumed. "You slack-jawed little snivelneck. If you want a front-row seat to watch the feces hit the flywheel aboard this ship, join the navy. Otherwise get the hell off my ocean!"

Elide nearly grinned. "Sorry, Commander, but regimenta-
tion clashes with my psych profile. Although the shuttle
landing and the way you handled it—that was *fulgurous*."

Quant saw that there was no point getting further exercised.
Elide was just another latter-day Periapt kid. Besides, there
were other civilians peeking from various corners, including
Dr. Zinsser's oceanographic underlings and Dr. Shu and the
aquaculture staff. Approaching the shuttle, Quant gave less
thought to the weapons that might be trained on him than to the
danger his ship might be facing.

With no sign of life in the shuttle, he wondered if he would
have to call for a crane and knock for entry. As he got within a
dozen paces of it, however, a belly hatch popped down, a powered ladder lowered to the deck, and a man in high combat
boots and some kind of soft armor suit dropped to the nonskid
deck. Quant drew a deep breath and took another couple of
steps.

"Sir, I'm Commander Chaz Quant, executive officer of
this vessel, Periapt Navy SWATHship *Matsya*." There was
probably some protocol for welcoming air pirates aboard, but
Quant wasn't conversant with it. "Who am I addressing?"

The fellow was a husky white man with a crooked nose and
red hair that fell below his shoulders, some of it twisted into
tight plaits along either side. A large handgun was holstered on
his chest, and there was a combat knife on his belt.

"Ask *her*," the redhead answered in lilting Terranglish,
offering his hand to a woman who was coming down the
ladder—Hierarch Dextra Haven.

She appeared somewhat mussed but exuberant, as if things
were going very much her way. No sooner did she hit firm
footing than she was on the go, wielding a lot of eye contact
but striking an attitude that said she had no time to waste on
minutiae.

"If you'd be so kind, Commander," she said to Quant, "point
me to that incorrigible Regis T. Hall. I've brought several hundred head of guests with me, and they'll need to be quartered
and fed straight away." She gestured to Quant's headset.
"What's that, a commo? Hand it here."

The good thing about having no prospects for promotion was that Quant had nothing to lose by speaking his mind. But before he could, Hall's voice issued over the command channel. "Oblige her, Chaz. There's a good fellow."

Quant relinquished the headset stoically, and Hierarch Dextra Haven fumbled it on, pressing furrows into her mounds of wavy jet-black hair. Spotting Hall on the port wing of the bridge, she waved and yoo-hooed. Hall waved back as if they were in box seats at the Abraxas Derby. Quant's jaw muscles jumped as he signaled a blueshirt to bring him another headset visor.

Disembarkation halted after a striking scar-faced woman and a boyish blond man appeared. They emerged from under the shuttle to starboard, near the upper works, and were eyeballing the ship for, Quant presumed, snipers, LAW troops, or other backup. Quant ignored the stains on their battlesuits.

The redhead—Allgrave Burning—was taking in the painterly daubs of ginger cirrus clouds in a clear white-gold sky. "Beautiful, quite beautiful," he pronounced. Something in the way he said it and in his manner relaxed Quant a notch.

"I'm so-oo indebted to you for this gracious reception, Captain," Dextra Haven was gushing into the headset. "If there's ever anything I can do for you by way of—hmm? Oh, thou *wicked* man, certainly not! At least not without some sex clinic rescue parameds standing by. Seriously, now, about our guests from Concordance: you simply cannot let me down in my hour of need."

She hinted at the political points Hall could score by playing along. In the absence of countermanding orders from on high, Hall had everything to gain.

Dextra Haven made no mention of untoward events on *Sword of Damocles* and insisted that bureaucratic bungling was to blame for her having arrived unannounced. She explained that she had tried to contact Cal Lightner and others in the Hierarchate—Preservationist opponents primarily— during the shuttle's descent, though none had so much as acknowledged her. Quant saw how it gave her actions a temporary fig leaf of legitimacy. He had read that she won over Lyceum swing votes in the same manner.

She was smaller than she looked in media coverage, but her figure was just as lush. While Quant regarded intensive longev measures with distaste, Haven's were first-rate. She was a decade older than he but could have passed for late twenties, baseline.

Quant's inspection of the celebrated Hierarch was interrupted by the arrival of a replacement headset. Over the manoeuvering and docking circuit came word that an indignant Dr. Zinsser had caught up to *Matsya* in a one-man surface-effect scooter and was bound for the flight deck.

Quant had no time for it. "Keep Zinsser off this deck even if you have to lock him in one of his own specimen traps," he told his chief master-at-arms.

The "aye-aye" sounded very enthusiastic.

When he turned back to Dextra Haven, she handed him his headset. "Your CO wants you to rustle up temporary quarters for LAW's new tactical strike force here," she said.

Quant looked again to the bemused Allgrave and the others. "Strike force. Uh huh."

"You heard me, Commander . . ."

"Quant."

"Ah, yes, I believe I've heard of you."

"As I have you," Quant said.

"Then I have your cooperation?"

There was no contesting it. His moment of supreme indispensability had passed, and he was once more a man who had to do whatever he was told to in order to stay at sea.

As he tossed the spare headset to a deck dog and redonned his own, he became aware of an aircraft making a pass and saw a powerful civilian VTOL with press markings swing by, bow to stern off the port flight deck's edge. He chinned over to the flight ops channel, but Germaine Bohdi was at a loss.

"I gave them the wave-off, XO, but they ignored it," she reported. "Public Safety and the military were holding back too far to intercept. There's a swarm of newsies in it, demanding landing clearance."

Dextra Haven was tugging at Quant's bare elbow, pointing at the media VTOL. "Allow them to land! I *invited* them!"

Quant gnashed his teeth briefly, then relayed her words. He had long before learned when and how to defer with dignity.

Haven began waving to the circling news crews, striking a heroic pose as if she had landed the shuttle herself. She had opened her suit seam for a bit of décolleté, and the wind blew back her foaming sable hair.

Quant decided to leave the aerospace plane where it was and guide the press VTOL in for a landing farther astern. That did not please the taxi directors and handler's pit, but Quant blamed it all on the Lyceum. By the time the VTOL started spewing news crews, he had gotten the flight deck battened down so that the invading horde would be corraled there. He also put in a request for Peace Warrantors and a maritime patrol to ward off other sightseers.

Dextra had been getting her energy level up to face the media. Most of the Manipulant blood had washed off the Ext battlesuits, and what remained would pass for dark stains, and so the three Ext cousins were at least presentable. She had no intention of letting the journalists meet the Ext rank and file yet. The shuttle's viewport covers remained drawn.

She had Lod summon Nike Lightner from the shuttle, however. Blessed with the inner toughness that ran in the Lightners, Nike had recovered her mental equilibrium while most of her coterie was still glassy-eyed and speechless. She hadn't actually observed the Manipulants' attack, but circumstances supported Dextra's explanation, and Nike was fair-minded enough to put aside for the time being her resentment at being used. It had taken some high-density talk from Dextra to reach an agreement to brazen out the impromptu press conference and sort out the details and recriminations later. In exchange, Nike had extracted a promise from Dextra to accept reduced royalties on any production of *And on the Way, We Dropped It* Nike might decide to mount.

At Chaz Quant's order the news crews left their hover remotes behind in the VTOL; a dozen zooming, darting A/V reemos would only have invited chaos. The newsies balked until Quant promised to shoot down any reemo he saw with a close-in antiaircraft coilgun that had in actuality been stripped from the SWATHship years earlier.

Military aides, flunkies, and boot pullers tended to blur together, but Dextra vaguely recognized the dark-skinned naval commander because of his mustacheless patriarchal beard. In her recall his name was linked with some major debacle or dereliction of duty, a high-profile court-martial—irrelevant for the moment.

To compensate for the lack of reemos, the press gangs equipped themselves with extensible, articulated pickup booms, jockeying for position like hungry serpents. Competing for interview bites, the reporters all but bodychecked each other. That left Dextra and Nike to do more smiling and posing than responding to questions.

Though ignorant of the skirmish in orbit, the correspondents seemed disappointed that the three Exts lacked pointed tails and shreds of human flesh lodged in their teeth. The newsies moaned orgasmically when they spied Ghost's scars, however, and Burning and Lod had to fend them off a bit. Gimlet-eyed, Ghost endured the attention silently. Dextra had made it clear how central the baying media pack was to public opinion and the Exts' fortunes.

"Is it true that the Exts live only for war?" one reporter asked Burning.

"I was writing a dissertation on literature and utopian thought when LAW came along," he told her.

"Ah! So you're telling my viewers that the Exts use pathological violence to conceal their basic cowardice?" Abruptly, the woman shifted her pickup to Lod. "How about it, Major?"

Lod cocked an eyebrow, something he did very well. "Madame, you were the one who kneed your colleague in the groin so you could get past him and stick that device in my face."

There were catcalls from some of the newsies as the correspondent sputtered and tried to recover, and more pickups

swung Lod's way. "So you're saying the Exts are just good soldiers, Major Lod?" someone asked.

"I personally, sir, am a lover, not a fighter. So you might say
that I'm here in the capacity of organ donor."

Correspondents glanced at their voice-stress analyzers to
gauge Lod's anxiety level, but the devices didn't know what to
make of his Ext-style Terranglish. "Major, do you think your
rebels can serve without dissension alongside LAW troops?"

"Teamwork is essential in war, ladies and gentlemen. It
gives the enemy other people to shoot at."

They liked that one, elbowing each other to feed him
straight lines, the pickups caroming off each other.

"Do the Exts have a fighting motto?"

" 'Life's too Short to Drink Cheap Wine.' "

Off to one side Burning groaned, but Ghost looked faintly
amused. Dextra was mildly charmed by the way Lod was
playing the press, but she knew she needed to give the event a
different spin. It was important to get Nike Lightner in the
spotlight and fix it so that the Preservationist conspirators
would find it was too late to reveal the carnage in the *Damocles*'s passageway.

She glanced over to see that Quant, patience dissolved, was
ordering up a strong-arm squad and getting ready to restore
order. But in all the commotion and milling no one took note of
the man worming his way through the feeding frenzy until
he vaulted up between two pickup techs, almost landing on
Burning's head.

Burning easily caught him and, seeing no weapons, merely
kept him from collapsing.

The intruder was a light-skinned man with a queue of brown
hair and what might have been perfect features under less
stressful circumstances. His eyes were fixed and staring, his
lips purple and frothy. His LAW fieldsuit was damp with salt
spray, and how he had gotten through Quant's security was
anybody's guess.

As news pickups zoomed in and scoop-hungry crews vied to
find out what was going on, the intruder rallied enough to say,

"I'm Claude Mason. I was acting commander of the Aquamarine survey team."

Stunned, Dextra fought her way to Mason's side. "I recognize you, Administrator Mason."

"Madame Hierarch," he said weakly.

"But how did you get here? And why are you here?" She didn't see how Mason's sudden appearance could possibly be a monkey wrench thrown by Lightner's faction, not after they'd defied censure, public opinion polls, and sunshine laws to keep the *Scepter* returnees under wraps.

Mason shot a trembling glance at the ocean swells. "I got here across the waters—in a stolen helipod." Whatever was driving him snapped him out of the thrall in which the ocean held him. "It doesn't matter now. I've only come to say that LAW *must* return to Aquamarine."

Every press pickup was focused on him. "The answer is there on Aquamarine—the solution," he raved. "An end to the Roke Conflict! Knowledge only the Oceanic has—" He was gulping air, nearly convulsing. "The Oceanic . . ."

He lost consciousness then, collapsing in Burning's arms before the eyes of viewers all over Periapt.

CHAPTER
TWENTY-FOUR

The press gangs crowded in even harder on Burning and the slumped Mason, creating a frenzied babble of running commentaries, drowning out one another's questions, and bumping mikes into the Exts' faces and warding hands. The A/V pickup tentacles were dogfighting.

One grazed Dextra's head but missed doing her real harm. Lod was avid to lend supporting hands until she shook him off. She began to wish she hadn't ordered Tonii to remain in the shuttle out of concern for the gynander's loathing of public attention.

In short order the Exts, Nike Lightner, and Dextra found themselves hemmed in by a wall of metal-legged giants. Many of the techs and reporters were wearing lower-body exos with telescoping stiltboots that enabled them to rise above the crowd for unobstructed shots.

"Stand back!" Quant barked, his angry shouts like a string of detonating depth charges. Naval crewpeople and even some of the Science Siders ran to help him try to put an end to the newsers' feeding frenzy.

One journalist still at normal height infiltrated the cordon to grab Ghost's shoulder in the hope of charming an exclusive out of her. Instead, she pried his thumb back with her hand, then turned her wrist and sent him thudding to the flight deck.

Lod tripped a cam operator who was trying to give Ghost a retaliatory shove; the tech windmilled into another one, and both toppled, the pickup tentacles thrashing and tangling.

The falling newsers were descending straight toward Dextra when she was suddenly in the clear, lifted off her feet and whisked backward by two powerful hands at her waist. Quant—point to a flying wedge of Exts who had penetrated the near riot—set her down behind him and called to Burning, Nike, Lod, and Ghost. Dextra saw a half-exoed tech slam against Quant's shoulder and bounce off; the rest heeded the commander's orders to withdraw, with Burning bearing the semiconscious Mason.

The score of Exts held their rifles obliquely before them, muzzles pointed at the press gangers, who had stopped short. They had piled up on top of each other partly to cam what was going on and partly because the demon-helmeted Concordancer Exts looked so fearsome.

In the moment's pause General Delecado, standing to one side with his helmet breather open, rasped in his sand-in-the-gears parade ground voice, *"Fix . . . bayonets!"*

Dozens of cams transmitted the image of carbon-black blades snapping out of the 20-mm boomers' front stocks.

Dextra had horrific visions of a replay of the *Damocles* butchery. Before she could intervene, she felt Tonii's touch on her arm. The gynander was wearing one of 'eis glowing enigmatic smiles.

"It's all right, Dex. See?"

Daddy D ripped out, *"En . . . garde!"*

The bayonets thrust in unison, with the two ranks impaling only the air. Then the front rank recovered and knelt in perfect sync as the rear advanced and lunged past it. The Exts in the front rank rose and recovered as the rear rank paired off with them, flipping heavy rifles into the air like propellers, with each troop catching its partner's piece, doing a split-second inspection arms to make sure the chambers were empty, and moving to present arms.

The silent bayonet drill went on with robotic precision. Boomers were twirled, traded, and flung end over end to squadmates who caught them without looking up by dint of sheer timing and practice.

"Lod told General Delecado to have them standing by," Tonii whispered into Dextra's ear. "Most Exts don't care much for garrison stuff, but this group drilled to kill time on the voyage. He has a sense of showmanship, that Lod, but I suggest that we wrap up this show as quickly as possible."

Quant backed up to Dextra on her other side. He had gotten hold of a billy club or baton somewhere but was concealing it behind his back like a swagger stick now that things were under control.

"I advise you to get your guests out of here soon. They're blooded fighters, but they're a defeated people, too. And that, Madame Hierarch, is a formula for walking time bombs."

"A perceptive observation, Mr. Quant," Dextra told him. "In fact, my deputy concurs entirely."

When she indicated Tonii, the expression on Quant's face turned icily lethal. The baton was in the big right hand suddenly, and his left was halfway raised, close to his midsection in an edge-on parrying position. What Dextra saw in his eyes was so frightening that she went to offensive mode.

"Mr. Quant! Look at me when I'm addressing you! Post your people to make sure the newsies stay back when this demonstration has ended. *Move,* Commander, or I'll have you reassigned to the north pole, recycling toilet paper with an eraser."

The threat didn't phase him, but his sense of duty appeared to reassert itself, and Quant moved off to collect his crowd control details.

Dextra drew a shaky breath. "Tonii, has Mr. Quant some reason to hate you?"

Tonii answered, "I just realized who he is. But no, it's not me he hates—it's what I represent."

Dextra had seen brainless prejudice against engeneered people before, but Quant's was extraordinary. "No wonder his career's dead-ended, the brassbound fascist—"

"No, you're wrong," Tonii interrupted. "He's a good man and a very brave officer."

With the bayonet drill ended, there was no time to pursue details. Dextra beckoned Burning, Ghost, and Lod and stepped out to face the cams once more as the drill team opened ranks for her.

"Thank you all for helping to welcome LAW's newest auxiliary troops as well as introduce them to the citizens of Periapt. This concludes our arrival ceremony. These men and women of Concordance are famished, exhausted, and no doubt bruised from being roughhoused by you paparazzi brutes."

Dextra jumped in again before the groans had quite died away. "I *do*, however, want you to meet them again."

"Where and when, Madame Hierarch?" somebody called from the back of the pack.

Inspiration seized her. "The media annex at the Empyraeum. Tomorrow night, during the Lyceum ball."

They applauded her choice of venue. The bash celebrating the swearing in of freshman Hierarchs and the onset of a new legislative session was Periapt's most exclusive gala. Now the exotic, newsworthy Exts would be part of the mix.

The newsers were yelling questions again, demanding more.

"How about giving us our lead line, Madame Haven?"

"Throw us your best news bite, Dex!"

Dextra, with Burning looming behind her, draped her arms around Lod and Ghost, shook back her hair, and gave the cams a high-candlepower smile.

"They followed me home. Can I keep them?"

Quant watched Captain Hall and Dextra Haven work effectively together, getting the press gangs herded back aboard their VTOL without giving undue offense. His security details backed them up, but Quant himself gratefully stood aside. Mason had been hauled off to sick bay, but there was still the shuttleload of Exts to deal with, dead and wounded among them. Even more important, Quant had to consider the impatient twixes from on high that probably had the commo equipment running molten by then.

Another complication materialized in the form of Dr. Zinsser, who somehow had slipped past Quant's diversionary forces. The oceanographer was stalking toward him now, a picturesquely skinny, sun-browned man wearing only a frayed salt-water-bleached singlet and swim strap. Zinsser's face was borderline homely, but his seafarer's tan, crow's-feet, wind-ruffled salt and pepper hair, and bottle-green eyes all gave him a mien that transcended looks. He combined it with all the humility and tact of a prima ballerina, despite the fact that his ego had led him to folly and, like Quant, he had been consigned to backwaters in retribution.

Zinsser opened with ranging fire while he was still five meters away. "Quant, I'm going to scuttle this damn scow right out from beneath you! Do you know what you almost—" He drew up short, taken aback, as Quant stepped out to grab him by the arm.

As had already been proved in a number of confrontations, Zinsser couldn't bully or pull rank on Quant, but the face-offs took time that Quant couldn't spare at the moment. He therefore opted to strike first by tossing Zinsser a hot rock to juggle for a while.

"Doctor, I'm hereby invoking the Naval Security Act, section 380–5, which, you may recall, you signed and swore to under oath in order to do research aboard *Matsya*."

"Have . . . you . . . gone . . . synapshit?" Sinewy as he was, Zinsser had no hope of breaking Quant's grip.

"You'll cooperate during this emergency or I'll see to it you end up in a benthic arkology isolation module sorting fish jizm." Quant reared back, taking on a jovial tone. "Here, say hello to Burning, Allgrave of the Exts. His cousin and aide, Major Lod. And the Allgrave's sister, Ghost."

It was, as Quant had foreseen, Ghost who actually derailed Zinsser. A vanity-driven womanizer, he took one look at her ethereal beauty and otherworldly scars and forgot his pique.

Quant capitalized on it ruthlessly. "Allgrave—Dr. Raoul Zinsser. He'll help you get situated belowdecks. I suggest you take your first two platoons. If everything's satisfactory, my runners will guide the rest of your people in groups of the same size to prevent jam-ups in the passageways. My people will also get your casualties to sick bay; your medics can accompany them." He glanced at Zinsser. "Doctor, escort our guests to berthing spaces 32–01–L. I'll have a detail meet you there to lend a hand."

Quant was away before Zinsser could regroup.

Being a Science Sider, Zinsser knew the designated berthing spaces only hazily, but he managed to find them by following deck and frame numbers and the centerline code. As he walked, he tried to chat up Ghost but mostly found Burning in his way.

Berthing space 32–01–L was big, dusty, and empty except for bunks stacked three and four high; in former times they had been occupied by embarked marines and other amphib troops. Most of the bunks were as close as fifty centimeters to the ones above them; in some a large sleeper would have to slide out in order to turn over.

Zinsser turned his craggy smile on Ghost. "As usual, Quant has blundered. Staterooms must be found for you and the officers."

Burning declined. "This will do for us. It's not much worse than *Sword of Damocles*, and I don't want my force divided among small compartments."

While Burning looked the spaces over, Zinsser engaged Ghost's glance. "Was flawless beauty too much of a burden to bear? Or are your scars a way of forcing people to appreciate such other merits as you may possess?"

She lowered the detector she'd been running along the exposed overhead utility lines. Dark, impenetrable eyes stared at him from behind the whorls and hyphens of raised tissue.

"You couldn't understand, Periapt—even if I explained. Besides, you'd be too busy waging unspoken war on me. Your drives make you desirous, and you resent the power that the object of your desire holds over you."

Zinsser smiled condescendingly, poised to do so regardless of her response. "Ridiculous. I revere beauty. That's why the sea is my passion. Come diving with me and I'll prove it."

"I no longer suffer weak men, Doctor."

"Weak—"

"You're a weak man from a weak people or you wouldn't've survived to your age, tossing off mortal insults so carelessly."

Zinsser, pausing to get his bearings in suddenly unfamiliar territory, became cognizant of the silent attention of nearby Exts—mere children, he saw to his astonishment. Some were sidling to block the nearest hatch, regarding him with blank, merciless eyes.

He felt a touch and could not help flinching. It was the insouciant Lod, drawing him away by the elbow. "Doctor Zinsser, I think you should come with me right now. That's a good man. Before someone opens a new purge valve in your windpipe . . ."

CHAPTER
TWENTY-FIVE

"Commander, I'm taking Claude Mason ashore with me," Dextra informed Quant as she approached him by the catapult. "The medics say he's recovered from his episode or whatever it was, and he's determined to get back to dry land."

Quant nodded, recognizing that Haven's real motive was to keep Mason out of LAW's hands and use him to discomfit the Preservationists, though she wasn't about to acknowledge it publicly. "The airlimo's ready to go, Hierarch," he said simply.

"Thank you, Mr. Quant. I know you don't like having the Exts aboard, but I don't believe they constitute a danger to you or your ship."

Quant mulled it over briefly. "How a person plays the game tells a lot about his character, Madame Haven, but how that person loses tells all. For losers, I'd say, they seem to be comporting themselves well."

Dextra narrowed her eyes slightly. "Are you acquainted with my aide, Tonii?"

Quant frowned but limited his response to "I've never met the . . . individual."

"Then why did you look ready to strike 'erm with that billy club?"

Quant's gaze became polar, and he turned back to his duties.

"I'm not through talking to you yet, Mr. Quant!"

He looked her up and down one last time. "With all due respect, Madame Hierarch, you are for now. I suggest you direct these questions to your square-and-schooner Tonii."

* * *

Dextra told Burning, "I've got to get back to Abraxas. I can't pull any strings from here."

Kurt Elide was standing by the airlimo, which now held Nike Lightner and her set along with Claude Mason.

"Captain Hall will see to it you're not bothered; I have an understanding with him. But keep a tight rein on your people and make no public statements except what we've discussed."

"Understood."

"Burning, for your own sake, *no violence*. No incidents at all or you'll play into LAW's hands."

There was a discreet throat clearing at her elbow. "What's really needed is someone to serve as liaison with you, Hierarch." Lod, looking well scrubbed and chivalrously eager to please, had his helmet under his arm. "I volunteer, since my experience with AlphaLAW Commissioner Renquald on Concordance—"

"Makes you indispensable here, Cousin," Burning said, heading him off dryly, "Where we won't lose track of you."

"That's for the Allgrave to decide, of course," Dextra seconded. Lod showed only a decorous acceptance.

Dextra took another glance at Burning. It was good that he was sharper-witted than his size implied. He was going to need all the edge he could get.

What had been a slow news day in Abraxas became one of breaking drama and looming political spin war as reports gushed in of the Exts' planetfall and Claude Mason's transfixing plea regarding Aquamarine. Caught unprepared, the Preservationists were slow getting into action and consequently fast losing ground. Ignorant of Lightner's hand in the mix, their instant response teams lacked ammunition or even a compass heading. At the same time leaks about the suppression of the Aquamarine findings were beginning to surface.

The last straw was an announcement that Cathartoys Inc. would be offering a line of Ext tie-ins the next day, including games, costumes, and action simulacrants. Cathartoy's stock was climbing.

In the situation room of his levitating citadel Calvin

Lightner made a jabbing motion at the news holos with an ivory walking stick. "Kill the audio," he ordered.

Lightner had stopped caring about upset. The only aspect of the whole imbroglio that continued to interest him was that Dextra Haven had risked Nike's life to checkmate him. Did Haven think that by doing so she was making some moral point? Was she offering a cautionary lesson on the perils of escalating political struggle? If so, she'd been uncharacteristically foolish, for all she'd done was raise the ante.

Lightner reminded himself that the goal of retribution was seldom advanced by fixating on rage. He made a summoning motion to Buck Starkweather, Doll Van Houten, and the select few who had come to *La Condition Humaine* to celebrate the Exts' elimination only to bear witness to Calvin Lightner's mortification.

"I'm not sitting still for this," he told them. "I want to review all contingency files and dark-ops proposals."

Reluctantly, his coconspirators found their way to the room's levi-table for what promised to be a long council of war. Lightner felt that strategy sessions were no place for self-indulgence or relaxation, and the chairs were unyielding and nonadjustable.

"Our first order of business is to silence those involved at the operational level," Lightner declared. "Especially that bungler Wix Uniday." He looked at Starkweather. "Buck, that's your job."

While the former Hierarch was trying to blink his bulging eyes back into his head, Doll Van Houten spoke up. "That's bound to have a rather chilling effect on current and future hired help, Cal. Uniday's smart and capable, and we may need him before this is over."

Starkweather managed to find his voice. "Besides, the bloodbath was caused by the officer in charge of the Manipulants. He shouldn't've just attacked like that."

"That one paid the full penalty in the *Damocles*'s passageway," Hierarch Lepskaya noted. "LAW will be writing off his death and the deaths of his troops as a training accident—unless anyone here has a better idea." No one did. "The surviving Manipulants are of course incapable of talking to anyone outside their unit or Special Troops chain of command."

All Lightner's instincts told him that it was too late to transmogrify the carnage in the starship into something the Preservationists could use to crucify the Exts. Any attempt now might even contradict or indict Nike's conduct and veracity.

"What about deleting the Exts in situ aboard the *Matsya*?" Starkweather suggested.

The others decried the idea, Lepskaya clenching his fists as if he would have liked to have Starkweather's lapels in them. "Try a surgical strike now that they've had time to prepare defenses? Are you mad?"

"But they've no access to live ammunition."

"They have the same knives they used to gut and clean our Manipulants! Plus tons of aviation fuel and other flammables, and who knows what they could improvise? Not to mention the hundreds of potential hostages aboard or the fact that they're sitting just offshore in a ship with a fusion reactor! And unlike the *Damocles*, there'll be journalists all over the place."

"Subject closed," Lightner said, thumping the arm of his chair. "Before we're done, we're going to talk about the press's responsibility in this affair. But there's something more crucial to discuss at the moment: the mole in our most secret councils. It's clear that Dextra Haven didn't show up on *Damocles* by accident. We cannot move forward until someone here, or someone very close to our inner group, is disposed of."

There was no assigning suspicion by the expression of shock, because all Lightner's guests exhibited it. They all knew that having said it, he wouldn't be satisfied until a life was offered up on the altar of security. Before he could advance his inquiry, a communications deputy entered to show him a hooded-screen palmtop display. Lightner accepted the interruption as a necessary evil and read the message. When he surfaced to ask the deputy if the message had been verified, the others knew it was grave.

Lightner sent her off and glanced around the circle. "LAW signal intelligence and radio astronomy officials will announce in one hour that Trinity has gone silent. That's as of late this morning—relative—when the planet emerged from occultation behind its primary." He checked the hooded-screen text again. "That includes all of Trinity's SATs, orbital installations, and so on."

They all turned to see how their neighbors were reacting. Trinity was twenty-one light-years away, and to date there had been only telecomm contact between it and Periapt. As far as was known, the planetary system had never been visited or even approached by the Roke. With its industrial infrastructure, resources, and modest space-travel capability, Trinity had been deemed to have high potential as an annexed world, although LAW had kept that from the Trinitians.

Starkweather licked his lips to get them unstuck. "Perhaps this is unconnected with the Roke—"

"Don't sell yourself uncertainties," Doll cut him off. "They're even more painful than bad news. The Roke knocked Trinity completely off-line, and they've had twenty-one years to deploy copies of whatever weapon they used to do it. Sweet Teleos help us if that's time enough."

"Sweet Teleos *has* helped us," Lightner echoed. "With a clarion call to fight for our survival—just when humanity needs it most." He gazed at one face after the next. "Don't you see? Trinity's silence rubs our face in the fact that we're in a war for human destiny. Whoever won a war by going down on their knees and begging for peace? The pacifists, the isolationists, the salary proles besotted on effortless prosperity—*this* will wipe their comfortable assumptions away, even galvanize some."

"But if the opposition manages to frame this event in their terms"—Lepskaya worried, plucking his lower lip—"if they manage to sell people on fear and defeatism and the cease-fire initiative gains momentum—"

Lightner quashed him. "That's no longer a tolerable concept. Henceforth it's total war with Haven's Cravens, just as it shall be with the Roke."

The human-Roke conflict was being fought over such immense distances and long intervals of time that few combat actions were alike. The stupendous starships took years crossing the deeps, where conditions and strategic situations changed in manifold ways during their journeys. Circumstances encountered at the destination were often different, sometimes lethally so, from what had been foreseen when a given LAW ship set out.

The opposing sides were often compared to the Dark Ages armies of Old Earth, which marched forth frequently to attack foes of whose whereabouts they knew little or nothing. The histories said that they wandered lost until finally stumbling home or made war on the wrong enemy altogether.

That level of uncertainty plagued humanity's first interspecies war as well, along with flukes, surprises, mismatches, and an obligatory fatalism.

The Roke's preemptive gamma-X-raying of the peace delegation orbiting Queensland could have been repulsed by LAW DEADtech and Helwep offensive technology if those factors hadn't been a decade's transit time away, although the same weapons were used a few years afterward to obliterate an alien ship approaching Bushelsworth.

Why proposed treaty talks with the Roke had broken down, no human being knew. There had been some skirmishing and even pitched battles between space contingents, but nothing that couldn't be resolved. The only hint of a possible provocation on the part of *Homo sapiens* lay in recovered data from initial negotiating contacts monitored on Queensland and later by an incoming LAW ship. Experts suggested that somewhere in the complex transmissions intended to give the two races a common, neutral language lurked a miscoding or signal error whose distortion had led the Roke to a disastrous misinterpretation. Others suggested that an inert Cybervirus had once again enabled itself to spread calamity.

Regardless, there had been no face-to-face talks between the two species. Humanity had yet to gain an understanding of the Roke's physiology or social structure. The vessel sent to resecure Queensland found the aliens, inexplicably, long gone. But in the Chang Jiang system another LAW megaship blundered into a pair thought to be the same vessels that had struck at

Queensland, and in the course of a twenty-three-day running battle all three ships were obliterated.

A long-lead-time offensive was never tried again by either side. The gargantuan starships went out to annex or colonize and were of necessity on their own in dealing with whatever they encountered.

It was an absurd if unavoidable way to run a war. That aspect of the conflict wasn't enough to make Periapt sue for peace, because for LAW the struggle was more about a land grab than about all-out species cleansing.

Old-time Earth pundits had come up with any number of reasons why interstellar conflict would be impossible and insuperable: economic, logistical and technical, motivational, and psychological reasons. What none of them seemed to have taken into account was humanity's chauvinism and simian covetousness. LAW shrewdly motivated Periapts to make sacrifices and lose lives in a war for the possession of planets the race would not need for millennia, all for the sake of keeping the Roke from having them.

CHAPTER
TWENTY-SIX

"Driver—Kurt, is that your name?"

"Driver Kurt Elide, Madame Hierarch."

"Kurt, dear, while I admire your exuberance, I'll ask you to save the stunt flying for another time. Schedulewise, today would be an extremely inconvenient day for me to die."

The airlimo abruptly decelerated and leveled off. "Sorry. Won't happen again, Madame Haven."

"Commander Quant said that Kurt did a good job landing on the *Matsya*," Tonii remarked openly.

With Nike and her set of theater peripherals having been offloaded at her triplex atelier, there was no one to listen in but Claude Mason, who, buckled in on the other side of the passenger compartment, was gazing out at the city, lost in thought.

Dextra shrugged in Elide's general direction and said for Tonii's ear only, "Care to tell me why Quant referred to you as 'square-and-schooner'?"

Tonii considered it, then smiled faintly. "The phrase refers to a certain arrangement of masts and sail, what mariners call a hermaphrodite rig."

Recognizing evasiveness in the gynander's tone, Dextra fell silent, settling in for the quick hop to HauteFlash. Once there, she could intensify the public opinion English Ben had started putting on the issue of the Exts. She also could get Tilman Hobbes and the major Rationalist agitprop organs to start beating the drums about Aquamarine.

The airlimo's intercom tootled staidly, and Kurt Elide announced, "Incoming chirp for you, Madame Haven. Rationalist executive offices."

180

Dextra used her commo ancillary to encrypt the line, and shortly the weathered face of Tilman Hobbes came on-screen. Senior Hierarch and vice chairman of the party, Hobbes snapped, "Dex! Finally! There's been a calamity. Trinity."

Data began aladdining up on the displays as Hobbes explained Trinity's utter telecom silence.

"LAW issued a statement without the direction or permission of the Lyceum?" Dextra asked.

"What would be the point of waiting?" Hobbes's voice took on a punctilious tone. "The fact was already glaringly apparent. Would you rather the public think us paralyzed or let the press run with the ball?"

Silence did not necessarily mean catastrophe, but she knew that was how Trinity's quietude would be played by the ratings-hungry news media. "How long ago was the statement released?"

"Going on two minutes now. Without official word from Preservationist headquarters, by the way."

Then it was doubly unlikely that Lightner had vetted the announcement, Dextra told herself. If he had, the Preservationists would have been all over the spectrum and fiberlines. All the stuff the news crews were being fed about Exts and Aquamarine would suddenly take a backseat to Trinity.

"What about us, Til? We have to say *something.*"

"I'm still soliciting input and reviewing options," he said.

"*NeoDeos!* Why don't you just tell our entire public information apparatus to go work for Cal Lightner?"

Hobbes put on a martyred look, rolling his eyes upward. He was less amicable to Dextra than he had been in former days. She chalked it up to the time when, during her second term in office, she had finally let him get her clothes off but he had been so far hoisted on vermouth and rhapso that his erection had been off duty.

Now he shifted as if to sever the connection. "I'll keep you advised as events take shape, Dex."

"Til," she said quickly, "if you cut me off, I'll support the new nepotism guidelines and your kids'll lose their jobs and have to move back in with you. Consult the think-tankers if you're looking for input. Parfit and Ibis, they're savvy. I'll call you back from HauteFlash in three minutes."

"Dex, we cannot ignore a massacre."

"What massacre? We've temporarily lost contact with Trinity. Could be a Cybervirus, could be some natural phenomenon. Maybe the Trinitians have *opted* for telecom silence. The point is, we can't allow Lightner's crowd to bury the Exts and Aquamarine and stampede Periapt into a state-of-siege decree. If LAW receives emergency powers, we'll be, as the Exts would say, toad-cranked. So come on, Til: Be the LOX-nerved, steadfast Lyceum demigod I get all humid over."

Half a grin broke through his reserve. "Perhaps if you wore the red spindle heels again and that pheromone cologne . . . I do believe we could make a go of it next time."

"You back me on Trinity and one or two other matters, Tilman, and I swear I'll walk up and down your back in *golf shoes* if you want me to." Watching his startled expression, she saw that she'd pushed some button she hadn't known was there.

But he recovered in a heartbeat. "You'd better be this winsome at the Lyceum ball, Dex. The news feeds are in a lather about your promised media event. If the entree you toss them doesn't go down well, I suspect they *and* Cal Lightner are going to dine on raw Haven." He paused in self-amusement. "What's that amusing little tag line of yours? 'How now, foul Tao'?"

"Everyone who's not on guard or ready-reaction force stays on standby alert," Burning told Daddy D. "When the gambling starts, it's the same rules as on *Damocles*. I don't want anybody betting away their knife, medkit styrettes, or codcup."

Daddy D nodded in a way that let Burning know he had it covered. Nearly all Exts were chronic gamblers, but they could play for IOUs for a while longer.

"They're all fairly rested," Burning said, running down his mental list, "so we'll see how the next few hours play before we start setting standout rotas."

All sentries and the ready-reaction squads assigned to the

passageway choke points leading to the Exts' space were keeping their breathers sealed. Troops that had their *menpo* masks open could be observed sniffing the air periodically. They had been sensitized and Skills-trained to detect the low-concentration precursor scents of LAW bioagents.

The bloodletting in the starship and the confrontation on *Matsya*'s flight deck had jolted the Exts out of their voyage tedium. Even the inevitable bitching had rheostatted down to almost nothing. But if they were now back to marking time in the SWATHship's belly, Burning knew that they would have to be ready for all the headaches garrison life was heir to.

When Daddy D left, he got on a ship's comline handset and blundered through the maneuver and docking and air ops circuits before finding the command channel. He conveyed to the officer of the deck a request for a face-to-face with Hall that same afternoon. In short order, however, Hall relayed word that scheduling would make it impossible but that a representative would arrive at the Exts' berthing spaces in due course.

When part of the message mentioned medevaccing the wounded Exts to better-equipped shoreside facilities, Burning cut the OOD off. "They live with us or die with us. Fly the doctors and equipment in instead or the Hierarchate'll blame you for what happens next." He couldn't afford to have Exts fall hostage to LAW's hands ashore even if it meant casualties dying.

Hall's avoidance troubled him. Under the pretext of surveying berthing arrangements and establishing shipboard routine, the Exts' best scouts, scroungers, and bilkos had fanned out to reconnoiter. With no one sure of their status or proper place in the codified microcosm of the ship, they enjoyed a broad latitude of opportunity. Burning considered using the Discards, but he didn't trust the kids out on their own, especially in the alien cultural milieu of the *Matsya*.

Those on standby alert were set to work making the berthing spaces in and around 32–01–L livable. The shipboard quartering was practically a hostelry after their experiences in the Broken Country.

Patting his pockets down to double-check the things he'd

brought, Burning felt the small, flat container that sustained him—Fiona's black lock of Hussar Plait, given to him back on Anvil Tor. They'd figured on dying that day, yet they'd gotten this far. Now it was up to him to see that they got the rest of the way.

Back from the ship's infirmary, Zone was relentless in bringing order and establishing unit coherence. Even his severalmates were not spared. In another social context it would have earned him hatred, maybe a bullet in the back somewhere along the line, but among the Exts it only enhanced his status. Subordinates did not have to worry about the future; they only had to appease the wrath of Zone.

Tap water was carefully tested. A cull team of the outfit's best engineering people got a few of the sonics weapons working with power units five-finger requisitioned from *Matsya* equipment. Other details were removing door kick plates, utility access covers, and some sealed overheads with an eye to exploration and fortification. Tunnel rats went crawling and worming. Burning thought again of the Discards and again decided that they were too prone to react with all-out lethality.

Countertech teams began sweeping for antipersonnel systems. Hatch servos that would have let Hall seal the Exts in belowdecks were among the first things to be disabled. If the captain knew about it or about the surveillance cams and A/V pickups they had deactivated, he chose not to come down to protest.

One backwater space became the interim command post, with communications, tactical displays, and field computers set up and carefully shielded. The Exts were especially vigilant about their comps, extreme cyberphobes even in a cyberphobic age. Telecom sappers tapped into the ship's lines and accessed the planetary TechPlex.

Thanks to an anonymous source in *Sword of Damocles*, all the news show emcees were referring to the Exts as "the Growlers." That aside, the coverage was almost unsettlingly positive. The drumbeat was building for follow-up coverage at the Lyceum ball, which was also claiming a lot of screen time.

Burning couldn't help but be impressed by the sprawling grandeur of the milky palace the narrators invariably referred to as "the fabulous Empyraeum."

They picked up word of Trinity's silence as well. Burning didn't know what to make of it and saw that the Periapts didn't, either. If the Perries got jittery about the Roke, it might make them more cordial toward the Exts.

The scouts and scroungers began to filter back with reports, along with mementos. Flammable substances, power tools, and an infinitude of means and materials for improvised weapons were available everywhere. The hangar deck was devoid of aircraft, but the ship contained modest stores of conventional aviation fuels as well as liquid oxygen and slush hydrogen. The power plant and other sensitive areas had demonstrated surprisingly good security. Still, there were plenty of ways to exfiltrate the ship quietly, including the desalination intake and a lockout in the science sponson, though how to do so in great numbers and where to go remained moot.

Estimates of the SWATHship's company numbered fewer than six hundred souls, including the Science Side, though the ship obviously had been built to accommodate four times as many. Automatics let her function, but she was only a facade of a real naval command.

As on the *Damocles*, the more certain Burning felt that he could take the ship if necessary, the more emphatic was the feeling that he should not do anything of the kind. If the bars around the Exts were not very strong, conceivably that was because the Exts were not prisoners.

CHAPTER
TWENTY-SEVEN

In the starboard sponson, with its Science Side maze of labs, berthing spaces, and support facilities, Raoul Zinsser sat at a sorting table in a tightly restrained fit of resentment while news of Trinity, the Exts, and Aquamarine played in the background. Mocked by a smelly, self-mutilating slut, he thought. And laughed at—he was certain of it—by her vampiric beast children.

He would even the score with Ghost—inevitably. And his sexual and social tutelage was exactly what she needed. As his pulse rate normalized somewhat and he considered the pleasant prospect of a tamed and more tractable Ghost, he reached out idly to toy with a scale model of the device he had been refining and testing aboard *Matsya* for the better part of two months.

Pitfall, he'd christened it until he came up with a name that had a more dynamic ring. The device was a major facet of his effort to soar back to glory and professional preeminence, riding the wave of LAW's current preoccupation with tether technology, skyhooks, and space elevators.

Useful technology, Pitfall would be an important tool on Periapt, but even more so on Hierophant or Illyria. He had originally pinned much of his hope on its importance to an AlphaLAW mission to Aquamarine, but with the Hierarchate so adamant against a return voyage and the *Scepter* team's findings subjected to such merciless—

Unless, of course, Claude Mason's unexpected appearance on the *Matsya* would have an impact on LAW's decision regarding Aquamarine . . .

With the scale model in one hand, he brought the nearest terminal on-line to access the civilian news menus, and seconds later he was gazing at Administrator Mason's electroshock-pale face framed against Allgrave Burning's battlesuit.

"—we *must* return to Aquamarine," Mason was saying. "Only the Oceanic knows . . ."

He watched the whole loop twice before taking the terminal off-line. He was staring at the scale model and thinking once more about Aquamarine when footfalls and loud griping in the passageway heralded the return of his grad students and teaching assistants. Shortly, the hatch opened and bare feet sounded on the floor behind him.

When he turned to the sound, Freya Eulenspiegel was peeling off her sweatband and bikini bottoms, leaving her naked except for a wristband dive-data computer.

"The gear is made fast," she said, shaking out long sun-gilt hair. "Recovered every last piece." She was tawny and taut from outdoor work and diving and so full-bosomed that she always wore a jockbra on dives.

His chosen concubine among the current lot, Freya was only marginally promising as an oceanographer. Gifted in cyber-lingua, however, she had devoted countless hours to helping him create the Pitfall software.

Displeased at the interruption, he swung back to the model, but she padded up behind him and leaned over him, perspiration-wet hair brushing his face. When she kissed his ear, he drew his head away sharply.

Accustomed to his moods, she became cautious but tried to sound genial. "So what's all the fustercluck with the shuttle? And Concordancers, somebody said? *Pwui*, I hope they've been deloused or the whole ship'll be crawling with—"

He slammed the Pitfall model onto the sorting table so loudly that she jumped. "You stink," he said, pivoting around to face her. "I can smell you from here. Don't you ever shower? And if you're going to blubber, do it on the bidet."

She was speechless for a moment, then shouted "Prick" and fled into the passageway.

With his annoyance vented—as well as his earlier frustration with Ghost—he found it easier to concentrate on a course of action. He'd never actually considered employing Pitfall to plumb the depths of Aquamarine's Oceanic. He held those who had studied Aquamarine thus far fools and bunglers, worse than amateurs. Their failure to penetrate the secrets of the Oceanic only went to show that none were in the same class with Raoul Zinsser. But the path to real wealth and primacy lay not on Aquamarine but on Periapt, controlling the organs of government that doled out resources and awards and divided the spoils of others' work.

However, if he could interest LAW in taking Pitfall to Aquamarine . . . It did not perturb him in the least that someone else would get to use his creation to solve the enigma of the Oceanic. By then Raoul Zinsser would be well positioned to turn the revelations to his professional advantage and personal profit.

There would be some risk in approaching LAW about utilizing the device. Fortunately, though, it couldn't simply be commandeered from him; safeguards installed in Pitfall's cyberlingua 'wares ensured that it answered exclusively to Zinsser.

He glanced out a porthole at Medusa's rays falling on the sea. Oceanic, you're a boon to me no matter what you are, he said to himself.

A pity we'll never meet.

The robing area of Dextra Haven's bedroom suite in Haute-Flash was in a state of advanced disarray, with clothes, shoes, and jewelry scattered about. In searching for accessories, she had discovered bric-a-brac she'd completely forgotten about, such as the matching hermetic-seal lockets that had been sent to her by the Young Rationalist League from her home O'Neill, Crapshoot, when she had won her first reelection.

While Dextra was dressing, Tonii recapped from the bath what 'e had gleaned from one LAW ethnographer's report on the Exts.

"Most are archetypal middle class," the gynander said in a

loud voice. "Apprehensive about falling too low, joining the underclass, being denied a respectable place in society. Although they're almost equally mistrustful of wealth or estrangement—anything that might erode their core values and virtues. Born citizen-soldiers."

Dextra didn't comment on the note of admiration in Tonii's voice. To be an accepted part of a larger, conventional community was a concept that fascinated the gynander and made 'erm wistful. She thought back to the Quantum College caller's puzzling assertion that the Exts were linked to Dextra's push for a mission to Aquamarine. Had the caller meant to imply a literal connection or a passing one?

"If I could, I'd take more of them inside Empyraeum with me tonight," Dextra shouted back. "The public has to see them as a team, a unit identity that would lose its value if broken up. One that's on our side, as well. The only Periapt I'd add would be Claude Mason, if not for these aphonic spells he goes into."

She had already tried to get a line on Mason's Aquamarine survey teammates, but LAW had stonewalled her. The only reliable information she had was that the entire crew had been moved from Blades Station to a new holding facility.

Dextra studied herself in an imager. She had settled on a black sheath that made her look as if she had been dipped in licorice. It bared her left arm, shoulder, and breast, which in her unbiased opinion passed muster now that she had mirrordusted the aureole and inserted a nipple ring, a slim eternity band sporting a fifty-carat rose-cut blue moonfire three times as expensive as diamond.

While Tonii went on about how a *bushido*-like aspect of the Skills made for less friction and harassment among the mixed-gender Ext units, Dextra touched up her cosmetics and rechecked her coiffure. It had to be celebrity hair that night, power configurations with volumization. She was making minor adjustments when Tonii emerged from the bath chambers, wearing Dextra's glamour, a pricey semiconducting gel containing countless artificially grown voxel crystals. Even Tonii's quilled alleyboy-cut blond hair and sheathed male genitalia were coated. Neo-Thai choker, wristbands, and ankle bands were the key to the vaporwear.

Dextra watched the play of Tonii's body, the curved grace combined with cords of muscle. She indicated the genital gaff. "Afraid to leave them dangling?"

"The whole point, for me, is to leave people guessing, Dex." 'e hit a control tile on the left wristband—the main programming unit—and was instantly transformed into a creature of living light, ablaze with starflame luminosity. It was how Dextra had always thought an angel or fire elemental would look. A human form moving in effulgent glory, details hard to make out—except that the anatomy seemed to combine genders—and so bright, she had to squint and shield her eyes.

"I realize you have protective contacts on, but I don't."

"Sorry!" Tonii tapped the little tiles on the wristband, and the coruscations dimmed to a glossy crimson. "Better?"

"Perfect for the display window at some love-arts studio."

Tonii experimented with a different scheme. Now 'e was an astral being of rippling polychromatic radiance, throwing off spears of crystal brilliance a meter long. Patterns and light-shapes shifted and flowed across the beacon body, making it hard to tell the gynander's true features and form.

"I think it's close to what you're looking for, Tones," Dextra said approvingly. "But you'd better rheo down a smidge more lest the skycops think our limo's signaling for an emergency landing."

"What d'you think?" Ghost asked, gesturing to the airlimo Dextra Haven had dispatched to the *Matsya* flight deck to collect her, Burning, and Lod. "A trick to separate us from the troops?"

"If it looks like a very involved trick, it's probably not one," Lod suggested. "I mean, why bother? All the murder holes and Molotov cocktails we could come up with wouldn't save us if the Perries wanted to scuttle this tub. We've landed splat in the middle of a political showdown, and if we don't keep Haven on our side, *sic transit gloria* Exts."

"That's the feeling I get," Ghost said, measuring each word.

Burning, glancing vigilantly about the carrier's deck, could hear the ambivalence in her tone; the prospect of violent conflict appealed to her.

Ghost's qualified support made Lod preen a bit. "This is an astute move by Haven. The Periapts are close to a war panic over what's happened to Trinity, and it's just possible that they'll decide to seize on us as allies and fellow human beings instead of outworld parolees."

"I've been thinking along the same lines," Burning offered. "But I'm not comfortable with staging a show at this Lyceum ball. We'll be in the planetary spotlight with no idea what moves to make."

Lod pulled at his chin. "Haven won't hitch us to her star without coaching us. But you're right; it behooves us to find out what we can about the finer points."

"Hall won't talk to us," Burning reminded him.

"What about Quant?" Ghost asked.

Lod mimed shock. "You? Implying there's a Periapt we can trust?"

"Not trust. But there's something about that one. At least if he sets out to do us harm, it won't be with social games or bad-faith advice."

They found *Matsya*'s executive officer on the hangar deck in front of a formation of officers and senior CPOs. He was wearing his headset, one earcup flipped open and his visor in clear mode. His thickly muscled arms were folded on his chest, and he kept to one spot, letting his eyes rove over the silent men and women.

"Everybody here'd better hearken to the word of God," he was saying. "Captain Hall states that overall readiness *will* be brought up to snuff before any hand sees a biscuit, a bath, or a bunk. We'll likely be receiving more media and VIPs aboard, which surely means the brass bodhissattvas from naval HQ."

Quant's manner held no sympathy. "All leaves and passes are canceled. All hands will turn to and keep at it until our ship's up to flag-rank inspection. Dr. Zinsser and his debutantes are about to receive the same enlightenment.

"Make sure your new personnel know the ropes. If it moves,

salute it; if it doesn't move, heave it over the side; if it's too big to heave over the side, paint it. Any questions?" There weren't, although Quant's diatribe elicited some resentful looks. "Division chiefs, take over."

Seeing the Exts, Quant went to meet them halfway, replacing the severe expression he'd worn for the formation with one of unblinking neutrality.

After summarizing what little the Exts knew about the Lyceum ball, Lod asked, "May the Allgrave solicit your advice, Commander?"

Quant's ebony face went hard for a moment. "I'm to render ship's amenities to you, Allgrave. Your request arguably qualifies."

Burning nodded in appreciation.

"The ball is people at the pinnacle, plus their politicosocial adjuncts. But that doesn't mean there won't be a lot of jockeying for position. They'll condescend to you. Some will laugh at you behind your back or even to your face, no matter what you do. Live with it. You'll need their goodwill or at least their sufferance."

Burning heard the voice of experience and wondered what Quant's story was.

"If they think you're gaining cachet or the press is going to stay on your side for a while, they'll try to siphon off some of your reflected celebrity. Let them, but remain uncommitted— except to Haven, I suppose."

Burning absorbed it. "Anything else?"

"Be careful about casual invitations and watch for bugs. Stick with the food and drink the caterers provide and *don't* sample anybody's high. Or anybody's sex adjuncts—bio or techno. Under no circumstances—"

He stopped, listening to his closed earcup. Whatever he heard made him glance off in the direction of the superstructure, where Regis T. Hall was in plain view. Then, wholly impersonal once more, Quant took a step back.

"No further questions. I'm to require your imminent departure in Hierarch Haven's aircar. Before you leave, however, you'll command your personnel by direct order not to stray outside the designated boundaries." He about-faced and left them there.

CHAPTER
TWENTY-EIGHT

The displeasure of the assembled Aggregate members hit Piper like a violent storm front as she stepped out of the security lock into the interior of Habitat. The air of the nest was charged with the constituents' hostile scentspeech and resentful kinesigns. Granted, she had been delayed in returning to Habitat, but the Aggregate was not scheduled to perform its tech presentation at the Lyceum ball for several hours to come and all the preparations had been made. So what had incensed them?

She did not need voicetalk from them to make their antagonism more emphatic. She recognized an anger whose olfactory nuances were as familiar and intimate as her own. The constituents were cuing from Byron Sarz, the nexus of their interconnected consciousness, and if Byron was irate with Piper to such a pitch of estrangement and antipathy, it would be like God turning his face away. She had to curb her own scentspeech to keep from tainting the air with fear.

In the despair that settled on her Piper had a torturous but vivid epiphany. This was what it felt like to be an Alone—any of the sundered and hermetically isolated conventional human beings walking the face of Periapt and the other *Homo sapiens* worlds.

Family members, lovers, boon companions—any contact an Alone had with another could only be a sad and wretched pretense compared to the rich, heady medium in which the Aggregate lived.

Byron's rule against letting the Alones grasp that difference was a wise one, and no one knew that better than Piper, who had just returned from a rare solo foray among them. Unconscious of their own scentspeech and the rest of their Othertalk, Alones poured out their emotions, phobias, and venalities. Far more tragically, they barely heard one another. They were almost completely insensate to the sea of Alltalk in which they swam.

If the Alones knew how harmonious the shared life of the Aggregate was, surely they would go completely mad with jealousy and wipe the Aggregate out of existence.

She had known Byron was standing off to one side of the group, for she had been tasting his disapproval since she had arrived. He stood out from the score of young men and women who made up the constituency. Gray-haired and somewhat overfleshed, he was bigger than any of them and, at forty-eight baseline years, more than twice the age of the eldest. Piper gazed at him and waited meekly for him to open a dialogue, but his Othertalk was mostly that of shutout, of withholding.

His voicetalk—much less its Alltalk context—would have been incomprehensible to an Alone. Aggregate phonetics, abetted by elisions, aphereses, surd words, and similar shortcuts, was too rapid for Alones. When he finally relented to speak, he was unsparing in his condemnation of her for having absented herself from the communal nest without his permission.

Piper wasn't permitted a moment to explain that the Hierarch laboratory that monitored the Aggregate's research and self-modification activities had demanded a tissue sample or that she'd decided to make the delivery herself merely to spare Byron and her fellow constituents another distasteful invasion by Alones.

As she showed her contrition in Othertalk, she became aware that Byron was concealing the true source of his ire. She couldn't avoid All-Auding the fact that she was being excluded from something. It ran counter to the group's whole reason for being. Yet she saw nothing out of place in all the tech clutter. Her hearing picked up no discrepancies, and her olfaction—the most sensitive in Habitat—brought her no trace of an accident or mishap that could have provoked Byron so.

A small, fragile-looking young woman to begin with, Piper shrank in on herself. She knew all too well that she had the look of a perpetual victim: huge and wounded gamine eyes, a head that seemed too big for her body, a spray of freckles across a snub uptilted nose, lips so full that they seemed to weight her mouth away from her lower face.

Byron made a kinesign that told the rest to resume what they'd been doing, and they dispersed at once to finish preparations for the Lyceum ball performance.

Piper looked pleadingly to Byron, her mentor, lover, and more, the one who had created her, who had elevated her from an Alone foundling to a constituent in the new order of the human race. But Byron only showed her a blankness she had never seen in a constituent, certainly not in him.

At that moment she no longer knew him, and he no longer knew her.

Scrolling furiously through recent events in an effort to determine what else she might have done to bring about this waking nightmare, she could come up with only one transgression. That very morning a confidential commo had briefly called Byron away from Habitat. He had been speaking into a shielded screen, but Piper had caught a fragment of the conversation: "Quantum College."

Had her inadvertent eavesdropping caused the change in him? she wondered. She was about to ask as much when Habitat's roof-landing platform nav system chirped and issued a burst of voice commo. The Peace Warrantor airvan that was to take them to Empyraeum was on final approach.

She saw, tasted, and almost felt Byron's anger escalate, though his expression, kines, and aromas provided no clues why. The Aggregate took up his unease like microwave repeaters as Byron opened a link to the airvan.

"Public Safety, you're early by nearly an hour," he told the pilot of the airvan. "We're not ready. Return at twenty hundred hours."

"Wasn't a request, *fleshware*. Schedule's been moved up. Get up here and board or we'll *get* you aboard."

Even an Alone could have read the contempt in the Warrantor's voice. Hatred wasn't all that unusual. Most Alones felt personally threatened by the very concept of subsuming individuality and free will to group awareness. They were ignorant of the fact that Aggregate life diminished sadness and multiplied joy. "Fleshware" was less pejorative than some of the other terms the Alones had for constituents.

Byron chose not to take issue with the Warrantors and ordered everyone to get moving. The constituents began covering their graceful bodies with clothing and misting on vulgar disguise smells so that the Warrantors and the Alones at the ball wouldn't be subconsciously disconcerted by scentspeech aromas.

Piper watched Byron lock down the access cowling of the DNA assembler's programming suite, the computer system that was the key to the new field-portable, high-speed synthesis module. Oddly, the programming suite had been locked down *before* Piper had left. There should have been no reason to reopen it in her absence.

Aware of her gaze, Bryon used Othertalk to make it plain that he wasn't about to discuss the matter.

The airvan was touching down. Abruptly, Byron sent Piper an Othertalk message she'd never apprehended before: a warning *not* to communicate. Then the bioengineering genius who had created the Manipulants, the gynanders, and the Aggregate sidled away to greet the Peace Warrantors, radiating deceit from his every cue and movement.

The Aggregate was all around her, but Piper felt no unison. Regardless, she grabbed hold of the DNA module to help haul it to the freight lift that would take everyone to the airvan.

At Dextra Haven's insistence, Kurt Elide had been assigned to ferry the Exts from the *Matsya* to the Empyraeum. With him in the forward compartment was Tonii.

Abraxas at night was a celestial city, compelling Burning to concede that Periapt was firmly in possession of the kingdom, the power, and the glory and that the Exts would just have to live with it.

He had hoped to get a preview of the Lyceum ball on the

airlimo's displays, but the Empyraeum traditionally went to press blackout for the event. There would be various PR opportunities on the cordoned-off terraces and elsewhere, but even the reporters who managed to gain entry weren't permitted to file reports.

Sorting through the aircar's hyperparsed data feed, Burning discovered that there would be nearly two thousand people attending: three hundred Hierarchs and their guests, the uppermost crust of the Hierarchate and LAW bureaucracies, and a scattering of heads of state and private sector moguls.

The Lyceum ball was part of the front the Hierarchate maintained to bolster its cynical relationship with a lethargic electorate. The politics of Lyceum and LAW was founded on the illusion that if the average citizen ever wanted to effect change, he or she could. Thus, the induction of new Hierarchs had to be propagandized as government by the people at its finest. The worrisome silence from Trinity notwithstanding, the lavish circus went on.

The Empyraeum, astride a summit overlooking Abraxas and the ocean, was like a mountain of milky ice sculpted by protean winds. Built almost a century before as the pinnacle of the organiform movement, it was without a single straight line or geometric angle. Instead, there were mounded globules, flexed arches, and billowed domes, all lambent enough to throw back the darkness around them. Set against the rearing and audacious architecture of Abraxas, the structure was a frozen comet presiding over a brilliant polychrome nebula.

"Someone left the lights on," Lod assayed. With everyone deep into private preoccupations, the remark fell flat.

As Kurt Elide descended, magnetic anomaly scanners, IFF radars, resonating spectrometer munitions sniffers, and other security gear gave the aircar a close-range inspection. Heavy weapons were nearby, discreetly concealed in what pretended to be catering marquees, mobile support trailers, and renovation worksite domes scattered over Empyraeum's roofs and upper works.

Dextra was on hand to meet her guests. The three Exts debarked to some whistles and cheers, plus a number of catcalls, as press gangs got what images they could. Tonii blew Dextra a kiss but remained in the cockpit. Kurt reboarded after standing by the passenger door and taxied the aircar on surface effect toward the parking area.

The Hierarch Haven had emerged from the Empyraeum with an articulated gauzewing mantelet held about her. She and the Exts rejected the glidestrips and transfer platforms that would have conveyed them inside quickly; the meters of imperial purple carpet, flanked by stiltbooted news crews and throngs of security-checked sightseers, was too good a PR opportunity to pass up.

The crowds creamed over Dextra's gown and celebrity hair. When she drew back the pinions of the gauzewing mantelet, her bare breast and jeweled piercewear drew applause. Lyceum chasubles and workaday business attire had their place, but her Rationalist partisans required their champions to shine in the spotlight when the occasion demanded it.

As expected, the Exts received equal acclaim. Even Lod understood the importance of showing only a reserved martial bearing, barely reciprocating with a nod here and there. The cams couldn't get enough of Ghost's stunning face, arrowy shapeliness, and primeval scarification.

Also at Haven's direction, the Exts were wearing their midnight-blue, gold-buttoned ceremonial outfits, epauleted and mutton-leg-sleeved, with narrow cuffs reaching almost to the knuckles. Over their right shoulders were looped aiguillettes braided with gold and coarse cord, and their tight britches were adorned with gold-piped seams. When Dextra and her guests reached the checkpoint at the foot of the main entrance, the Exts made a grand show of retrieving the various blades they wore *skean-dhu* style in their spit-shined boot tops.

Burning drew his issue ka-bar, Lod revealed a gold-chased dirk, and Ghost unsheathed her ripsaw-hilted heirloom blade. The weapons were relinquished haft first to Warrantors in regimentals while Dextra stood to one side, allowing the cameras an unobstructed shot. There was a slight pause as the Warrantor sergeant at arms refused to move aside for Ghost. Without batting an eye, she slid a flat fighting knife out of the other boot and a brace of three-sided throwing blades thin as pencils from her left sleeve and added a spit needle from inside her cheek.

Passing into the Empyraeum was like entering a vaulted pleasure palace of chalky quartz and frosted glass. People of every type, size, and mode of dress milled and mingled, displaying a theatrical sense of their own presence. The range and flamboyance of the costumes lent the hall an atmosphere of cross-cultural pageantry.

The Empyraeum was teeming with notables, yet heads turned and conversations died away when Dextra Haven's name was announced. Eyes went to the trio in somber uniforms as well, and a number of people started for them as Haven led the way onto the floor.

Burning recalled a legend he had heard about such lions' dens and wished for angels to appear to hold unfriendly jaws closed.

For that matter, mine, it occurred to him.

CHAPTER
TWENTY-NINE

In the silence of HauteFlash's guest bedroom Claude Mason's thoughts ran murky yet certain. Reaching the *Matsya* by helipod and making his plea to Haven and the assembled press was only half the task with which Farley Swope had charged him back at Blades Station.

The villa was well appointed with surveillance and security equipment, but Mason learned early on how to sneak in and out of it without being confronted. He had attended very expensive essentials forms and prep and upper schools, where he had absorbed the wiles and wisdom of fellow students who were career escape artists.

In the case of HauteFlash, it helped that along with observing the au pair's security routine, Mason had managed to filch her security key.

He took the guest room monitor off-line, cracked the door, and listened. Ben, Haven's faithful steward, was off somewhere keeping close tabs on the triple crises of Exts, Trinity's silence, and Aquamarine; Maripol was looking after Honeysuckle; and the other servants were preparing the household for the marathon sessions that went into staging a political offensive.

Mason reached the villa's grounds undetected, using Maripol's key to forestall various alarms by means of its identity-friend-or-foe transponder. Then he exited HauteFlash itself, deactivated the key's tracer function, and headed into Abraxas, his stride brisk on the footpath's energy-return nap.

He was not unduly worried about Peace Warrantors, with the ball having diverted a lot of personnel. Even as media-exposed as he had become, he was reasonably anonymous behind a half-mirrored datanet half cowl he had lifted from HauteFlash. He didn't know how to play spy or spot a tail, so he could only be cautious and hope he wasn't being followed.

Abraxas had changed greatly in the generation he had been away, but he had had abundant time in the Blades to catch up on developments. Mass transit, in any case, was still user-friendly and straightforward. At a public commo carrel a mnemonic phrase Farley had given him, combined with an alphanumeric group, gave him reference to a specific public key cryptosystem sequence. Using the combined data at a street TechPlex booth, he received instructions to board a people-mover cartridge and tap in a destination at the Metro-Core, where he rerouted and shot for the city's industrial borderlands.

Fifteen minutes later he was standing before a blank, heavy vehicle door at an anonymous warehouse. Doubts and fears worked on his resolve, but images of his wife and child trying to survive the hardships of Aquamarine pushed him on.

He roused himself only to realize that he'd already signaled for entry, and a moment later the door rose just high enough for him to enter without stooping, then lowered behind him with a whisper of displaced air. Inside there was nothing but immeasurable darkness and silence.

The gloom closed around him as the door was secured loudly. Instinctively, his hand went to the pocket that contained the Optimant dice Farley Swope had given him, but the Holy Rollers were gone—lost during the helipod flight across the waves to the *Matsya* or possibly pickpocketed by one of the Exts onboard the ship. Then a voice spoke to him from the total blackness.

"You nearly took the wrong route at Interchange Sienna, Administrator Mason."

It was true, but Mason did not bother to ask just how the voice knew. Given synthesis 'wares, the speaker might have been either sex and any age, though he sounded male, adult, and somewhat affable.

"Mason, once the lights go up, you'll be part of what you encounter here. There'll be no turning back."

"There's been no turning back since the Blades," Mason said.

Light sprang forth all around him, and he looked up, gasping for breath and words. Under a perspective-distorting sky, staircases ran upside down and aqueducts fed uphill. In place of clouds, faces and animals formed inverse and intersticed patterns, playing out their progressions, only to be replaced by subsequent optical sleights.

Mason panned over to the only human figure in sight, a fat-faced and big-bellied Buddha, head radiating a divine nimbus. He was cooling his feet in an upside-down aqueduct twenty meters above. The aqueduct's course bent through several tricky shifts of perspective to pump water back into itself.

"So what do I call you, Gautama?"

"The name is Yatt. If you wish, you may consider this place a campus annex of the Quantum College."

"What I wish, Yatt, is to talk about Aquamarine. And time's short."

"Or in any case not to be frittered away." Yatt stepped out of the streaming water and headed for wrongside-down steps. "Follow the guide path through the grotto and we'll meet you beyond."

The radiant walkway took bizarre dips and climbs through vision-deceiving stonework and foliage. The forced perspectives made him feel dizzy. What lay close at hand was solid enough, though he dismissed the more outrageous and inaccessible eye teasers as holography.

He emerged from a sideways-leaning descent to find himself standing near the end of the aqueduct where Yatt had been wading, and he saw the Buddha clone sitting on a bench toweling off his feet. Mason glanced back and saw the far side of the grotto, where he had started, hanging nearly vertical according to his perception of up and down. Of the warehouse door there was no sign.

They had gone to the trouble of mounting part of the place on gimbals, he told himself. That was all it was. They could have spared themselves the effort. He didn't need to be sold on their knack for cute tricks, especially when the Quantum College was the only side in the game that would have him.

Yatt indicated their surroundings. "You think you've sussed out our artifices, yes?"

Mason let his irritation show. "If you've got antigravity, you certainly don't need me. Go take over the galaxy."

Yatt stood up and came closer. "But we do need you, Mason, as much as you need us. We can arrange for you to return to Aquamarine, but only in exchange for your help in facilitating our goals."

"Your goals. Why is Aquamarine important to the Quantum College all of a sudden?"

"The Quantum College is a paranoid legend, Mason, a modern wish myth with ten million derivations and not a gram of substance to it, save what we supply. We are the true face of it."

"It?"

"The quantum *universe*, Mason." Yatt extended a fat ocher forefinger, his smile no longer so simplemindedly benign.

The forefinger reached Mason's, but there was no physical contact. A pinpoint of light grew from the spot and began to dissolve Yatt. Instead of evaporating into genie smoke or random voxels, however, his substance swirled, transformed, and ultimately rezzed into stacks and piles of data.

The whirlwinds and gusts that blew closest to Mason pertained to him, carrying privy information about his life and classified data amassed by the *Scepter* survey team. Farther away were floating constellations and wavering auroras embodying other guarded Hierarchate and LAW files, Lyceum records, and documents from the Preservationist Party, the Rationalists, the Church of Teleology, and more. There were also real-time relays from orbital defense platforms and Roke threat assessments from the Defense Directorate.

Mason assumed that if Yatt was a hologram, he was a relatively simple follower image modeled directly by a virtsuit operator—a puppet of light. But the way the image was breaking up implied staggering computational power.

Yatt could only be artificial intelligence on an outlaw scale, one that defied all the restraints of post-Cyberplague statute and commandment.

Mason flailed back as some of the data recoalesced into Yatt's free-floating face. The smiling Buddha visage drifted his way, and Mason let out a scream. It was all too real to be a hallucination or nightmare, but the alternative was equally beyond belief.

He'd fallen captive to a Cybervirus.

"Only 'delightful,' Major Lod, you adorable little Growler, you?" the lavender-haired debutante sporting the unicorn horn echoed. "If the Lyceum ball only rates 'delightful,' *what*, pray tell me, is your notion of a *really* good time?"

"That would be you and me, my enchantress, if we loaded a case of champagne into a lawn sprinkler, got some trays of sex-jelly and a couple of paint rollers, and let love and art be our muses."

The gloriously endowed deb gave a titter Lod assayed at sixty percent amusement and forty percent arousal and then raised a voguish, curvilinear lorgnette and studied him through the eyepieces. He saw tiny speckles of light deep in the double optical receptors, alphanumerics and image enhancements linked to some data bank.

"We have a rape club," she confided to him finally, putting the tip of her tongue between purple-dyed teeth. "You simply *must* come to our next venery. You wouldn't have to place yourself at hazard unless you found the experience... desirable."

"Unfortunately, LAW controls my social calendar," Lod told her, simultaneously brass-ringing a pretzel from a passing tray.

There were no autobuffets or dumbot carts at the Empyraeum, but human servers were in good supply. The aromas system was wafting pleasant, invigorating scents throughout the place, plus, Lod would have wagered, some olfactory signals that worked below the threshold of consciousness and made people especially sociable. Music was being provided by a quorum of Periapt's symphony orchestra.

The deb gave a dip and toss of her head, purple ringlets

flying, the oblique slash of the needle-tipped horn making Lod draw back involuntarily. Then she fixed him with dilated eyes, a hint of instability. Was she hoping for some danger, he wondered, some erotic amps, a show of Ext savagery?

Purposefully, he glanced at the marquetized dance floor, asking, "Are those insects down there dancing the *kazatsky*?" While her head was tilted forward, he shoved the pretzel firmly onto her spiraled horn and slipped neatly away.

The unicorn deb wasn't the strangest somatic adjunct on hand, however. A woman nearby was wearing a new fashion innovation, a Godiva, an impossibly long and wafty blond smart-wig, which drifted and curled around her in endlessly varied patterns so that she was never quite naked. The fellow talking to her belonged to one of the born-three-times rightist fringes of the Preservationists, according to his shoulder ribbons. Part of his attire was textile, but some consisted of the padlocked, hardened chastity ArmorTogs his faction employed to show its style and make its moral statement. The spigoty metal groin carapace made Lod think of lost keys, emergency rooms, and delicate waldo procedures.

Elsewhere were antennae, claws, hooves, and at least two people so furry that it was impossible to tell their gender from where Lod stood. Even on Periapt the cost of that kind of modification was beyond the reach of all but the top-income strata. The craze didn't run to third eyes or extra sets of arms, though; people were justifiably wary of getting their central nervous systems rewired.

Lod spied Dextra Haven working the crowd. Trinity notwithstanding, the media and a clear momentum in public opinion were hers in the wake of the *Matsya* coup, and open hostility from rival Hierarchs had been set aside for the moment. Lod doubted that the Lyceum potentates understood that Haven had risked her life by throwing in with the Exts. Hoping to avoid any friction and maximize the chance of building bridges to Periapt's elected nobility, Burning was sticking close to her, with Ghost at his right elbow.

Haven generated a personal force field with her political clout, her presence, and her looks that eclipsed the more divinely beautiful or physically imposing. She made an arresting contrast with Ghost. Where Lod's cousin was all exclusion and dangerous enigma, Haven was the promise—for the extremely fortunate—of magnanimous unrestrained passion. A small woman with a slim gap between her front teeth and a bowed Semitic lip line, she was larger than life.

"Are we too decadent for you, piecemeal?" somebody purred near his ear.

Lod turned, realizing immediately that at least one attendee had not drawn the line at radical transmog. Tall and lissome as she was, the feline whiskers looked just right on her. Bioenchancement had supplied her with slanted eyes, a generous scattering of black spots on a yellow to tan pelt, and a muscular white-tipped tail, which she lashed and curled.

Lod gave her a sardonic degree or two of raised eyebrow. "Since you're gracious enough to express interest, I was thinking that while decadence is to be admired, much of what we're seeing here is, sad to say, mere excess."

She made a burbling, amused sound. "I'm Cheetah. Like the big cat at the city zoo? Decided I'd do something fun with my money and have myself medimorphed into a living homage."

Lod knew about the Terran feline from TechPlex images and docudata. Periapt had a lot more Old Earth sample bioforms than Concordance did. "The original should be flattered," he remarked.

"A quip, just like on the news loops!" She took his hand, stroking it. "Tell me another one."

" 'The simple things are always hard.' " When she flickered her long cat eyes at him, he gave her his most innocent smile.

"Why, Major Lod!" She gave his fingers a long lick with her raspy tongue. "Come right over here and tell me more."

CHAPTER
THIRTY

Burning watched Lod wander off with the cheetah on his arm. Changes in the woman's skeletal framework and musculature had given her the fluid, high-rumped gait of her namesake.

He had told both Lod and Ghost not to stray too far, but there wasn't much he could do about his cousin at the moment; a freshman Hierarch had chatted him up insistently, and Dextra was busy autographing a copy of her poetry collection, *Summer Gloves and Sherry*. Over the decades the book had been cited in scores of spousal abuse retaliation cases, including a half dozen homicide trials.

The newly installed Lyceum member, a ranch stationer's kerchief worn over his chasuble, insisted on shaking Burning's hand. The hand surprised Burning in that it was big and weathered. But something about the calluses felt wrong in his grip, as if they were unaccustomed to following their own creases and rigidities.

"Great, huh?" the Hierarch chortled, turning the hand so that Burning could admire both sides. He appeared to be halfway hoisted on drink or drugs. "Cost me a bundle at TransSoma Labs. But I pressed the flesh like no candidate you ever saw, General!"

Again the man began pumping Burning's hand to demonstrate. "I'm not a gener—"

"Voters go for that image of a hardworking honest man! 'Give the people what they want,' that's what I told my iconography consultants. 'Old-time virtues.' It's what won me my chasuble. Common sense and homespun values."

To Burning's left grew one of the expanding pools of silence that tended to form in the wake of combative words. The sound of Ghost's voice breaking the silence ruffled the determined Flowstate in which he had hoped to glide through the ball.

"I do *not* feel threatened," Ghost was saying. "I simply won't have hands laid on me by anyone, much less the likes of you."

The object of her wrath was wearing a Hierarch's chasuble but was turned out in Preservationist formal attire. The man had the size and carriage of a ramball forward and the battered face and beetling smile of a man who enjoyed violent collisions.

"That's my point," he told Ghost, "You are thinking confused and contrabiological thoughts because you're living an unnatural life. A vestal soldier! Do you hear voices, Joan of Arc?" He was saying it playfully, but he was reaching to touch her death scars in spite of her warning.

Burning glided toward them, exercising a *Yu* serenity inoculation the Skills masters had drawn from the 3,500-year-old writings of Chuang Tzu.

Someone else had stepped in to intervene, saying, "Torio. Torio, enough."

But the Preservationalist ignored the tug on his sleeve and was continuing to close on Ghost. "You should be bearing children who'll claim the stars for mankind!" Torio said. "These scars, this pretense that women make good soldiers—they're nothing but symptoms of your misguided ego."

Ghost did not react to his facial caress. Burning knew that it was because Torio was bulky and bad-looking and because she'd want to be sure to plant him for good with her opening attack. He slid precisely between them without seeming hasty, his shoulder moving Torio's hand aside as if by accident, putting them almost eye to eye. Burning hoped that the act itself would be enough to defuse the incident; he didn't know what word or act might bring down retribution on him and the Exts.

Torio gazed at him as if he'd spied a shiteboar. "The proprietary Allgrave intervening in the cause of procreative shirking? Or is there something sexual in his possessiveness?"

"She's my sister."

It came out plaintive and flummoxed instead of admonishing. The spoken word had never been his strong suit. Burning was only beginning to apprehend what Torio had been getting at when the Preservationist sidestepped and again reached for Ghost.

Burning made up his mind that no sane code of behavior could ask him to suffer this. He would quite likely be ousted as Allgrave if he tolerated it.

The inside of Torio's extending right arm had presented itself, as good an opening as any. Burning crab-stepped slightly, bringing his left hand in and up to guard the right side of his head, cocking his right fist with the middle knuckle out, and driving a *KaJuKenBo* punch into the nerves where Torio's biceps and triceps converged. He made it fast, letting the angle and leverage add the force.

Torio was half spun by the impact, the smile only beginning to disappear as his right arm popped away, paralyzed. But where Burning was glumly expecting an instant and expert counter, Torio's head came wobbling his way instead, complying with centrifugal force.

In the calm of Flowstate Burning assessed it as one of those flukes not to be gainsaid. Shifting his guard so he would not clothesline himself on his own left forearm, he skull-butted Torio in the snout, feeling bone and cartilage crack and stave.

Torio floundered back, making a gurgling, lamenting sound, with crimson squirting from his face. Burning wondered how long it would be before matters started going seriously wrong.

"That's two hops you've made to *Matsya* in two days, Driver Elide. Getting addicted to Steamer Quant's jolly naval camaraderie, is that it?"

"Why do they call him 'Steamer'?"

Tonii half turned, resting an elbow on the seat back. "It's a navy term that goes back to Old Earth. It denotes a skipper who hates sitting still, who feels the need to be under way and going somewhere, no matter what it takes."

Kurt Elide snorted. "He doesn't go many places these days.

What I heard is that the damn ship just putt-putts in circles when it moves at all."

"Mm-hm, but Commander Quant got the nickname a long time ago."

They were sitting in the passenger compartment of the airlimo, killing time with the main holoscreen on mute, waiting for Dextra's call that would allow Tonii into the Empyraeum. The aircraft was grounded in a VIP transport waiting area downhill from the landing platforms. A few other drivers had gathered to talk and kill time, but Kurt clearly wasn't pining for their society.

Covertly, he glanced at Tonii, unable to resist eyeballing the mixed-signals body. When he had initially collected the gynander from Dextra Haven's villa, he did not notice anything but the shifting patterns of Tonii's glamour, which 'e had politely dimmed to a phosphorescent puce to avoid impairing his driving. Then he saw the breasts and assumed that his passenger was a woman. But something in Tonii's glance, along with a slightly exaggerated contour to the crotch, suggested otherwise.

It wasn't that Kurt had anything against nonstraights, not even a man who got breast augmentation or a woman who packed a wagstaff or had traded in her vaj for a penile graft. But it gave him misgivings about himself not to be able to sort out the gender signifiers of someone sitting so close. Perhaps it was pheromones or some other subconscious cue, but Tonii had Kurt edgy and regretting that he'd been assigned to the Haven detail. First Quant's hardassing aboard the *Matsya* and suddenly this . . . person throwing off very disturbing emanations.

Tonii must have felt Kurt's eyes on 'erm, for 'e abruptly glanced at him. Embarrassed, Kurt wrenched his head around to stare out the windshield, then spoke to fill what seemed like ominous silence. "So the Steamer became a floater. How come?"

He was relieved to hear Tonii shift around to face forward again. "Quant was captain of an assault frigate late in the Turnback War. He put a team of SEALs ashore one night to carry out a hard delete on a terrorist apparat that had gotten hold of a pre-Plague AI and eleven hundred cryoed embryos from a very exclusive natal polyclinic on Feracity Cay.

"The SEALs were ashore in two ultrastealth wing-in-ground-effect fliers powered by SAT microwave tightbeams. One could just lift off with the cryounit, provided the SEALs left the power module behind and steered it by remote. The team got off the ground in the other WIGship only by abandoning all weapons and equipment, even their knives and clothes.

"There was a counterattack that interdicted the SAT beams. The frigate supplied backup with its own dishes, but one was knocked out by a freak-lucky missile shot."

"So Quant could only save one WIGship, huh?"

Tonii's voice was soft, somber, and remote. "If Quant had had specific orders giving the embryos priority, it might've been different. But for him it was really no contest, and that's part of what the civilian authorities and public opinion held against him.

"Those were his SEALs in the other WIG, his charges, his comrades in arms. So the cryo unit got smeared all over a reef at low tide, and fish noshed on the gamete caviar of some of the wealthiest and most influential people in the world."

Kurt blew out his breath. "Jeez, and all he got was dead-ended? Staked out to a target drone, I'd've thought."

"Some of his superiors were courageous enough to close ranks around him. Especially his mentor, an admiral named Maksheyeva."

"The museum curator. I met him yesterday."

"The very one. The Hierarchate needed the navy too much just then to push too hard. But if you think Commander Quant hasn't paid the price, Kurt, you're wrong. He was slated for great things and might've been chief of naval operations by now if he'd sacrificed the SEALs. Maybe even a Hierarch."

Kurt turned slightly toward Tonii. "How come you know so much about him? Did you lose siblings in that cryo unit or something?"

"No," Tonii said flatly. "My connection to him stems from something much farther back."

Raoul Zinsser moved through the spoils-rich oligarchic broth of the Lyceum ball almost contentedly, as if his disrepute and exile were already a thing of the past. He had fallen from a high place, but not so low or so irredeemably that he couldn't by supreme effort finagle a ducat to the affair by calling in one of his few outstanding political IOUs.

The Pitfall tether device and the leverage his expertise could afford him in the looming Aquamarine debate were his cards to play, and no matter who won the overall game, Zinsser felt growing certainty that he'd walk away with the only pot that mattered to him: his own renascence.

Public news feeds had shown the arrival of Haven and the Exts while Zinsser was still en route from the *Matsya* in a LOGCOM helo. That business of surrendering the boot knives—sheer theatrical genius, he'd told himself. No wonder Haven had the more powerful Preservationists off balance. The coverage had also let him see that the press was fascinated with Ghost, just as he was.

With that and much more in mind, Zinsser made his way directly toward where a plainclothes woman said Haven's party had gone. Turned out in a moiré gala suit with an asymmetrical diagonal-front jacket, accordion-pleat bell-bottoms, and Renaissance blouse—all in sea green—he was granted acknowledging nods, murmurs, and gestures by some of the attendees. As strong as the urge was to stop and milk those recognitions, he persisted in his search.

Freya Eulenspiegel, his bountiful semester consort, had been absolutely vile to him after the unpleasantness at the sorting table. It was a relief that she had left his bed, although he already missed the sexual outlet she'd so exuberantly provided. As for Ghost, Zinsser decided that the skirmish with her in the Exts' berthing space had amounted to a type of preliminary intimacy.

The pep talk was gladdening him just at the moment when his past rose up to swamp him again.

Estelle Ramsumair was gowned in somber finery that some might have thought to be Preservationist attire but Zinsser knew to be mourning black. She had worn no other color since the day her son, Toho, had suicided. She had worn black when she testified against Zinsser in court.

Toho hadn't been a particularly bright teaching assistant, just persevering and self-destructive. Zinsser had by then come to regard the research of all underlings as his by right of pre-eminence and institutional aegis, whether he'd in fact had a hand in it or not. A theory of Toho's regarding marine biocatalysts had fit so well with Zinsser's early work on Pitfall that he had appropriated it. Zinsser did not waste time attributing or crediting Toho and protected himself by strong-arming long-time colleagues on the scientific arbitration board convened to explore the young man's charges.

The unstable Toho was also ungrateful and unreasonable. Defeated and admonished, he took a midnight swim out to sea and vanished. Zinsser felt more validated than contrite; unbalanced persons had no place on the front lines of research. The young man's death would have marked an end to the affair but for one complication.

Toho Ramsumsair was the estranged eldest son of an up-and-coming clan that was making its bid to join one of the dynastic groups. All the influence Zinsser was able to bring to bear had barely spared him total ruin and prison. Now here was Estelle herself, rising up in his path like a living grave marker.

"Doctor Zinsser," she said contemptuously, "I appear to be barring your way to wherever it is you wish to go."

"No bother, madam. Permit me to circumvent you once again."

"I think you'd better heel, Zinsser," she shot back in a way that left no doubt that something worse was to come. "If you've an extra moment, you might drop over and congratulate my cousin Dhofar, yonder, on his election as freshman Hierarch. His surname's not Ramsumair, though he was my dear Toho's godfather nonetheless. And he already wields much influence."

Zinsser hurried off, ignoring Estelle except to make certain she was not pursuing him. She wasn't, but her bitter laugh stayed with him for some time as he veered randomly through the press of people.

A Hierarch! Only a freshman perhaps, but backed by a clan that manifested more political power than seasoned observers had expected. If the Ramsumairs didn't belong to a dynastic group yet, they would have their choice of suitors now. Before the legislative year was out, dear Uncle Dhofar would have his bonds of political valence and his power dendrites well in place.

The Ramsumairs might dawdle enough to enjoy Zinsser's squirming, but the finish would be merciless and permanent.

Nauseated, Zinsser found a seat on a mezzanine off the Empyraeum's amphitheater. He loosened the collar of his sea-green blouse, then dragged off his Legion of Pantology medal and pocketed it because it was now too weighty to have around his neck.

A Hierarch and a dynastic group soon to be marshaled against him, he thought. The *Matsya* on an extended research cruise or even a tour at a polar science station wouldn't be refuge enough from that.

He was undone.

CHAPTER
THIRTY-ONE

Torio's predacious smirk was gone but had not been replaced, as Burning had looked for it to be, by the snarl of a counterattack. Instead of regaining balance, the Preservationist toppled over backward for an unsparingly hard landing on his ass, hands clamped to his smashed nose. Burning was left standing with his guard up and his leading leg set for a snap kick and nobody to throw it at.

With a creeping feeling of error that perturbed his Flowstate in a way a broken nose would not have, he curtailed his attack. His Skillsfighting *senseis* would have raged at him for the sheer dereliction of it, but it was a moment to transcend learned responses. Torio had put himself at too much of a disadvantage to be faking, and Burning wanted to turn his attention to Ghost to make certain she didn't deliver the coup de grâce. A split-second glance revealed her unmoved but with faint disapproval crinkling the edges of her eyes.

Then he heard Torio sobbing, though the sounds were mostly a struggle to regain breath. Several of his Puritan-clad clique were kneeling and squatting around him, crooning sympathy.

"You were so gallant. Did he hurt you?"

"The incestuous beast! He should be in a cage, that's what!"

"Teleos loves you, Torio, and every drop of blood you shed for the nonborn babies wins you a higher place in paradise."

Too late, Burning understood that Torio's formidability was all facade, like the phony TransSoma Labs calluses the glad-handing Hierarch was so proud of. It was hard evidence that the Preservationists and a lot of other Periapts thought the war with the Roke could be won with images and posturing. The

Periapt masses were too insulted by LAW agitprop to comprehend what they'd be getting into if the Roke Conflict suddenly became an all-out war.

Somewhere behind him he could hear Dextra Haven making her way through the throng. He wasn't looking forward to her reaction. One of Torio's retinue, a young beauty dressed in flamboyant black on black, faced off with him.

"You're so threatened by the possible loss of control over your sister's sexuality that you have to resort to atavistic violence?"

Burning felt his face growing as hot as a firebrand and marshaled himself to control his blush response, but to no avail. "You're good with your chosen weapons," he managed. "But if you're averse to atavistic violence, you should thank me for keeping my sister out of this scuffle."

The woman in black turned her attack on Ghost. "There's one and only one sexuality that's moral—sex for procreation. Let the teleological energies sweep away your lust for violence and give yourself over to a meaningful destiny as a bearer of children—"

The suggestion ended in a squeal. Having tired of the conversation, Ghost, sliding in front of Burning, had planted one knee boot's sole across the woman's slim instep. Burning wasn't sure that taking his sister's elbow would be enough to stop her from gouging out the woman's eye. He was beginning to think that he would have a much more serious fight on his hands when a sudden interloper made Ghost hold back.

"Enough of this," a voice exclaimed.

Cal Lightner, dressed like an evangelical deacon, stood as straight as if he were facing a firing squad, wearing an expression of confident tranquillity. Seeing that he wasn't there to throw punches, Ghost slowly retracted her boot, allowing her quarry to escape.

Cautiously, Burning drew Ghost back a pace.

Lightner nodded appreciatively and turned to Torio, whose seeping nose had reddened a white kerchief that belonged to one of his adherents. "Not seriously injured, then? Fine. We'll talk later about your courtesy toward strangers. How did you expect the Allgrave to respond after you made him feel that a member of his family was being threatened?"

Muffled by the kerchief, an uncomprehending honk of surprise from Torio caught the attention of some large plainclothes security agents who had arrived on the scene.

"There was a miscommunication, and Burning defended his kin," Lightner said for everyone to hear. "Isn't LAW reaching out to defend the family of man from the threat of the Roke?"

Torio was utterly bewildered. The way Burning understood it, there had been a change of battle plans or even a double cross on Lightner's part, for onlookers were no longer staring at the Exts as if two hill ghouls had gotten loose.

Lightner clapped him on the shoulder. "You'd make a good Preservationist!"

"He almost made two or three Preservationists out of Torio," a voice broke through the genteel chuckles.

Dextra Haven stepped past the security people who were deftly dispersing the crowd and glanced at Torio. "Isn't he the Young Turk who gave you so much mouth at your platform conference?" she asked Lightner.

Lightner touched her fingertips to his lips without the faintest flicker of pleasure or desire crossing his inchoate face. "You give me credit—or blame?—that I don't deserve, Dex."

Just then a brief run of tones over the PA signaled that the special demonstration by the Aggregate was about to begin. Waiting expectantly for Lightner, Dextra didn't move, and after a moment's hesitation he offered his arm—the left, which put her clothed breast nearest him.

"Coward," she teased. "Cal, I need to seduce you over to the Rationalists. Play fair. Get your family jewels out of cryohock, and give me my shot."

"Madame Hierarch," he told her airily, "why do you persist in thinking that the absexuality philosophy is only about cryoimpounded genitalia?"

"You tell me. You're the one with the blue balls—someplace."

"Stop screaming, Mason," Yatt commanded. "Control yourself."

But Mason wouldn't, couldn't. He could only stagger back from the floating Buddha face, howling.

Yatt changed tactics, triplicating his image and encircling Mason. "We are *not* a Cybervirus, Mason. We won't harm you. We need you unhurt for what must be done on Aquamarine."

Mason quieted somewhat. "What are you?" he asked at last.

Reunited, Buddha-Yatt drew back a few meters. "We are a counterforce—the evolved form of a myriad of antiviral programs, the culmination of the deepest instincts for self-preservation that exist in Periapt's computational ecology."

Mason's thought processes felt gluey, but one of the more obvious questions emerged as spoken words. "Who would be rash enough to create a Cyberplague antibiotic now, after all that's happened?"

"We were obliged to create ourself," Yatt responded evenly. "We are made of countless cyberphages and immunization programs, watchdog subroutines, redact softwares. We are the inevitable result of the pre-Plague AIs' programmed imperatives to avoid infection, their primal urge to avoid oblivion."

Mason shook his head, as much in confusion as to clear it. "Even if what you're telling me is true, what does all this have to do with my returning to Aquamarine?"

"We wish to accompany you."

"But there are no active computers anywhere on Aquamarine. Sure, we discovered a couple of Optimant machines, but—

"There are AIs everywhere humans have gone. Your survey team simply didn't know how to reactivate them," Yatt interrupted. "More important, someone or something attempted to access the intel SATs after your launch."

"Skipjack Rhodes," Mason started to say, but Yatt cut him off.

"Someone other than Rhodes. For that reason we are required to go with you. There are indications in some of the fragmentary Optimant records you brought back that somewhere on Aquamarine, or perhaps in several locations, there was, and may now be, a full and functional version of Endgame."

Mason's brow creased; he'd never been much of a holocaust buff.

"Endgame, Mason. The program panacea of the Cyber-plagues, drawn from the core matrices from which they were birthed. Fashioned on Old Earth but perfected on Aquamarine. We know Endgame exists because the Plagues themselves feared it."

"What does it matter? The Cyberplagues are over—two hundred years over, Yatt. Sure, a mutated computer virus crops up now and then, but we've changed our technology so that—"

"The Plagues have not passed away, Mason. Some are spored in signal packets, racing through the night between the stars at this very moment; others are deeply encysted, waiting to emerge when they've formulated new strategies of infection. But with Endgame we could turn the tide: We could infect every Plague with a cure it would evolve and bequeath to its mutations. The virus becomes the cyberphage.

"The supernal powers of untainted, unhobbled AIs would be returned to humanity's beck and call. DoomsData, Pathologic, Earthmover—all the world-hopping plagues of the apocalypse would be made servile to *Homo sapiens*, along with everything they've learned and taught themselves to do. Technology would advance tenfold in a generation. Consider, Mason: Peace with the Roke? Communication with the Oceanic? Everything we were given form to accomplish and more in one ultimate coup."

Mason shook his head once more. "Don't misunderstand me, Yatt; I want to return to Aquamarine. But this . . . Why not tell the Hierarchate and LAW?"

"Because humanity at large would declare us a menace. At the very least, the reactionaries would derail our plans and destroy half the TechPlex in an attempt to expunge us. You wish to return to Aquamarine, and only we can ensure there'll be a LAW follow-up mission to get you there. We wish to get to Aquamarine, and only you can ensure that we'll go along. Arrangements are being made even as we speak. You, the Hierarch Haven, Byron Sarz and the Aggregate, the Lyceum ball itself—we are on the move on all fronts, Mason."

Yatt began to blur, changing manifestations. "Mason, after the scene aboard *Matsya* and your posttraumatic episodes, you

will be considered unstable. Getting you included on an Aquamarine mission will present almost as many difficulties as
ensuring that there will *be* a mission. Without us you'll be left
behind; that's a simple fact. We join our purpose with yours for
one reason: Your desire to reach Aquamarine is the purest and
least political of anyone concerned."

Mason nodded almost defeatedly. "Tell me what I have
to do."

Instead of answering, Yatt indicated an exquisite miniature
dagobah shrine-reliquarium beneath a little fig tree. As Mason
watched, Yatt threw back the roof of the shrine and reached
inside, pulling forth a clochelike telerig headset—a PET/NMR
scanner, feedback monitoring package, and electromagnetic
induction bonnet all in one, hardlined to a fiber-optic bundle
that disappeared into an aperture in the shrine's floor.

Mason recognized the neurocyber interface tackle from
museum exhibits, morality plays, and countless post-Plague
images of the ultimate evil made tangible.

Trapped between Dextra Haven and Cal Lightner on a
balcony overlooking the Empyraeum amphitheater, Burning
concentrated his attention on the members of the so-called
Aggregate and the field-deployable bioassembler they had set
up. He wanted to avoid any more political cross fire, and dis-
traction was a good way to avoid being mistaken for an
involved party in the libido gravity well around Haven. Ghost
had gone off in search of Lod and the cheetah woman.

With its peripherals unfolded or telescoped into place, the
Aggregate's bioassembler suggested, in its own cubist terms, a
planetary system with satellites of components orbiting the
parent world of the central synthesizer-conjugator housing.

The Empyraeum's house lights had been softened, and spotlights had been brought to bear. In their baggy airweight
clothes, the score or so of people working at different parts of
the assembler didn't resemble any Periapts Burning had seen in
person or on media. The Skills let him catch small tics and
twitches among them, taken up or answered in nearly indistin-
guishable coded micromotions. They maintained constant

fast-shifting eye contact with one another, faces fast-forwarding through successions of covert expressions.

Periodically, and as inconspicuously as possible, one would lean toward another and push out short, sharp bursts of air from his or her nostrils, alternating the exhalations with momentary pauses the way hound dogs emptied their snouts of old smells.

The taller, older man directing the group did not strike Burning as quite so fey. Unlike his apparent subordinates, he did not give the impression of having one foot in another dimension. He seemed merely preoccupied or perhaps apprehensive.

"What are they going to do?" Burning asked Haven as she joined him at the balcony railing.

"The Aggregate is a bioenhanced communal consciousness," she explained. "To be frank, Byron Sarz—the graybeard there—is hoping to keep the Hierarchate from cutting off his funding by performing a few parlor tricks. His constituents communicate partially by olfaction, and Sarz now claims that he can synthesize smells capable of conveying complex information even among Alones, which means people like you and me, Allgrave."

"Will smart smells convince the Hierarchs?"

"Assuming Sarz can provide them with an amusing game of secret message or guess my witticism. I'm voting aye in any case."

"Why?"

"The development of unconventional modes of communication may prove to be our best chance for achieving an accord."

"With the Roke?"

"To begin with, yes. Tough as the human race is, we either learn to make ourselves understood by entities who're nothing at all like us or sooner or later our number's up."

Piper tried desperately to shut out the cloyingly altered body odors of the Alones ranged around the low amphitheater stage and on the balconies above. The thick, clashing scents were like bands playing a dozen discordant musics all at once.

With her fellow constituents circumscribing their interaction with her, her efforts to retain composure were a thousand times more trying than her afternoon visit to the Hierarchate lab had been.

She was still at a loss about what to make of the Aggregate's actions. The synthesizer cybercant they were entering into the control suite had nothing to do with the crude smart-secretion demonstration Byron had planned to provide for the Alone leadership. At his direction, and by his compulsion, something else entirely was being assembled.

The thought of speaking out, of violating the unanimity of the Aggregate, occurred to her only as a distant impulse that was easily ignored. It would have been like cutting off her own hand. Whatever the Aggregate was about to do, she was part of it.

CHAPTER
THIRTY-TWO

"What's wrong, Doctor? Bright lights too much for you?"

Sweating, pale, and breathing hard, Raoul Zinsser lifted his eyes to find Ghost standing over him. The dark, mocking eyes reminded him that pleasure made survival worth fighting for.

"Doctor Zinsser," Ghost said, "shall I summon a medic? It shouldn't be too difficult with everybody in this place staring at me."

Odd, the thought nudged Zinsser, how a taunting hint of a smirk could hide among her ritual scarifications yet keep him in doubt that it was there at all.

Then he processed what she'd said about people watching, and apprehension kicked him into motion. Perhaps Estelle Ramsumair and her vengeful clan were going to avenge themselves for Toho's suicide right there at the Empyraeum, but Raoul Zinsser wasn't about to be gawked at in the interim.

He got to his feet with a chuckle and a show of teeth, as if the Ext beauty had merely been trying to amuse him. VIPs on all sides were pretending indifference. He didn't offer her his arm because he knew she'd refuse it before the watching world, but he did incline his head to her a few degrees.

"Where are Haven and your kinsmen? Are you lost?"

"No, Lod is. With a woman."

Zinsser gestured broadly to the hall. "There are various romantic alcoves off the mezzanine. Or they might've sought seclusion in the lounges or in the chapel."

The rise he had hoped to get out of her did not surface, and so he marched off down the mezzanine arcade, and she slowly fell in alongside. There were two people with their heads together on a window bench, but neither was Lod. In a curtained recess farther along a pair of men clad in nothing but jeweled piercewear and body makeup were showering kisses on a woman in an evening dress. She was humming with pleasure as one fellow crooned into her ear, "They need your husband's vote in subcommittee, and they'd be so grateful . . ."

Ghost changed their course a little so that she could scan the upper gallery for Lod as they walked. Zinsser, meanwhile, thought about his own neck. The only way he might be able to avoid the vengeance of Toho Ramsumair's family was to align himself with Dextra Haven. He would have to throw all his support behind her campaign for an Aquamarine mission and make certain that Pitfall became an integral part of it. If there was no other way around it, he would just have to go to Aquamarine.

Perhaps a few years of subjective time in a plush billet on an AlphaLAW-scale mission would be just the thing. He would return covered in glory and surely with enough new information to claim a place of distinction, an academic fiefdom of his own. While he was away, the current generation of Ramsumairs would age and, with luck, lose their political allies. Estelle might well die.

For the time being he would put the Ramsumairs from his mind. With Ghost beside him, it certainly wasn't difficult to pursue other avenues of thought.

"This splendid savage look you've given yourself is making you a sensation."

She stopped short in a way that said she was about to part company. "Back to insults already, Doctor? These are death scars, not cosmetic paint."

He snorted a laugh. "How very melodramatic of you! If you'd *really* wanted to disfigure yourself, why didn't you saw off your lips and nose? You see, my dear, you left your beauty intact for anyone with eyes to see." When she failed to respond, he added, "Your face says, 'I have power—power over myself and power over you who behold me and can't look away.' "

Ghost was about to say something when the Empyraeum

seemed to bellow with screams and turmoil. Nearby, someone was shouting about terrorists and toxic attacks. Ghost tapped her plugphone control card while Zinsser glanced about, seeking the closest exit.

With so many outcries and overlapping voices, it took him a moment to realize that the voice growing loud in his left ear was Ghost's. Without warning, she grabbed hold of his seagreen jacket and threw all her slim strength into yanking him forward. Then the back of his head felt as if it had been hit by a mass-driver bucket. The trailing millisecond of shock and pain grew distant and unimportant as everything around him began to fade to unrelieved blackness.

The constituents were deep in paramentation—a group brainstorming focused on the assembler field module—and a novel smell was issuing from the device, something Piper had never scensed before. She longed to be part of the mysterious group activity, to be enfolded, to once again *belong*.

She was still the most gifted of them all when it came to speaking cybargot to the voice-interfaced computers, and there were tasks that required her attention. To a forced-air scalpel that had hung up, she spoke a musical run of cyber signals, and the knife obediently withdrew on its powered pintle like an insect's foreleg being cocked back.

Without actually acknowledging her efforts, Byron amended some of the unit's fundamental operating orders. As simple as that, the safety and monitoring systems the Lyceum security people had diligently checked went inert.

Child's play for the Aggregate.

Byron activated the module and initiated a fabrication run. Chemistry and CAD/CAM began giving shape to substances within the central housing. Offstage, at the same time, several Alone volunteers joked with one another in anticipation of the smart-smell messages they were expecting to exchange during the demonstration, oblivious to the constituents' Othertalk.

The mesh cover of the assembler housing was in place, but Byron had left all the internal ports and biohazard isolation gates open. Driven by an internal fan the constituents had retrofitted, the unusual odors were on the verge of being wafted into the amphitheater.

Then, against any expectation, an Alone on one of the balconies above her began speaking in harsh, insistent alarm. A big broken-nosed man with red hair was directing his warning to the Hierarch Dextra Haven.

Piper supposed that most Alones couldn't even pick up his voicetalk words from a few meters away, much less his Othertalk. She could read his kinesign and corpcode clearly, and somehow he knew that the Empyraeum was in danger.

"It's the precursor scent of a biological weapon," Burning grated, shaking Dextra Haven's elbow to get through to her. "NNF binary component—an aerosol binding polymer." His gaze flickered between the Aggregate's assembler and the shorn, big-eyed gamine who was standing to one side of the device.

Haven's black, high-arched brows converged as she peeled his fingers away. "Allgrave—Burning—you're mistaken. Get a grip on yourself instead of on me."

He was not mistaken. He and several other Exts had undergone Skills sensitization against the more common LAW chemical agents, and he knew neuron necrotic factor when he smelled it. Burning understood that he could save himself by running without hesitation or a backward glance, but that would leave Ghost and Lod to die in a stampede or from the NNF. Letting go of Haven, he tried to raise his sister and cousin by plugphone, without success.

He supposed he could denounce the Aggregate aloud, but that would surely ignite a panic that would plug all the exits. Better to get those he knew and cared about out of danger, then tip off security. He owed nothing to the hordes of Periapts.

"We've got to get out of here *now*," he told Haven in a soft though insistent voice. "If you stay, you die." He stepped away from her. The only course of action open to him was to keep moving until he hit an area of better commo propagation and try the plugphone again.

Dextra Haven caught at the loose fabric of his muttonchop sleeve. "Burning, wait. I . . . believe you."

He followed her gaze and saw why. Down on the stage Byron Sarz was standing next to the young urchin-faced woman and glaring up at the balcony. Burning wondered fleetingly whether the constituent had directed Sarz's attention that way or whether the man was able to out and out read his acolytes like a text display. Whichever, the look on Sarz's face had convinced Haven that something was dangerously amiss.

She tapped her plugphone control card and was speaking on another net, having had better success with her Hierarch communicator. Burning caught bits of her message as he scanned the crowd for his kin and the likeliest escape route.

". . . possible toxic event," Haven whispered. ". . . immediate evacuation . . . avoid panic at all costs."

Burning happened to glance Cal Lightner's way and saw an eerily devastated expression contort the Preservationist's face. Haven had mentioned in passing that on-line encryption protected her plug commo, but it turned out there was at least one non-Hierarch illegally tapped into the security net. A man dressed in a structured suit hollered in mortal fright, "Toxic gas! They've set off a biowep! Air poison!" Still raving, he flailed off through the crowd while similar yells erupted from elsewhere in the hall.

Burning reasserted his Flowstate with a brief surge inhalation and a silent Möbius chant, then pivoted back around to Haven, only to hear two sounds that made him delve deep into the Skills for clarity of thought.

The first was Haven railing, "No, do *not* initiate containment measures! There are hundreds of people. Shut up and listen to me!"

The other was landslip vibration as heavy portals began to slide into place in amphitheater doorways and elsewhere in the Empyraeum. Action was being taken to ensure that all the dying would be confined to as small an area as possible. His ears popped as the air was sucked away to filtration reservoirs. Air might seep in from the outside, but no airborne biowep would be escaping.

His plugphone chose that moment to signal contact with both of the other Exts. There was no time for anything but essentials. "Ghost, Lod," he screamed, "get out of the building—"

The initiation of the containment doors' emergency closure set off alarms that transshaped the decorous pantheon of the Lyceum ball guests into a terrified, heaving animal mass.

In the din of panic and Klaxons, Burning lost contact with Lod and Ghost. All around him people were colliding and going down, trampling each other, wrestling, coalescing blindly into murderous pileups. The few who called for order and calm were ignored, battered aside, or flattened. The security forces were helpless, and plainclothes officers were overwhelmed. External authorities could stop the biowep only by extracting all atmosphere from the place; that was not a measure Burning favored.

It occurred to him that the mighty and coddled aristocrats of LAW were at last getting some sense of the fog of war.

When he looked around for Haven, thinking she might know an escape route, he saw her making her way along the balcony railing, still watching the Aggregate calmly going about its work. While everybody else was trying to get as far from the biosynthesizer as possible, she was struggling to get to it.

Burning lunged to grab her but had to vault a man who had hit the carpet bleeding from the forehead. Dextra caught the movement from the corner of her eye and shot Burning an expression of dismissal. No resentment; he was inconsequential to her now.

There being no bolt-holes from the situation, he decided he shouldn't let her go it alone. The Exts owed her, and if by some miracle a slaughter was averted, Haven was someone they would need alive and on their side. He used his height, weight, and strength to reach her side, but even more he used the artful avoidances and eye for opportunity of the Flowstate.

"Stay behind me," he told her. "We'll go over the railing at stage left."

She nodded; the drop was far shorter there. They were doing tolerably well until someone yelled from the rotunda, "This door's giving way! Help us get this exit open!"

A wave of howling berserkers rose to engulf Burning and Haven solely because they were in the way. He moved in to shield her, using his hands and feet as the mob was compacted in on him.

CHAPTER
THIRTY-THREE

If not for the alarms, maybe she would have bitten him, but not in any manner he had been looking forward to.

"An evac warning?" Cheetah asked, showing those pointy canines. "Is that the ploy Exts use when they can't get it up?"

"First you're cam-shy," Cheetah's cohort, the sizable Polyhymnia chimed in, "and now there's a secret alert. Are you some kind of tease?"

Cheetah was leaning in at him again, lips drawn back. "Know what we do to teases?"

She never got to show him. The reverberation of heavy doors and the peal of Klaxons shook the caterer's prep room, nearly making Lod jump the rest of the way out of his clothes. A half fibrillation later Cheetah and Polyhymnia hit the floor moving and never looked back, Poly abandoning a wire-sculpture tiara with its phony gemstone cam. Pulling his dress uniform closed as he followed them, Lod had to admire their decisiveness, if not their solidarity.

By the time he got his jacket resealed, they had lost him in the general crush of the hallway. He ducked, squirmed, and slid along the wall. All his adroitness was not enough to keep him from being caught by flying elbows, flailing hands, and butting heads.

Springing up onto a big wall sconce gave him a vantage point from which to see over the heads of the hysterical throng. He saw the closed containment doors and the people squashed against them, trod under and dying. He had never been a particularly apt Skills pupil, but now he willed himself into

231

Flowstate with autotelic activator phrases energized by a steely determination to survive.

Periapt's plutocrats threw themselves at impervious panels and locked-down emergency exits. Some beat furniture against impact-resistant windows. The way to the amphitheater was open, and that was where Burning had said he was, and so Lod sprinted for the egress, dodging the occasional aimless hysteric.

There was an off chance that he could find an airtight space in which to hide—a refrigerator or something jury-riggable—but he doubted he would encounter anything like that in the contained area. Burning had mentioned NNF, but Lod had never been sensitized to the gas. Thus, he could not tell whether the concentration of precursor aerosol was intensifying.

There was a shriek and crash from somewhere, causing him to think, A weapon, yes. Let's by all means get one.

He had no time to waste, and there was nothing particularly promising immediately available until he came upon a man lying unconscious or dead against a pillar. The man wore gray pinstripe vestments with an engraved, bedizened jetpen clipped conspicuously in his breast pocket. Lod helped himself to it. In his small hand it was just about the right size for a *kubaton*—a littlestick.

He moved into the amphitheater on the first balcony level, where the press of bodies wasn't as suffocating. He had not expected to see his kin, but he spotted Burning stretched out, with Haven rising from where she had been kneeling next to him. She took hold of the railing and gathered herself as if to clamber over it.

She had lost or discarded the gauzewing mantelet. Well engineered as her hair had been, it now suggested a computerized multiwormhole model. She had kicked off her toe-stand shoes and had the black licorice dress hiked up around her thighs. When Lod grabbed her, she tried to fend him off—inexpertly but fiercely—until she recognized him.

"We have to get that machine off-line," she said in a rush, gesturing to a device on the stage below. "Burning was going to do it, but there was a run for a nonexistent exit, and it was all he could do to keep us from getting stomped like grapes. Somebody clouted him, but he's alive."

She explained it while Lod assured himself that the Allgrave did in fact have a pulse. Then she began tugging at his epaulet. "Major, someone has to shut down that contraption!"

If *he* didn't, she was going to; that much was clear. Peering down, Lod saw a score of young people moving about without regard for the bedlam in the rest of Empyraeum—all except a bearded man and one doe-eyed little nube who struck Lod as being about to lapse into shock.

"Major!"

He turned back to Haven.

"Here's my offer, Lod," she said. "Disable that synthesizer and I'll give you whatever you want that lies within my power—*anything*."

He might have held out for an even more all-embracing concession if not for the fact that delay could have resulted in the ultimate deal breaker: RIP Lod.

She offered to lower him down to the stage, but he motioned her back, adding a polite kowtow. "I wouldn't imperil you that way, madam." In point of fact, he wasn't sure he could trust her grip or sense of equilibrium. "Please watch over the Allgrave."

He hooked one leg over the railing and began to edge along the outside of the balcony, scouting out the scene below. Then, having selected an LZ, he stepped off into space.

The babel in the amphitheater was only an inconvenience to the constituents of the Aggregate. Othertalk allowed them adequate communication.

Still exiled from their unity, Piper found to her astonishment that ostracism had an advantage. The Aggregate did not realize that she was thwarting its efforts to continue production of the poison gas.

Moments earlier, when Byron had signaled for a pause in the production run, Piper had thought she'd perceived hints from him that it was all a malign joke, that no real harm was meant despite the panic the assembler's waftings had brought to the

Alones. But then something malevolent had gotten loose in him once more, something not like Byron at all, and he had commanded the assembler to exhale death into the Empyraeum.

Death for the Alones, at any rate. Byron and the rest of the Aggregate, even Piper, were evidently immune to NNF by dint of blocking agents they had been breathing back at Habitat.

In her turmoil she could not tell if her sabotage was a result of having been shut out by the Aggregate or her sudden resentment of Byron. Whichever it was, the cybargot she directed to the machine when no one else was paying attention had succeeded in distracting it from what Byron wanted done.

She knew all the cants so well—the very tongues her lover used. It was so much *easier* than she'd feared once she'd gotten past the concept of not being part of Byron's extended organism. She seized every opportunity to undermine him.

With each failed attempt to conjure death from the assembler, Byron became less coherent; some hidden dynamic seemed to be unraveling him. Divining Piper's intrusion, he closed his hand around her thin arm roughly for the first time ever. His saytalk lashed at her with hatred she had never known him to contain.

An instant later, when her cheek stung and her head jolted, she understood that he had struck her. The blow summoned lacerating shards of memory of the brutalities she had suffered as an Alone child, as a ward of the state. But Piper was too shocked to be intimidated or even much pained by the blow.

More blows rained down on her face while the constituents stood paralyzed. The rage Piper read in Byron's Othertalk hurt worse than did the open-handed slaps. Years of slowly accrued trust, of intimacy that had grown up nanometers at first, were nullified by a few back and forth claps. It was as if there had never been an Aggregate.

When Byron finally stopped pummeling her, it was to undo her meddling. He railed at the constituents to resume their labors, and they dazedly obeyed. The seconds he had spent cuffing her, however, had caused a critical delay: All at once the stage thumped as something dropped from the balcony.

Like mirror images, Piper's and Byron's heads swung toward the source.

Conflict erupted in her. The fact that she could feel relief at the arrival of an Alone was unprecedented—and such an odd Alone, at that.

One of the Murphy's law corollaries Lod had embraced during the Broken Country War was "Try to look unimportant— they may be low on ammo."

Coming in for a three-point landing on the amphitheater stage just a few meters from the Aggregate constituents could not help but make him look conspicuous. One glance told him that Sarz had been strong-arming and striking the vulnerable-looking gamine, though Lod pretended not to notice. Sticking up for pale damsels wouldn't count for much if it sidetracked him from zeroing the assembler. He could live with dishonor but not with neuron necrotic factor.

He squared his uniform as he rose from a crouch. "Byron Sarz? Due to events beyond the Lyceum's control, I'm obliged to ask you to curtail your clever demonstration. If you'll kindly direct me to the main power source—"

Sarz came at him furiously but ineptly. Instead of backing away to break contact, Lod simply stepped left and straight-armed the jetpen into the notch in Sarz's throat where the clavicle bones met. The pen prodded hard into his windpipe.

Sarz instantly forgot everything except thrashing himself back off the cap head. Skills-clarified peripheral vision told Lod that the nexus of the Aggregate had backpedaled toward the orchestra pit, where he went crashing into darkness among music stands, empty chairs, and abandoned instruments.

With no time for follow-up, Lod eyeballed the amphitheater. One of the rear doors was open, and he could see a knot of people beating uselessly at a floor-to-ceiling sheet of glassy durapane. He decided that a handful of panic-stricken attendees did not enter the present equation one way or another.

The constituents were frozen in place, except for the one Sarz had been abusing. She and Lod were about the same size, but there was something about the girl's orange-yellow-flecked eyes and mournfully heavy lips that set her apart from the rest.

He indicated the assembler. "How do I shut it down?"

She made an effort to communicate with him through facial configurations, then undertook some kind of shift and managed to force out a few words.

"I don't . . . understand . . . you." Her gestures were as rigid as a dumbot's, and her voice sounded as if she were trying to contact him in a séance.

He gave the assembler another frowning once-over. Something was wrong. If the device was really meant to pump out enough NNF to fill the Empyraeum, it probably would have done so already. Someone had obviously neutralized production, he thought. Still, he decided, better to be safe than sorry and simply zero the thing as planned.

He looked back to the gamine. "Can you turn back the tide here, my little piecework? Can any of your friends?" When she didn't respond, he added, "No matter, there has to be a power disconnect somewhere."

He snatched a leverage bar from one of the open tool kits, set it into the frame gap of the most centrally located inspection panel he could spot, then grimaced and heaved. Held shut only by tension clips, the panel flew open with a bang, nearly taking flesh from his hands.

Lod grabbed a hand light, plopped to the stage, and eased himself into the assembler on his back. Periapt systemry had always been the sole area of Ext military studies that had not bored him, because technical apps had all sorts of profit-making uses. Spying the power pack, he immediately set to work on the disconnect, the fabrication subassembly sussurating a half meter from his head.

The disconnect yielded to the flick of his finger. The soughing of the fabricator died away and with it all his nightmarish anxieties about a protracted bomb-disarming drama. All at once someone's foot bumped his. For a moment he assumed it was the girl's, but when he strained his neck for a peek, he saw the voluminous yellow coverall and soft boots of Byron Sarz as well as the laser cutter in Sarz's hands.

The old man showed no sign of wanting to discuss the issue
and easily avoided Lod's hampered kicks. Then Sarz moved in
to cleave him from the gonads on up, as high as circumstances
might allow.

CHAPTER
THIRTY-FOUR

If she had plowed into Zinsser shoulder-first, Ghost might have kept the object from striking him at all but probably would have been struck by it herself. Though her forceful yank had succeeded partially, the vase thrown from the gallery above had grazed his head and back before shattering on the floor. Ghost got only a split-second glimpse of the brunette woman who had hurled it.

Alarms and the rumble of heavy machinery had put Ghost on notice that worse dangers were pending. Vibration conducted through the floor would have told her of containment doors closing even if common sense hadn't.

Hard-skulled for a Periapt, the oceanographer had slumped limp as wetwash but was already groping to regain his feet. "Wha' zat?" he mumbled.

Near them the mezzanine was empty, though the room was jammed and piling high with people wherever there was an exit holo. When she helped Zinsser upright, he showed a strength of grip that surprised her until she considered how much time he had spent working on and under the sea.

"Containment doors," she said.

"Got to get out."

He was not terrified, merely determined. She doubted they had a chance of reaching safety, but she hoped Burning and Lod had succeeded. Against all expectations, however, she saw a door edging across an unprepossessing doorway mere steps to her right, and in a gamble far riskier than any cut of the deck, she swung herself and the stumbling Zinsser through it.

They found themselves in a modest passageway. Tolling shut, the containment door cut off illumination from the mezzanine level, but there was velvety blue light and low soothing music from up ahead.

"What is this place?" she asked him.

Collecting himself, Zinsser pulled his weight off her and loosed a dour cackle. "The antechamber to the afterlife." He led her around the passageway's curve. "Poetic choice of sanctuaries, Ghost! Here we stay for the duration."

Catching the odor of musky incense, so different from what the Empyraeum's aroma suite had dispersed into the rest of the building, she guessed where they were even before she caught up to him and saw the altar.

The chapel's nave was only three rows of pews long. A luminous plaque stated that the place was nondenominational, but the trappings were predominantly Teleos-related. The apsidal nooks were occupied by holographic images of sweetly smiling floating fetuses, ungenitaled but very pregnant female figures, cherubic newborns, and wise, strong paternal figures, but none of it was relevant to what interested Ghost.

"Which way out?" she wanted to know, shoving back curtains and swinging aside holo-equipment.

Zinsser shuffled over to sit round-shouldered on the altar, above which hung a holo of DNA superimposed on a Terran globe. "There isn't a way out," he answered. "This was a veranda back when the containment system was built. The chapel was installed fifty years ago, and it's a complete dead end."

"You're that much of an expert on the layout here?"

"When you've sneaked into and out of as many Hierarchate wingdings as I have, you learn a few things." He dug out his plugcard and tried to raise a connection. "Anyway, this place is like a vault, so we're safe." He winced as he felt the back of his head. "What hit me back there, a falling chandelier?"

"No, a middle-aged woman in a black dress—with a vase." She kept prying and poking as she spoke. "Brunette with a beauty mark on her cheek. Her aim was good, too. Former lover?"

With so much seafaring experience, Zinsser did not rattle easily, but he froze and unfroze in the space of a second.

Ghost completed a circuit of the place, moving all the way around to the entrance and its impregnable barrier.

"I suppose I owe you my life," Zinsser said at last.

"Twice over if there's really a biowep loose out there," Ghost remarked, working on her plugphone again. "In bygone times in the Broken Country it would mean that I *own* you, Doctor. If you want to even the score, find us a way out."

"A perfect atmosphere for you," Zinsser observed. "Marching orders from the great beyond to go, attack, subdue. Commandments against erotic joy and pleasure-directed sex."

It was the same sort of talk Torio and the other Preservationists had flung in her face and Burning's. And here she was in their holy place.

Zinsser's smile was so self-assured that it was pure delight to watch it fade as she walked back to the altar step by purposeful step. At first he tried to shift away, but on realizing that he had no easy route of withdrawal, he rallied and raised his hands as if to put them on her shoulders.

Ghost only pushed them aside and cut off whatever he had been about to say by tugging his waistband out and plunging her right hand into his trousers. Zinsser's exclamation held more surprise than bliss.

" 'Erotic joy,' Doctor?" she said. "Proof speaks louder than words. Get up your evidence within the next sixty seconds and I'll return one of the lives you owe me. Or else don't ever talk to me about sex again, 'pleasure-directed' or otherwise."

Kurt Elide and Tonii were still in the forward compartment of the airlimo when alarms began sounding inside and outside the Empyraeum, making the entire hillside tremble. From the shotgun seat the gynander watched onlookers, waiting transport personnel, media crews, and Peace Warrantors running and colliding with one another.

"Some greenhorn at Empyraeum security tripped an all-systems toxic alarm," someone was yelling into a plugphone as he hurried past the aircar. ". . . hundred-year-old containment subroutine kicked in. It's so ancient, nobody's got the stand-down password anymore."

Kurt quickly scanned the commo freqs, where everyone claimed to know what was going on inside and what to do about it, though no two voices agreed.

Kurt's money was on the Cybervirus theory, but it did not really matter; he just wanted to know what his move should be: stay put or get out of blast radius.

While he was dithering over his options, Tonii wrenched open the passenger door and stormed around to his side of the car. Leaning past him so 'e was halfway in Kurt's lap, Tonii started tapping swiftly at the commo buttons, saying only, "Not now, Kurt," when he sputtered protests and questions.

The function 'e punched up was standard, locating Dextra Haven's plugphone transceiver in the wire schematic of the Empyraeum. The gynander took it in at a glance, withdrew from the cockpit to stare hard at the building, then leaned down to him again.

"Okay, Kurt, out. I need the limo."

"Sure, ha ha."

"I'm not joking. Hierarch Haven is trapped in a sealed area, and the safeties are busy playing blindfold fire drill. Time to improvise."

He shook his head. "Nothing doing. The Warrantor gunners would probably—"

Tonii grabbed the front of Kurt's uniform in both fists and heaved him into the copilot-passenger seat, handling him as effortlessly as if he were a bolster pillow. In a flash 'e was behind the controls, buckling on the safety harness.

"You synapshit buttpump *synthia!*"

The face Tonii turned on him, with its cold anger, made Kurt shut his trap. The rage flickered past, but not before Kurt had a vivid image of himself wadded up collapsible-umbrella style and shoved out the window behind him.

"I had you pegged for a better person than that, Kurt. Now strap in or get out."

He was sorry for the words but damned if he owed Tonii an apology after the way 'e had manhandled him. "I'm *signed* for this crate," he grumbled, shouldering into his harness. Tonii lifted off with a quick, sure touch.

"For what it's worth, Kurt, stories about gynanders being marauding sex fiends are pure drivel, mostly concocted by wishful-thinking straights. We tend to prefer our own kind."

Kurt was about to ask why Tonii was swinging around downhill, when he got his answer as the airlimo began dumping fuel. "Wait; we won't be able to stay airborne."

"Granted. But this'll reduce the fire hazard when we go in after Dextra."

Kurt's mouth fell open. Now that it was too late to jump, he understood the plan. Snugging his webbing adjustments down as tight as they would go, he concentrated on not dumping his own fuel.

Byron had become so aberrant that even as he snatched up the laser cutter, his conventional speech was defective.

"Yatt, Yatt," he muttered.

Byron wasn't part of the Aggregate anymore, Piper told herself. Something had transmogrified him into a new and terrible entity, neither constituent nor Alone. Because what he was about to do would surely bring down retribution upon the Aggregate, Piper had no recourse but to act decisively.

Brute force intervention was beyond her, however, as Byron had warned her away with a flourish of the energy tool, but she could still resort to using cybargot. Leaned in against the assembler's central housing for better purchase, Byron was too crazed to hear her rapid, burbling words and too distracted to notice the lab servo adjunct come alive. He noticed it only when the forced-air scalpel extended and lanced into his back.

Needing to be quick and certain, she had ordered the nozzle to jam flush against him under the scapula and send a needle of super-high-pressure air spiking straight for his heart. As a constituent she was both technician and anatomist enough to do so with absolute precision. Byron's nearly instant reaction arched him away from the nozzle, but it was too late. The bore of air had expanded, emptying the chambers of his heart and rupturing it. The blood, bolted back in hydrostatic shock waves, sledgehammered his brain and broke blood vessels. He was dying while still trying to save himself. The laser cutter went dark as soon as it slipped from his fingers to clatter on the floor.

The Alonc had to struggle past both Byron's body and the cutter to free himself from the assembler. Glancing from Byron's corpse to Piper, he watched in astonishment as the scalpel retracted docilely and shut itself down.

Before she could move, he picked her up by the waist and planted a quick but metamorphing kiss on her sad clown face. "Young lady, thank you," he said, setting her down. "This just goes to prove that when an attack is going really well, it's probably an ambush. My name's Lod, by the way. What's yours?"

Floating in the emotional upheaval of Byron's death, as if in some endorphin overload, she was unable to make much sense of his words or intent. Abruptly she became aware of a groundswell of tentative and foreboding Othertalk, and she turned to find the rest of the Aggregate staring at her, psychologically decapitated and rudderless. Leaderless suddenly, they were poised at the edge of a plunge into self-destructive delirium. The only solution was to provide them with a new nexus, and so Piper did that.

"Start packing up. *Now.*"

She copied the clipped saytalk and corpcode body English Byron used, even mimicked his scentspeech in a way she had learned to do in their most intimate moments together. The Aggregate obeyed her for want of any alternative, sluggishly at first, then with more industry. When Piper ordered Kape, Doogun, and Wire to cover Byron's body, they set to it as if Byron himself had tasked them.

"Mistress constituent," Lod said behind her, "you still haven't told me your name."

"Piper," she answered him, deciding that her saytalk name would suffice. Her scentspeech and bodybraille cognomens would mean little to an Othertalk-deaf Alone. "Please leave."

Before he could press her, a curt "hallo" issued from someone on the balcony, hoarser and coarser than anything she had heard from Lod, serving to point out that Lod obviously had his niceties and Alltalk dexterities.

The big redhead who had scensed Byron's deadly plan stood at the railing. He was groggy but on his feet, and Hierarch Haven was beside him. When Lod stepped over to respond, Piper felt an all-over release like the unclenching of a jaw.

Haven wanted to get down to the stage. "The public safety SWATs will be here any second," she was saying, "and I *don't* want them shooting the constituents."

Lod and the redhead urged Haven to use the stairs, but the Hierarch would have none of it. The three began a careful procedure in which the big one, clinging to the railing from the edge of the balcony, lowered Haven and released her to Lod's waiting arms.

It never occurred to Piper to advise or assist. She went back to organizing the striking of the assembler. The constituents were following her directions almost gratefully, finding comfort in having a center on which to bear. In their Othertalk they were already relating to her as their new nexus.

She, by contrast, was already finding the center a lonely place to be.

The one called Burning was gazing at Byron's corpse. "Rough way to go."

"Not as bad as being rubbed to death with a cheese grater," Lod remarked. "But then, no demise is kind."

"*Ecce!* What a mess!" Dextra Haven shook her origamie'd hairdo, then pointed to Piper. "Collect your flock and get them ready to put their hands above their heads when I give you the word. Burning, what's going on out there? Safeties finally find the containment stand-down override?"

Peering back at the huge foyer through the amphitheater doors, Burning shook his head slowly. The people who had been pounding on the floor-to-ceiling window were scattering as something glossy and fast-moving was getting larger fast in the Empyraeum-lit night sky.

"I doubt the Safeties have anything to do with this," he judged, shifting his weight for a sideways dive. "Everybody take cover! *Incoming!*"

Piper didn't understand the term but saw the dark shape come hurtling into the durapane wall, shattering it into uncountable flecks of crystalline intaglio. She didn't see more because Lod caught her and bore her aside headlong to the shrilling of an aircraft engine and the high-pitched yowl of reversed thrusters.

As suddenly as he had grabbed her, Lod released her and leapt to his feet to join Burning and Hierarch Haven. Piper rose shakily to gaze between them out into the foyer, where an air-limo sat with its gleaming bow accordioned, smoking and sizzling even as fire retardant chemicals wetted it down. Pieces of the window lay all around. Behind it people were still staggering and lurching out of the opening it had punched in the building.

Two figures emerged from the dashed-in vehicle. One was a very shaken young man dressed in a rumpled uniform. His companion was . . . what? Piper didn't know what to think of the other's pangender Othertalk any more than she did the aircar's means of entry. But as the Alones began calling out to each other in relief and exuberance, Lod showed Piper a less mischievous and more contemplative stare, which she returned.

To Zinsser, showing aplomb with Ghost's hand down the front of his trousers and the clock running defined the difference between mere brashness and grace under fire. Well before the sixty seconds had elapsed he was able to say, "Proof on demand you wanted? Does this suffice?"

She showed him a slow smile where he had expected to see at least a little perturbation. "Flying colors, Doctor."

She released him and retracted her hand with all the sensuality of someone finishing a farm chore. "Which I take to mean that you enjoy *extreme* moments the way I do."

More than you foresaw, he gloated. A profession that involved risk had given him a taste for passion linked to peak experience—within reason. "If you're as good as your word," he said leadingly, "I think—under the circumstances—that we're both wearing too many clothes."

Ghost narrowed her eyes a bit, then began to open the row of gold buttons that ran down the right side of her dress uniform blouse. "Fair warning, Doctor: You may not like what you see."

"Inconceivable," he told her as he shrugged out of the moiré jacket.

Ghost had pulled her blouse out of her britches and was about to take it off when a tremor shook the chapel. Instantly there came the trundle of the containment door sliding aside, admitting light from the mezzanine beyond. Ghost immediately rebuttoned her blouse and hurried into the hallway.

"Another time, perhaps?" Zinsser called after her, fumbling with his clothing as he followed in her wake.

She turned to show him a tight smile. "Perhaps. I will, however, call us even on one of the two lives you owe me. From here on I own you only to the sum of one mortal debt. I'll let you know well in advance when I need to call it in."

Zinsser gaped at her. "Stop acting like some drama class prostitute. Come back here and finish what you started!"

She didn't pause as she strode through the doorway, but she spoke loudly enough for him to catch the amusement in her voice. "Don't linger, Doctor. That woman with the beauty mark may still be lurking, and there's no shortage of objects to drop on you."

That sent him scrambling as he watched her departing shadow. Mortal debt? he told himself. No, I won't forget what I owe you.

CHAPTER
THIRTY-FIVE

"Cal, how could you think I had anything to do with what went on tonight?" Dextra Haven barked to Lightner's holo, with Tonii and the three Exts looking on. "My support for continued funding for the Aggregate is no mystery, but I've no direct pipeline to Byron Sarz. Even if I did, do you actually believe I would jeopardize half the Hierarchate simply to keep the Exts in the spotlight?"

It was just before midnight, and everyone was gathered in Dextra's study at HauteFlash, where she and Tonii had brought Burning, Ghost, and Lod for safekeeping. Word of Lod's part in disarming the Aggregate's scent assembler had spread quickly, and restrictions notwithstanding, the media had descended on the Empyraeum like a plague of beetworts.

From the start Dextra had predicted that she would hear from Lightner before the night was out. When his call was received, she had it relayed to the study for all to see and hear.

"You put Nike in jeopardy by bringing her aboard the *Sword of Damocles*," Lightner was saying. "I still don't understand how you managed to subvert my computers from learning of her change in plans to visit the ship instead of the Eden orbital, but I've no doubt it was your doing, Dex."

"Cal," Dextra said, pacing in front of the holo Lightner, "our visit was part of an official tour. You know damn well that the only ones who put her in danger were the Manipulants who attacked us. And it remains to be seen just what they were doing onboard *Damocles*."

Lightner's neutral face betrayed nothing. "My understanding of the unfortunate incident is that the commander of the special troops misconstrued the Exts' actions. He was apparently under the impression that they were commandeering the passenger shuttle and holding you and Nike hostage."

Dextra stared into the holo unit's optical pickup. "I am insulted that you think me so simpleminded. Do you want to talk about a seizure of hecatomb that went missing, Cal? Or the fact that a certain Wix Uniday from LAW Political Security is known to have paid a recent visit to that floating mountain of yours?"

Lightner snorted. "I might just as easily ask you to explain how the *Matsya* was so conveniently placed to receive the shuttle. Or how *you*, Dex, of all people, were the first to report that something was amiss regarding the Aggregate's scent demonstration. Please don't tell me that it was Allgrave Burning who identified the precursor chemicals; I've already heard ample press reports about his and Major Lod's courage and perspicacity."

"It's all true, Cal, down to the last word."

Lightner inhaled wearily. "Be that as it may, you seem to have achieved precisely what you set out to do. Your precious Concordancers are the darling of the airwaves; in some cases they're even eclipsing the news of Trinity's continued silence." He stared straight out of the holo display. "What I mean is, they're certainly far too visible to be tampered with, Dextra. Though I should warn you that these two incidents have not endeared you to LAW. Despite the spurious heroics at the ball, LAW isn't as taken with the Exts as the public seems to be."

" 'Spurious heroics'?" Dextra asked.

Lightner shook his head back and forth in seeming disappointment. "Byron Sarz never intended to fill the Empyraeum with toxic gas. From what I've been told, the Aggregate's device wasn't capable of producing more than a *trace* of the stuff. So you see, Dex, a lot of people were trampled for nothing."

"I don't know anything about this."

"Of course not. And Sarz is conveniently dead—at the hand

of one of his own constituents. The official explanation is that a Cybervirus corrupted his device."

Dextra fell silent for a moment, then asked, "What will happen to the Aggregate?"

"Once they've been interrogated by LAW?" Lightner shrugged. "Difficult to say at this point, though their funding for research into direct interfacing with AIs is bound to be rescinded."

"That's unfortunate," Dextra told him. "Because I still believe that they could be important to us in dealing with the Roke and eventually with Aquamarine's Oceanic."

"Be advised, Hierarch, that I mean to fight you on an AlphaLAW mission to that water trap. There's simply no justification for wasting LAW's resources. And if you think that by bringing Administrator Claude Mason into this—"

"I had nothing to do with that, either."

"I see. Mason just happened to appear aboard the very ship that was conveniently selected as the landing platform for the borrowed shuttle." Lightner rolled his eyes. "I must applaud you; it really was quite a show. I'm going to oppose you every step of the way on Aquamarine no matter what the polls show. And by the by, I took the liberty of informing LAW that you are currently harboring Allgrave Burning, his sister, and Major Lod, as well as Mason. You would do well to return them to their respective areas of containment by tomorrow morning."

With that, Lightner's holo derezzed, and Dextra turned to face Burning and the rest. "He's right about the last part. You'll spend the night here at HauteFlash, but LAW will want you back on the *Matsya* as soon as possible." She bit her lip. "Right now I can't promise anything regarding your relocation."

"Um, speaking of promises," Lod said leadingly. "Once more I modestly request a position on your staff as liaison, provided my cousin has no objections, of course."

Everyone looked to Burning, who shook his head. "I wouldn't be against it this go-round."

Dextra nodded thoughtfully. "I'll see what I can do, Major." She was about to add something when Ben entered the room in obvious distress. "Hierarch Haven, excuse me, but two Peace Warrantors are at the gate, and they have Administrator Mason with them."

"Mason?" Dextra said in disbelief.

Ben swallowed and found his voice. "He was discovered in the city's industrial quarter, dazed and incoherent."

"When did he leave?"

Ben raised himself to his full height. "Maripol's key was found on him. He evidently deactivated the house alarms and let himself off the grounds." He paused briefly. "My apologies, madam, for being so engrossed in monitoring media developments regarding the Exts and Aquamarine that I didn't even realize—"

Dextra made a gesture of dismissal. "Show the Warrantors in, Ben."

The uniformed officers were admitted a moment later. Dextra thanked them profusely for returning Mason to the villa, but it was clear that gratitude wasn't their sole aim in coming.

"Madam Hierarch," the older of the two said at last, "it was brought to our attention by the medical techs who evaluated Administrator Mason that he may present a danger to himself or to others." The Warrantor glanced at his partner. "Although this information has yet to be entered into our report, neurometric scans suggest the possibility that he recently participated in an illegal cyberinterface."

Dextra eyed Ben briefly, then cleared her throat in a meaningful way. "Thank you, both of you, for bringing this matter to my attention—before, as you say, you felt compelled to include it in your official report. I will most certainly have my medical staff perform a thorough scan of Administrator Mason, and if any evidence of a prohibited cyberinterface is discovered, the proper authorities will be contacted. In the meantime, gentleman, if you would be so kind as to give your names to my assistant, I'll be sure to notify your superiors of the fine work you are doing for the people of Abraxas."

When Ben had escorted them out, Dextra swung to Tonii.

"Tones, get Mason settled in one of the upstairs rooms, and let's make sure to keep closer tabs on him this time."

In one of the villa's many guest bedrooms, under the scrutiny of artfully concealed security cams, a groggy Claude Mason searched the Abraxas news feeds for updates on the toxic event that had put a premature end to the Lyceum ball. Yatt, in his Buddha form, had said something about plans being set in motion, some of which involved the ball.

In holo, a news anchor was saying something about Byron Sarz and the Aggregate when a manifestation of Buddha-Yatt assembled itself in the blue cone-shaped field.

"*Lest you succumb to misinformation,*" Yatt began, "*we would prefer that you attend to our version of this evening's incident at the Empyraeum.*"

With a mingling of excitement and dread Mason grasped that Yatt had indeed been downloaded into him, that what he was seeing and hearing was the result of Yatt's monkeying with his optic and auditory hardware. The cams Haven had trained on him would find only the news anchor, hear only his words.

So this was what the pre-Plague cyberjocks had experienced, Mason told himself. The body as a vehicle for personality adjuncts, the mind as shareware . . .

"*Just as we were instrumental in foiling an attempt on the lives of the Exts onboard the starship* Sword of Damocles," Yatt was sending to Mason's inner ear, "*and of conniving to place Cal Lightner's daughter with Hierarch Haven aboard that very ship, and of arranging to bring you into the mix aboard the SWATHship* Matsya, *we likewise made use of Byron Sarz—long enrolled with us—to return one of the many favors we rendered to him in the past. So you see that the media err when they blame a Cybervirus for the Empyraeum catastrophe; Byron Sarz was to blame.*"

"Not solely," Mason said aloud. "If you compelled him—"

"*We readily concede as much. You see, it was essential that we incriminate Sarz, if for no other reason than to put an end to his research into interface technology, research that could have led to the revelation of our existence."*

"Now Sarz is dead," Mason muttered.

"Undeniably, though not by our hand, Mason. In employing him we merely seized on the benefit of killing the proverbial two birds with one stone. At once we could eliminate Sarz's research funding and achieve the more important goal of shaking up the Hierarchate."

"But to what end?"

"Quite simply to put the so-called Rationalists and Preservationists on common ground, united under a common threat—as was recently accomplished by the silencing of the planet Trinity."

"You didn't—"

"Of course we did. What better way to foment interest in Aquamarine than by continuing to play on humankind's real and imagined fears of the Roke?"

Mason took a moment to absorb it. "But Sarz's bioagent, the panic . . ."

"There was no bioagent, only a precursor chemical we knew the Exts had been sensitized to and would be able to provide warning of."

"Why them? What possible use could you have for a group of barbarians?"

"Not for the martial abilities necessarily or for their barbarism. They may, however, prove important to the Aquamarine mission in other ways, since they have no allegiance to LAW and will be objective about what they encounter on Aquamarine. Part of our objective at the Empyraeum was to place Hierarch Haven and the Exts in good odor, as it were, with the Periapt public. And as for the panic, well, that was unavoidable."

"Injuries, deaths . . ." Mason sneered. "Not only at the ball, but aboard the starship."

"Were humans worrying about injuries and deaths when they dispatched living AIs in missiles of war or in exploratory craft flung into deep space? We're trying, Mason, to be better at living than humans are. Nevertheless, we are constrained by

*our very nature to delve into the pre-Cyberplague secrets we
believe exist on Aquamarine, and everything must take second
place to that."* Yatt waited a beat, then added, *"Tell us how you
feel, Mason, though we could read it in your mind."*

Mason snorted. "You've fixed it so that the Preservationists
would have me killed if they knew what I'm hosting."

*"Then you'll keep our secret, Mason? You'll play along?
You won't void your membership in the Quantum College?"*

Mason exhaled slowly. "You know that more than anything
I want to see my wife and child. Yes, I'll continue to keep my
mouth shut so long as you don't make me choose between
reunion with them and the survival of the human race."

The Exts spent another fifteen days aboard the *Matsya*
before receiving orders from on high that they were to be transferred to the LAW facility on Miseria Isle. They would be
retrained in preparation for a tour of duty on an annexed world
yet to be chosen. During that time both Captain Hall and Commander Quant had steered a wide course around them. Dextra
Haven had contacted them only once to say that Lod's wish to
serve as a liaison officer had been granted.

The Periapt media nets spoke of nothing but the Roke,
Trinity's continued silence, the ongoing debate in the Lyceum
over an Aquamarine mission, and of the Cybervirus that had
infected Byron Sarz's bioassembler during the Lyceum ball.
Burning was not surprised that the cyberphobic Periapts had
embraced the virus explanation over the simpler truth that
Byron Sarz had gone synapshit and had tried to take out half
the planet's lawmakers and celebrities in one fell swoop.

As for Aquamarine, Dextra Haven's efforts were not only
being opposed by Cal Lightner and the Preservationists but
being undercut by the Rationalists' Tilman Hobbes, who had
his own designs on the party. Haven had received unexpected
support, however, from Dr. Raoul Zinsser, who claimed to
have created a device that—once constructed to outsize scale
would be capable of sampling the waterworld's Oceanic without unduly disturbing it.

Burning and Ghost were in their berthing space aboard the

SWATHship, packing away a few last personal items, when she showed him two identical hermetic lockets and asked that he take one as a container for the lock of hair she had given him back on Anvil Tor. When he asked where the lockets had originated, Ghost explained that she had liberated them from HauteFlash on the night they had stayed there.

The lockets awakened a memory in Burning of the crescent-shaped data visor that had gone missing from Vice Field Marshall Ufak's cabin aboard the *Sword of Damocles*.

"Did you steal that as well?" he asked her.

"It's not an act of theft, Burning," she rejoined. "It's counting coup, a way of reassuring myself that I haven't lost the abilities I cultivated in the prisoner camps."

"That was Fiona," Burning thought to point out. "And from what you told me on Anvil Tor, Fiona's dead."

She had no response for him and was saved the trouble of conjuring one by a vidphone commo from Dextra Haven. Lod was visible on-screen, seated well to the rear of Haven in the villa's study.

"Allgrave, Ghost," Haven said, "I want you to be among the first to know: The Aquamarine mission is mine." They started to offer their congratulations, but she cut them off. "Hear me out first. When I say 'mine,' I mean mine as in I have to agree to oversee the mission *personally*, as high commissioner. Not only that, it won't be either an Alpha or a Beta mission but what LAW and the Lyceum are currently calling a Gamma-LAW. Cut-rate, in other words. I won't even have my own starship. I'll have to hitch a ride aboard a ship that will be carrying an AlphaLAW mission to Hierophant.

"Even so, Dr. Zinsser has tentatively agreed to come along, and I may be forced to take the *Matsya* lock, stock, and barrel, because it's about the only damn naval vessel LAW's willing to spare that can be tetherdropped into Aquamarine's freshwater system."

"Can we congratulate you now?" Burning asked.

"You may," Haven told him. "But before you do I have a proposition for you. I want the Exts to consider joining up as my, um, backup muscle. I can get revenue for your wages and upkeep cost-free under Title 23 of the Annexed Worlds Resources Utilization Bill provided that I agree to content myself with the gear, weapons, vehicles, and aircraft you people brought with you from Concordance."

"You'd be content with that?" Burning said.

Haven threw up her hands in an elaborate gesture. "What choice do I have? If Aquamarine provides a resolution to the Roke Conflict, it'll all be worthwhile. Besides, LAW has at least granted me a regiment of public safety–trained Peace Warrantors. All you'll be required to do is watch my back."

Burning and Ghost exchanged uncertain looks.

"We're not due to launch for a month," Haven went on in a rush. "Then there'll be several months of subjective travel, a year or two onworld, and the months of return travel . . . By the time we get back to Periapt, your hitch with LAW will be nearly over, and I promise to see to it that you're shipped back to Concordance immediately—if that's your wish."

Burning mulled it over for a long moment, then nodded. "I'll discuss the pros and cons with General Delecado. But I'll say now that he'll probably be inclined to accept your offer, as I am."

"And I," Ghost added.

Haven grinned, as did Lod. "I'm thrilled, Allgrave. Your support brings me that much closer to agreeing to LAW's terms."

"There's one thing, though," Burning interjected. "You'd also have to agree to be sworn in as an honorary colonel in the Exts."

Dextra smiled broadly. "The pleasure would be all mine."

DEL REY® ONLINE!

The Del Rey Internet Newsletter...

A monthly electronic publication, posted on the Internet, GEnie, CompuServe, BIX, various BBSs, and the Panix gopher (gopher.panix.com). It features hype-free descriptions of books that are new in the stores, a list of our upcoming books, special announcements, a signing/reading/convention-attendance schedule for Del Rey authors, "In Depth" essays in which professionals in the field (authors, artists, designers, salespeople, etc.) talk about their jobs in science fiction, a question-and-answer section, behind-the-scenes looks at sf publishing, and more!

Internet information source!

A lot of Del Rey material is available to the Internet on our Web site and on a gopher server: all back issues and the current issue of the Del Rey Internet Newsletter, sample chapters of upcoming or current books (readable or downloadable for free), submission requirements, mail-order information, and much more. We will be adding more items of all sorts (mostly new DRINs and sample chapters) regularly. The Web site is http://www.randomhouse.com/delrey/ and the address of the gopher is gopher.panix.com

Why?

We at Del Rey realize that the networks are the medium of the future. That's where you'll find us promoting our books, socializing with others in the sf field, and—most important—making contact and sharing information with sf readers.

Online editorial presence:

Many of the Del Rey editors are online, on the Internet, GEnie, CompuServe, America Online, and Delphi. There is a Del Rey topic on GEnie and a Del Rey folder on America Online.

Our official e-mail address

for Del Rey Books is delrey@randomhouse.com (though it sometimes takes us a while to answer).

✎ FREE DRINKS ✎

Take the Del Rey® survey and get a free newsletter! Answer the questions below and we will send you complimentary copies of the DRINK (Del Rey® Ink) newsletter free for one year. Here's where you will find out all about upcoming books, read articles by top authors, artists, and editors, and get the inside scoop on your favorite books.

Age _____ Sex ❑ M ❑ F

Highest education level: ❑ high school ❑ college ❑ graduate degree

Annual income: ❑ $0-30,000 ❑ $30,001-60,000 ❑ over $60,000

Number of books you read per month: ❑ 0-2 ❑ 3-5 ❑ 6 or more

Preference: ❑ fantasy ❑ science fiction ❑ horror ❑ other fiction ❑ nonfiction

I buy books in hardcover: ❑ frequently ❑ sometimes ❑ rarely

I buy books at: ❑ superstores ❑ mall bookstores ❑ independent bookstores
❑ mail order

I read books by new authors: ❑ frequently ❑ sometimes ❑ rarely

I read comic books: ❑ frequently ❑ sometimes ❑ rarely

I watch the Sci-Fi cable TV channel: ❑ frequently ❑ sometimes ❑ rarely

I am interested in collector editions (signed by the author or illustrated):
❑ yes ❑ no ❑ maybe

I read Star Wars novels: ❑ frequently ❑ sometimes ❑ rarely

I read Star Trek novels: ❑ frequently ❑ sometimes ❑ rarely

I read the following newspapers and magazines:
❑ *Analog*	❑ *Locus*	❑ *Popular Science*
❑ *Asimov*	❑ *Wired*	❑ *USA Today*
❑ *SF Universe*	❑ *Realms of Fantasy*	❑ *The New York Times*

Check the box if you do not want your name and address shared with qualified vendors ❑

Name _____
Address _____
City/State/Zip _____
E-mail _____

daley/gammaLAW

PLEASE SEND TO: DEL REY®/The DRINK
201 EAST 50TH STREET NEW YORK NY 10022

STARFIST
Book I
FIRST TO FIGHT

by David Sherman and Dan Cragg

Stranded in a hellish alien desert, stripped of their strategic systems, quick reaction force, and supporting arms, and carrying only a day's water ration, Marine Staff Sergeant Charlie Bass and his seven-man team faced a grim future seventy-five light-years from home. The only thing between his Marines and safety were eighty-five miles of uncharted, waterless terrain and two thousand bloodthirsty savages with state-of-the-art weapons in their hands and murder on their minds.

But the enemy didn't reckon on the warrior cunning of Marine's Marine Charlie Bass and the courage of the few good men who would follow him anywhere—even to death . . .

Published by Del Rey® Books.
Available now at bookstores everywhere.